A WOMAN OF WAR

Mandy Robotham has been an aspiring author since the age of nine, but was waylaid by journalism and later enticed by birth. She's now a practising midwife who writes about birth, death, love and everything else in between. She graduated with an MA in Creative Writing from Oxford Brookes University. This is her first novel.

A Woman of War

Mandy Robotham

avon.

Published by AVON
A division of HarperCollins*Publishers* Ltd
1 London Bridge Street
London SE1 9GF

www.harpercollins.co.uk
11

A Paperback Original 2019

A catalogue copy of this book is available
from the British Library.

PB ISBN: 978-0-00-832424-7
TPB ISBN: 978-0-00-833591-5

This novel is entirely a work of fiction. The names,
characters and incidents portrayed in it are the work of the
author's imagination. Any resemblance to actual persons, living
or dead, events or localities is entirely coincidental.

Typeset in Bembo Std by Palimpsest Book Production Limited,
Falkirk, Stirlingshire

Printed and bound in the UK by
CPI Group (UK) Ltd, Croydon CR0 4YY

MIX
Paper from
responsible sources
FSC™ C007454

This book is produced from independently certified FSC™ paper
to ensure responsible forest management.

For more information visit: www.harpercollins.co.uk/green

To the boys: Simon, Harry & Finn
And to mothers and midwives everywhere

Author's Note

Midwives love to talk, analyse and dissect; the post-birth babble in the coffee room is where we relate the beauty of a birth and the small dilemmas: How to relay to women the intensity of what they may go through in labour? Is it fair to describe in detail the two-headed agony and ecstasy of birth before the day? It led me to wonder at the bigger moral issues we might face, a point where we as midwives may not *want* to give body and soul towards the safety of mother and baby. And who and or where would that be?

For me there was only one answer: a child whose very genetics would cause ripples among those who had suffered hugely at the hands of its father: Adolf Hitler. Combining a fascination for wartime history and my passion for birth, the idea was conceived. Using real characters like Hitler and Eva Braun – both of whom continue to incite strong emotions almost eight decades on – tested my own moral compass. And yet, I retain the premise that all women, at the point of birth, are equal: princess or pauper, angel or devil, in normal labour we all have to dig deep into ourselves. Birth sweeps away all prejudice. Eva, in the moments of labour, is one of those women. So too, the baby is born free of moral stain – an innocent, entirely pure.

While using factual research material and scenarios, this is my take on a snapshot in history. There has been past speculation that the Führer and his eventual bride had a child, but *A Woman of War* is a work of fiction, my mind asking: What if? Anke too, is a fiction, yet an embodiment of what I sense in many midwives – a huge heart, but with doubts and fears. In other words, a normal person.

A WOMAN OF WAR

1

Irena

Germany, January 1944

For a few moments, the hut was as quiet as it ever could be in the early hours, a near silence broken only by the sound of a few feminine snores. The night monitor padded up and down the lines of bunks with her stick, on the lookout for rats preying on the women's still limbs, ready to swipe at the voracious predators. Small clouds of human breath rose from the top bunks as it met with the icy, still air – strange not to hear the women coughing in turn, a symphony of ribs racked by the force of infection on their piteous lungs, as if just one more hack would crack their chests wide open. Every thirty seconds, the darkness was split by pinpricks of white as the searchlight did its endless sweep through the holes in the flimsy planks, in the only place we could call home.

I was dozing at the front of the hut, knowing Irena was in the early stages. A sudden cry from her bunk next to the stove broke the silence, as a fierce contraction coiled within her and split her uneasy sleep, spilling through her broken teeth.

'Anke, Anke,' she cried. 'No, no, no . . . Make it stop.'

Her distress wasn't of weakness – Irena had done this twice before in peacetime – but of the inevitable result of this process, of labour. A birth. Her baby would be born, and that to Irena was her worst nightmare. While her baby lay inside, occasionally kicking and showing signs it had not sucked away its mother's life juices and still found wanting, there was hope. On the outside, hope diminished rapidly.

I was soon at her side, gathering the rags and paper we had been harbouring, a bucket of water drawn painstakingly from the well before curfew. She was agitated, in a type of delirium usually seen in the typhus cases. The name of her husband – probably long since dead in another camp – burbled through her dry lips time and again as she thrashed on the thin hay mattress, causing the wooden slats below to creak.

'Irena, Irena,' I whispered her name repeatedly, bobbing to catch her gaze while her eyes opened and closed. Unlike women in the Berlin hospitals, mothers in the camp often became otherworldly in labour, taking themselves to another place, a palace of the mind. I imagined it was a way of avoiding the reality that they were bringing their babies into this stark world of horror, creating a perfect nest in their dreams where life failed to provide it.

Much like third labours generally, this one progressed quickly. After simmering for several hours, contractions came one after another, spiralling rapidly. Rosa was soon by my side, roused from her half sleep too. She stoked the pitiful fire and put some of the water on to boil, while another woman brought an oil lamp, the fuel saved for such occasions. That was as much as we had, other than faith in Mother Nature.

The contractions were fierce and the waters broke during one particularly strong moment – a pathetic, meagre amount – but Irena was resisting. In any other scenario, the body would have been forced to bear down, the natural expulsion overwhelming and unrelenting. Women in their first pregnancies often worried whether they would know when it was time to push, and we as midwives could only reassure them – you *will* know, a power from within like no other, a tidal wave to ride instead of fight. Irena, however, was hanging on to her baby for dear life, a thin snake of mucousy blood just visible now as I looked under her covering. It signalled the body was eager, more than ready to let go. Only a mother's iron will was clamping the gates shut.

Eventually, after several strong contractions, Irena's womb won out; a telltale primal grunt, and with the help of the lamplight I saw the baby was on its way, his or her head not yet visible but a distinctive shape behind the thin, almost translucent skin of Irena's buttocks, rounding out her anatomy. She swished her head in distress, panting and muttering: 'No, not yet, baby, stay safe,' fluttering her hands towards her opening in a desperate attempt to will the baby back in. Rosa was at Irena's head, whispering reassurance, giving her sips of the cleanest water we could find, and I stayed with the lamp below.

Oblivious to its future, this baby was determined to be born. In the next contraction, black hair sprouted through the strained lips of Irena's labia, and I urged her to 'Blow,

blow, blow,' hoping to slow her down and avoid any skin tears that we had no equipment or means to stitch, another open wound the rats and lice would target.

Sensing the inevitable, Irena gave in, and her baby's head slid past the confines of its mother, corkscrewing its way into the world. For a moment or so, as with so many births I'd seen, time stood still. The baby's head lay on the cleanest rag we had, shoulders and body still inside Irena. Her sweat-stained head fell back on Rosa, a body convulsed with sobs of relief and sadness, and only a sliver of joy. The hut was silent – most of the women had woken, two or three visible heads to a bunk, as curiosity triumphed over the desire for sleep. Still, they only glimpsed, respecting what little privacy she had.

The baby had emerged back to back, looking up at me squarely, and I could see eyes opening and shutting like a china doll's, mouth forming into a fish-like pout, as if he or she were breathing. The seconds ticked by, but there was no worry, the baby's lifeline umbilicus giving filtered oxygen from Irena, far purer than the stagnant air around us.

'It's fine, all is well, your baby will be here soon,' I whispered. But nothing, I knew, would make Irena feel anything other than impending fear or sadness.

The contraction brewed, and she shifted her buttocks to make room as the baby's head made a half turn to one side, allowing the breadth of the shoulders to come through, and Irena's son slipped out, bathed in only a little more water, mixed with blood. He was a sorry scrap of a thing, a head too large for his tiny, scantily covered limbs and bulbous testicles. Irena had grown him the best she could on her meagre diet of almost no protein or fat, and this was the result. I took the next best rag and wiped off the fluid, stimulating his flaccid body that gave out no sound, and a small part of me thought: 'Just slip away now, child, save yourself the pain.' But I carried on chafing at his delicate skin, rubbing some zest into him, as part of our human instinct to preserve life.

Immediately, Irena was back in this world, panicked. 'Is it all right? Why doesn't it cry?'

'He's just a little shocked, Irena, give him time,' I said, feeling my own adrenalin peak then as I chanted in my own head: 'Come on, baby, breathe for her, come on,' while talking and blowing on his startled features: 'Hey, little one, come on now, give us a cry.'

After one more vigorous rub, he coughed, gasped, and seemed almost to take in his surroundings with even wider eyes. Instantly, I passed him up to Irena, and settled him next to her skin. The effort of labour had made her the warmest surface in the room and he began murmuring at her, rather than a lusty cry. Still, any sound was breathing; it was life.

For the first time in months, Irena's features took on a look of complete satisfaction. 'Hey, my lovely,' she cooed, 'what a handsome boy you are. How clever you are.' After two girls he was her first boy, her husband's desire. What everyone was thinking, but no one voiced, was that she was unlikely to see any of them grow into their potential, into people. Not a soul would burst her temporary bubble.

Without a word, Rosa and I went into our defined roles. She stayed with Irena and the baby, tucking him further under any covers we had, while I kept a vigilant eye on Irena's opening as blood pooled onto the rag. It was normal

– for now. But since I began my training, placentas had made me twitch far more than babies ever had. Sheer exhaustion could make the body shut down and simply refuse to expel the placenta. Beads of sweat began forming on my brow and at the nape of my neck. To lose a woman and baby at this stage would seem like Mother Nature really had no soul.

Yet she came through, as she had again and again, a constant in this ugly, shifting humanity. Irena's features, still awash with hormones of sheer love, crumpled with pain, as another contraction took hold. In another two pushes, the placenta flopped onto the rags, tiny and pale. The baby had stripped every ounce of fat from this pregnancy engine and it was a wrung-out rag with its stringy cord attached. Well-nourished German women produced fat, juicy cords that coiled like helter-skelters into blood-red tissue, fed well in their nine months. I hadn't seen anything other than meagre ones since coming into the camp.

Once I had checked to ensure the placenta had all come away – anything left inside could cause a fatal infection – we opened the door to the hut and threw it outside, away from the entrance. There was a fierce scrabbling as several of the rats, some nearing the size of cats, fought to be the first through their entry holes in the side of the hut, to the lion's share of fresh meat. Months before, there had been cross words among the women about feeding the rats in this way, since they could only get bigger, but these creatures were relentless in their quest for food. If they had none, they turned towards us, nibbling at the skin of women too sick to move, too lifeless to realise. If the creatures were distracted, or satiated, at least we had some respite from their prowling. I hated the vermin, but at the same time, I could admire their survival instinct. Vermin or human, we were all simply trying to live.

Rosa and I cleaned around Irena with whatever we could find, she enjoying skin-to-skin time with her baby – we had no clothes to dress him in anyway. He fed hungrily at her papery breast, his little cheeks sucking for dear life on almost dry flesh. The hormone release caused more cramping in her tired belly, but you could tell she almost enjoyed the draw on her body. Rosa brewed some nettle tea from the leaves we had saved, and Irena's face was pure joy for an hour or so. But as the dark diminished and daylight began licking through the cracks in the walls, the atmosphere in the hut became edgy. Time for Irena and her baby was limited.

Some of the women moved towards her, a low hum gathering as they encircled her bed, forming into a welcome song for the baby. In the real world, they would have brought gifts, food or flowers. Here, they had nothing to give, except the love squirrelled away in a protected corner of their hearts, some hope they occasionally let flutter; so many had already lost children, been parted, ached in every way possible for the smell of their babies' wet heads, siblings, nieces, nephews. They were all part of the longing. One woman offered up a blessing, in the absence of a rabbi, and they accepted the baby as one of their own. His mother named him Jonas, after her husband, and smiled as he became part of history, recognised.

Rosa and I sat in the corner, me as the only non-Jew in the hut, taking stock of the beautiful sound. I had one ear out for the camp waking up, the guards shouting their orders, the constant clumping of their boots on the hard, frosted

7

ground outside. It was only a matter of time before they entered our domain. Hiding the child was pointless. We had tried as much once before – a newborn's constant, mewling hunger cries were impossible to muffle. That time, it had resulted in the loss of both mother and baby in the coldest, cruellest way possible. If we could save at least one, it counted as something. Irena had children she may well find again. Unlikely, but always possible.

In the end, Irena managed almost three hours of precious contact with her newborn. At seven, the door was thrown open, a fierce wind whipping as the guards came in to make their roll call. This hut had been excused an outside count only because so many of the women were bed-bound and the guards grew dangerously irritated if they fell during the long wait. I had appealed to the camp Commandant for an inside count and been successful – a surprising and rare concession on their part.

It was the first guard who sensed the new arrival. I was almost sure this particular one had worked in hospitals before the war, possibly as a midwife; she looked at me with deep suspicion, a grimy furrow to her large brow, particularly when I was with the Jewish women, as if she could not contemplate even touching them. She had no qualms, however, about employing the butt of her cosh, a target she perfected in the base of their wizened skeletons to cause maximum pain. She also had a second, more sinister, speciality.

It was her nose that caught the coppery taint of birth blood, and not that of the second, shadowy guard.

'You've had another one, then?'

I walked forward, as I always did. The exchange had become a game I was almost certain to lose, but it never stopped me trying.

'The baby's only been born an hour,' I lied. 'It's not long. Just a little more time. It won't interfere with the count.'

She scanned up and down the hut, the sixty or so sets of eyes upon her, Irena's normally dull gaze the whitest I had ever seen. For a second, the guard looked as if she was considering a minor reprieve. Then, she sniffed and grunted, 'You know the rules. I don't make them. It's time.' The justification for ninety per cent of the degradation in the camp was the same – it's not our fault, we're only following orders. The other ten per cent was pure enjoyment.

It was then Irena burst out of her own birth world, clutching the baby to her bare breast, springing off the bed and backing into the corner near the stove, a trickle of blood following her.

'No, no please,' she cried. 'I can do anything. I *will* do anything, anything you want.'

The guard's granite reflection told Irena her bargaining power was worthless, so she turned on herself: 'Take me instead. Take me now, but leave the baby.' Irena aimed her frenzied voice at me. 'Anke? You can care for the baby, can't you? If I'm gone?'

I nodded a yes, but in reality I couldn't; the few non-Jews allowed to keep their babies had little enough milk for their own newborns, let alone another one scraping at the breast. The infants succumbed to malnutrition in a matter of weeks, and to glimpse a baby beyond a month was unusual. I wouldn't even need to ask – not one of these desperate appeals had ever worked. We all held our breath for Irena, a scene we had witnessed too many times, but which never ceased to feel completely surreal. A mother having to beg for her baby's life.

The female guard sighed, boredom apparent. The next step was inevitable, but every mother, if they weren't immobile or nearing an unconscious state, made the same unrealistic plea. It was a mother's reflex: laying down your own life to save a new one.

'Now come on,' said the guard, moving towards Irena, 'don't make it harder. Don't make me hurt you.'

She made a grab for the cloth, and Irena backed herself further into the corner. The baby's sudden howling almost masked the crack to Irena's body, and the guard emerged from the scuffle with the cloth and tiny limbs loosely wrapped. She turned, eyes narrowing to match the thin line of her lips. The heavy boots clomped as she marched towards the door, while we immediately crowded around Irena, as a protective field; if she ran out in pursuit of the guard she would almost certainly be shot by snipers on the lookout posts. She lunged like the fiercest of grizzly bears out of the shadows, broken teeth bared, a tornado of desperation, and we caught her in our human net. The high, shrill screams would have filled the air outside, and I imagined the camp stopping for a second, knowing the deathly protocol was about to happen.

Instantly, the women started up a song, a lament, the volume rising rapidly, as the group took on a unified swaying, with Irena at its core, a shield around her suffering. It was meant as comfort, but there was another purpose – to mask the sound of the baby hitting the barrel of water, as shocking as gunfire if you've ever heard it. Rosa caught my eye, nodded and was through the door in an instant, hoping to scoop up the pitiful body after the guard tossed it aside, in time to stop the rats and the guard dogs staking their claim. A placenta was one thing, but a human body – a person. It was unthinkable.

After several moments, Irena's shrieking died away, replaced with a low moan seeping from her heart's core, a consistent braying that was beyond words. I had only ever heard such a sound during summers spent on my uncle's farm in Bavaria, when the newborn calves were taken away to market. Their bereft mothers kept up a constant, needy calling throughout the day and well into the night, searching blindly for their offspring. I would lie in bed with my hands over my ears, desperate to block out the torturous mooing. As I got older, I always asked Uncle Dieter when it was time to take the calves to market and arranged my visits to avoid them.

I cleared up as best I could, and then busied myself seeing to some of the other sick women in the hut, changing a few meagre dressings, giving them water and just holding them as they coughed uncontrollably. At those times, I thanked the automated nurse training I had been through, where doing menial tasks required little thinking. I didn't want to give any thought to, or process, what had happened that morning, and many others besides.

I stepped out twice, once for some air – the chill brought me round a little – and once to visit another hut for non-Jews, where two women had recently given birth. There was little I could do for them post-birth, as I had no equipment or drugs, but I could at least reassure them their blood loss was normal and their bodies recovering. The stronger women in their own hut did the fetching and carrying while they tried in vain to encourage milk into their breasts.

My camp classification as 'German political', a red star instead of yellow stitched onto my armband, allowed movement around the huts as a nurse and midwife, since I was happy – as in peacetime – to attend any woman, regardless of culture or creed. The majority of women I cared for would arrive already pregnant, or somehow manifest a pregnancy once imprisoned. It was especially true of Jewish women, even though none of the guards were ever called to account. Rape was simply not in the camp vocabulary. It seemed ironic that a good portion of the babies born were half Aryan, and yet sacrificed in the name of the master race.

Back in Hut 23, unofficially dubbed 'the maternity hut' by guards and inmates alike, Irena remained in her bunk by the dying fire for several hours, constantly held by one of the women in the singing circle. I checked her bleeding wasn't excessive, and she opened her eyes briefly. They were swollen, blackened sacs beneath her wide pupils, crusted and completely wrung-out. She grabbed my hand as I drew it away from her belly.

'Anke, what was the point?' she pleaded, inky pupils piercing directly into mine, collapsing back in sobs of dry distress.

I was at a loss to reply because I didn't know what she meant. The point of what? Of pregnancy, of babies, this life . . . or life in general? There was simply no answer.

2

Exit

Just the words caused me to shake visibly: 'The Commandant wants to see you.' Eyes widened amid the gloom of the hut, and all movement stopped. There was no sound, just a stale breath of fear rising above the stench of humans as animals: urine and excrement, feminine issue, and the shadow smell of birth. My hands were wet with pus, and the trooper looked at them with obvious disgust. I scouted for a cloth not yet sodden, and it took me a moment in the darkness.

'Hurry!' he said. 'Don't keep him waiting.'

At that point, my thoughts were clear: I am going to die anyway, I might as well not hasten the event. No one was called before the Commandment for a friendly afternoon chat.

Ironically, it was the icy wind whipping through the holes in my dress that stopped me shaking, my body's remaining muscles tensing to keep in whatever warmth it could. Across the barren yard, more eyes settled on me, their gazes sketching my fate, as I struggled to keep up with the goose-step pace of the trooper. 'Oh, we remember Anke,' they would later say, in the dank of their own huts. 'I remember the day she was called to the Commandant. We never saw her again.' If lucky, I might be one of many such memories, a story to be told.

The guard led me through the scrub of the sheds, and then up to the gate to the main house, shooing me inside with a gruff: 'Go, go!' I had never seen the door to the house, and slowed to marvel at the intricate carvings on the outside, of angels and nymphs, no doubt the work of Ira, the wood-carver and stonemason, who'd died of pneumonia the previous winter. His pride in his work showed through, even at the gates of the enemy, although I glimpsed a tiny gargoyle sandwiched between two roses, a clear image of Nazi evil. His little slice of sedition gave me a hint of courage as I clumped up the steps towards the door.

Inside, my cheeks burned with the sudden heat and my top lip sprouted small beads of moisture, which I licked off, enjoying the tincture of salt. In the wide, wooden-clad hallway, a fire roared in a grate, fuel stacked beside it that would have saved a dozen of the babies I had seen perish over these last months. I was neither surprised nor shocked, and I hated myself for the lack of emotion. We'd become used to rationing feelings to those that could accomplish something; rage was wasted energy, but irritation bred cunning and compromise, and saved lives.

The trooper eyed my skeletal limbs, barking at me to wait by the fire, which I took as a small token of humanity. I stood outwards, letting it burn my bony rump through the threadbare dress, feeling it quickly sear my skin and almost enjoying the near pain. The trooper rapped noisily on a dark wooden door, there was a voice from inside and I was beckoned from the fireside to walk through.

He had his back to me, hair almost white blond – an Aryan poster boy. The trooper clicked his heels like a Spanish dancer, and the head swivelled in his chair, revealing the model man Nazi; sharp cheekbones, taut and healthy, a rich diet colouring his flesh pink, like the tinted flamingos I remembered seeing at Berlin's zoo with my father. Skin tones in the rest of the camp were variations on grey.

He shuffled some papers and set his eyes on my feet. A sudden, hot shame washed over me at the obvious holes in my boots, then a swift anger at myself for even entertaining such guilt – he and his kind had engineered those holes, and the painful welts on my leathery soles. His gaze flicked upwards, ignoring the wreckage between feet and head.

'Fräulein Hoff,' he began. 'You are well?'

We might as well have been at a tea party, the way he said it, a passing comment to a maiden aunt or a pretty girl. Irritation rose again, and I couldn't bring myself to answer. Absently, he'd already gone back to his papers, and it was only the silence that caused him to look up again.

I thought: I have nothing to lose. 'You can see how well I am,' I said flatly.

Strangely, there was no rage at my dissidence, and I realised then he had a task to carry out, a distasteful but necessary chore.

'Hmm,' he said. 'You act as a camp midwife? Helping the women, *all* the women?'

He looked at me with deep disdain, at my dark looks, which naturally straddled the German and Jewish worlds.

'I do,' I said, with a note of pride.

'And you worked in the Berlin hospitals before the war? As a midwife?'

'I did.'

'Your reputation is a good one, by all accounts,' he said, reading from sheets in front of him. 'You were in charge of the labour ward, and rose to the rank of Sister.'

'I did.' I was beginning to be slightly bored by his lack of emotion; even anger was absent.

'And my staff here tell me you have never lost a baby in your care during your time here?'

'Not at birth,' I said, this time with defiance. 'Before and after is common.'

'Yes, well . . .' He skated over death as if waving away the offer of more tea or wine. 'And your family?'

This was where my pride and bloody-mindedness deserted me, falling to the level of my holey boots. A well of hurt caught deep in my throat and I swallowed it like hot coals.

'I have a mother, father, sister and brother, possibly in the camps,' I managed. 'They may be dead.'

'Well, I have some news of them,' he said, accent shorn and clipped. 'You come from a good German family by all accounts – but your father, he is not a supporter of the war, as you know, and your brother neither. They are, of course, in our care, and alive. They know of your status too.' His eyes tacked briefly upwards to assess my reaction. When there was none, he turned back.

'You should know this because of the proposal I am about to put to you.' His tone suggested he was offering me a bank

16

loan, rather than my life. At that moment, I pondered on whether he hugged his mother when they met, kissed her with meaning, had sobbed on her like a baby. Or had he been born a callous bastard? I speculated whether war had made him like this, a vacuum in uniform. I was amusing myself nicely, my bones finally warming from his own fiery grate. I might die feeling warmth, and not with blue, icy blood limping through my veins. I would bleed well all over his nice, scrubbed floor, and cause him some grief, more than mere inconvenience. I hoped his boots would slip and slide on my ruby issue, a stain sinking into the leather, forever present.

'Fräulein?' It wasn't the urgency in his voice that roused me, but a single gunshot out in the yard, a crack slicing through the quiet of his office. One of several heard every day. He didn't flinch. 'Fräulein, did you hear me?'

'Yes.'

'You have been summoned, by the highest authority – the Führer's office, no less.' I expected a little trumpet fanfare to follow, the statement coated with such a gilded edge. 'They have need of your services.'

I said nothing, unsure how to react.

'You will leave in one hour,' he said, as a sign of dismissal.

'And if I don't want to go?' It was out of my mouth before I realised, as if something other than me had formed the words.

Now he was visibly annoyed, probably at his inability to shoot me, there and then in cold blood. As he had done many times before, so his reputation told us. The mere mention of the Führer's office signalled I wouldn't die here, not today, if I agreed to go. The Commandant's jaw set, the cheekbones rigid like a rock face, eyes a steel grey.

17

'Then I can't guarantee your family's safety or outcome in the present troubles.'

So that was it. I would attend Nazi women and help give life, in exchange for avoiding a final death for my own family. There was nothing veiled in his meaning – we all knew where we stood.

'And the women here?' I said, ignoring his dismissal. 'Who will see to them?'

'They will manage,' he said into his papers. 'One hour, Fräulein. I advise you to be ready.'

My body was immune to the wind chill again as I was marched back to Hut 23. Strangely, I felt nothing physical, not even the reprieve of emerging from the main house alive. My mind, instead, was churning – of the things I needed to pass on to Rosa, just eighteen, but to date my most competent helper. Rosa had been with me at almost every camp birth in the past nine months, soothing when needed, holding hands, cleaning debris and mopping tears when the babies were plucked from their mothers, as they so often were.

No Jewish baby made it past twenty-four hours of birth at their mother's side. The non-Jews were sometimes permitted to nurse their babes until the inevitable malnutrition or hypothermia took hold, but at least their mothers had closure. The Jewesses clutched only an empty void, their rhythmic sobs joining the whistling wind as it ripped through the sheds. Only one Jewish mother and baby had been ghosted out of the camp overnight, on the orders of a high-ranking officer, we suspected. We were divided on whether her fate was good or bad.

In the hut, the women greeted me with relief, then sorrow at my leaving. I had no belongings to pack, so that precious hour was spent in a breathless rundown with Rosa of the checks needing to be made, where our meagre stash of supplies was hidden. In sixty all too brief minutes, I did my best to pass on the experience I had learnt over nine years as a midwife: when shoulders were stuck, compresses on vaginal tears, if a bottom came first instead of the head, action to stop a woman bleeding out, sticky placentas. I couldn't think or talk fast enough to include it all. Luckily Rosa was a fast learner. The normal cases she had seen many a time, and we'd had few abnormal ones too. I took her face in my hands, parched skin stretched around her large, brown eyes.

'When you make it out of here, then you must promise me one thing,' I told her. 'Do your training, be a midwife, at least witness the good side of mothers and babies together. You're a natural, Rosa. Make it through, and make a life for yourself.'

She nodded silently. Her pupils were sprouting tears now, genuine I knew, because none of us wasted precious fluid unless it drew hard on our hearts. It was the best farewell she could have given me.

A hammering on the shoddy door signalled the hour was up, and I had no time to return to my own hut. It would be empty anyway, Graunia and Kirsten – my human lifelines – on work detail. With no time allowed to seek them out, Rosa was charged with passing on my love and goodbyes. I hugged several on my way out, eyes down to disguise my own distress. I was getting out, but to what? A fate potentially worse than the ugliness of the camp. I couldn't begin to contemplate what depth of my soul I might be expected to plunder.

A large black car was waiting, the type only Nazi officials travelled in, with a driver and a young sergeant to accompany me. The sergeant sat poker-faced, in the opposite corner on the back seat, his distaste at my physical and moral stench apparent, as a German with no allegiance to the Fatherland. Reluctantly, he pushed a blanket towards me. I hunkered into the soft leather, warmed by the luxury of real wool against my skin and the rolling engine, closing my eyes and falling into a deep – though uneasy – sleep.

Berlin, August 1939

They called us in one by one, plucked from our duties on the labour ward, into Matron's office. She stood, impassive, while a man in a black suit sat behind her desk, looking very comfortable. By my turn, he must have read out the same directive enough times to know it by heart, and he barely looked at the paper in front of him.

'Sister Hoff,' he began, in a monotone, 'you know how much the Reich values and appreciates your profession as gatekeepers of our future population.'

I looked solidly ahead.

'Which is why we are so reliant on you and your colleagues to help us in maintaining the goal that we have, the goal of purity for the German nation.'

I'd been forced to sit through enough lectures on racial purity to know exactly what he meant, however much the language shrouded the obvious. The Nuremberg Laws had made marriage

21

illegal between Jews and Aryans for several years and we'd seen a real decline in 'mixed' newborns in the hospital. Now that Jews were excluded from the welfare system, we barely came into contact with Jewish mothers any more, unless they were both rich and brave.

He went on. 'Sister, I am here to share news of a new directive that will now become part of your existing role, effective immediately. We require that you report to us – via your superiors – all children either born, or that you come into contact with, where disability of any nature is suspected.' Here he looked down at his list.

'These conditions include: idiocy, mongolism, hydrocephaly, microcephaly, limb malformation—' he took a bored breath '—paralysis and spastic condition, blindness and deafness. This list is, of course, not exhaustive, but acts as a guide only. We rely on your knowledge and discretion.'

Speech over, he looked at me directly. I continued staring somewhere between his temple and his oiled hairline while his eyes crawled over my face. I hoped beyond anything he wouldn't ask me for a decision.

'Do you understand that this is a directive, and not a request, Sister?' he said.

'I do.' In that, I could be honest.

'Then I am relying on your professionalism in working towards a Greater Germany. The Führer himself recognises your vital role in this task, and ensures your . . . protection in law.' He weighted the last words purposefully, and then continued lightly. 'However, we do understand it is a drain on your time and knowledge, and there will be an appreciation payment of two Reich marks for every case reported, payable by the hospital.' He smiled dutifully, at the generosity of such an offer, and to signal we were finished.

I wanted to howl inside, to take my too-short nails and gouge them deep into his tiny eyes set in too much flesh, made pinker and fatter by numerous trips to the bierkeller – sitting alongside his Nazi cronies, quaffing beer and laughing about 'filthy scum Jews'. I wanted to hurt him, for presuming we were all as dirty and disgusting – as inhuman – as he had become. But I said and did nothing, just like Papa had told me. 'Anke, there is diversity in defiance,' my wise father advised. 'Be clever in your deceit.'

The Nazi shuffled his papers and I saw Matron's skirts shift from the corner of my eye. I knew her thoughts. 'Keep calm, Anke, and, above all, keep quiet,' she would be willing me.

'Thank you, Sister Hoff,' she said smartly, and piloted me swiftly out.

I went back to the ward – in my short absence, a woman's fourth labour had progressed rapidly, and within the hour she was cradling her newest child, counting her fingers and toes and completely unaware that the efficient Reich would readily sacrifice her beautiful daughter if one such finger or toe were out of place. There was no mention of what would happen after we – as dutiful citizens – reported any disability, but it wasn't a great stretch of the mind to foresee. I had no doubt it was not to build and provide excellent care facilities for such 'unfortunates'. But in guessing their fate? I really didn't want to delve too far into my own imagination. The increasing numbers of Hitler's Brownshirts on the streets, and their open violence towards Jews, told us the boundaries were already breached. It was simple enough: to the Reich, there were no limits. No one – man, woman or child – was safe.

Every midwife, nurse and doctor had been spoken to, creating a strange conspiracy of silence. People were polite to each other – too polite – as if we already weeding out the dissidents, the non-committals among us. The labour ward was steady, but each birth brought a new question. Where once it was: 'Boy or girl? How much do they weigh?' now it was: 'Everything all right?' We were playing Russian roulette with an unknown number of chambers in the barrel – and no one wanted to be the first.

I thought back to a birth I'd attended a few years before, at the home of a Slovakian couple. The labour had been unusually long for a second baby, and the pushing stage exhausting. As I watched the baby's head come through, the reason became obvious – a larger than average crown, which pulled on every ounce of the woman's anatomy and spirit to birth. With the baby girl finally in her mother's arms, we all saw why: a disproportionately swollen head, with eyes bulging from a heavy-set brow, one eye ghostly and opaque, unseeing, the other eye turned inwards, likely blind as well. The body was scrawny by comparison, as if the head had swallowed all the energy the mother had poured into the pregnancy. And all she said was: 'Isn't she lovely?' The grandmother, too, cooing over the new life, content with what God had given them.

Beauty was never fixed so firmly in the eye of the beholder, as in that birth. I could only guess the mother might have shed private tears about the lost future of her beautiful daughter, or speculate about how long the baby survived. But I was even more certain that all babies are precious to someone, that we did not have the right to play judge, jury or God. Ever. I resolved firmly I would not be complicit. In the event it happened, I would find a way – I just didn't know how.

Just one month later, Germany was at war with Europe, and the fabric of a whole nation was swiftly put to the test.

3

The Outside

A distinct chill in the air woke me. It was dark, and we were still travelling – the big engine purring steadily, a few lights sprinkled along the way, houses only just lit. I was disorientated, having no idea which direction we had come in, but I guessed we were in the mountains and climbing gently. The air felt different – a crystal edge, a taste recalled from family holidays.

I was surprised. I had assumed we would be in Berlin, Munich, or some other industrial town, headed for a private maternity home, where the wives of Nazi officials and loyal businessmen would be doing their duty – the women of Germany having been charged with procreating the next generation as their 'military service'. Before I'd been evicted, posters had projected from every street corner in Berlin, recruiting to the ranks – blonde, smiling women with caring arms splayed around their strong, Aryan brood, ready to serve the Reich as rich fodder for the ranks. It was their duty, and they didn't question it. Or did they? You would never know, since loyal German women didn't speak out.

The sergeant startled as I moved, squaring his shoulders automatically. He spoke into the air. 'We will be arriving soon, Fräulein. You should be ready.'

I was sitting in my only rags and had nothing to gather, but I nodded all the same. In minutes, we swept left through wrought-iron gates, rolling steadily up a long drive, icy gravel crunching underneath. At the top was a large chalet house, the porch lit by a glow from inside. The style was distinctly German, though in no way rustic, with carved columns supporting the large wraparound veranda, wooden chairs and small tables arranged to take advantage of the mountain view.

For a brief moment I thought we had arrived at a Lebensborn, Heinrich Himmler's thinly veiled breeding centres for his utopian racial dream, and that my task was to safeguard the lives of Aryan babies, from appointed carrier women or the wives of SS officers. But this looked like someone's home, albeit large and grand. I mused on what type of Nazi spouse would live here, how important she was to have caught the attention of the Führer's office and the promise of a private midwife.

The imposing wooden door opened as we drew to a stop, and a woman appeared. She was neither pregnant, nor the lady of the house, since she was dressed like a maid in a colourful bodice and dirndl. I stumbled slightly on getting out, legs numbed from the extreme comfort. The maid came down the steps, smiled broadly, and put out her hand. Her white breath hit the chill air, but her welcome was warm. This day was becoming ever more bizarre.

'Welcome Fräulein,' she said, in a thick Bavarian tone. 'Please come in.'

★　★　★

She led me into an opulent hallway, ornate lamps highlighting the gilded pictures, Hitler in pride of place above the glowing fireplace; I had seen more welcoming fires today than in all my time in camp. I followed puppy-like through a door off the hallway, and we descended into what was clearly the servants' quarters. Several heads turned as I came into a roomy parlour, eyes dressing me down as the maid led me through a corridor and finally to a small bedroom.

'There,' she said. 'You'll sleep here tonight before you see the mistress in the morning.'

I was struck dumb, a child faced with a magical birthday cake. The bed had a real mattress and bedspread, with a folded fresh nightdress on the plump pillow. A hairbrush sat on top of a sideboard, alongside a bar of soap and a clean towel. It was the stuff of dreams.

The maid prompted me again. 'The mistress said to give you—' she stopped, correcting herself '—to *offer* you a bath before you have some supper. Would that suit Fräulein?'

Quite how they had explained away my dishevelment was a mystery – my dark hair had grown back and my teeth were intact but I looked far from healthy. This maid was either ignorant of my origins, or at least disguised it well.

'Yes, yes,' I managed. 'Thank you.'

She disappeared down the corridor, and the sound of running water hit my ears. Hot water! From taps! In the camp it had been scarce, cold and pumped from a dirty well. I couldn't take my eyes off the tablet of soap, as if it were manna from heaven and I might bite into it at any moment, like Alice in her Wonderland.

I sat gingerly on the bed, feeling my bones sink into the soft material, never imagining that I would spend a night again under clean sheets. The maid – she said her name was Christa – led me to the bathroom, shutting the door and allowing me the first true solitude in two years. Despite the sounds of the house around, it was an eerie silence, the space around me edging in, claustrophobic. There was no one coughing into my own air, sucking on my own breath, no Graunia shifting her bones into the crevice of my missing flesh. I was alone. I wasn't sure if I liked it.

I peeled off my thin dress, my underclothes almost disintegrating as they dropped to the floor. Steam curled in rings above the water, and I dipped in a toe, almost afraid to enter the water, in case a real sensation would pop this intricate dream.

Sinking under the delicious warmth, I wasted precious salt tears, when there was already water aplenty. When you saw so much horror, destruction and inhumanity in one place, it was the simplest things that broke your resolve and reminded you of kindness in the world. A warm bath was part of my childhood, but especially when I was thick with a cold, or racked with a cough. Mama would run the bath for me, sit talking and singing while she washed my hair, wrapping me in a soft towel before putting me to bed with a hot, soothing drink. I tried so hard not to think of them all, as I wallowed in the strangeness, but I hoped beyond everything they weren't in the hell I'd just left behind. Heavy sobs shook my wasted muscles, until I was dry inside.

Tears exhausted, I surveyed my body for the first time in an age; there were no mirrors in the camp, and the cold meant we barely undressed. The very sight shook me. I counted my ribs under parchment flesh and saw that the arm muscles developed through hospital work were now flaccid and wasted, my hipbones projecting through my skin. Where I had disappeared to? Where had the old Anke gone? It took a good scrub with that glorious bar of soap to cut through the layers of grime, and the water was grey as I stepped out, tiny black corpses of varying insects lying on the leftover scum. Christa had laid out a light dressing gown for me, and I purposely avoided any glimpse in the mirror. Tentatively, I padded back down the corridor in my bare but clean feet.

In the room, more treasures awaited. Clean underwear was draped over the chair, along with a skirt, stockings and a sweater. There was an undervest but no bra, though I had nothing to keep in check any more, with almost the look of a pubescent teenager on a prematurely aged body. Within minutes, Christa arrived with a plate of glazed meat, potatoes and carrots the colour of a late afternoon sun glowing along-side. Hunger was a constant gripe, and I hadn't noticed not eating throughout the day.

'I'll leave you in peace,' she said, with a sweet, natural smile. 'I'll bring in breakfast in the morning, and Madam will see you after that.'

My instinct was to go at that plate like a gannet, gorging on the precious calories, but I knew enough of my starved insides to guess that, if I wanted to retain it and not retch it up instantly, I needed to tread carefully. I chewed and savoured each morsel, quickly feeling the stretch inside me. Once or twice, my throat gagged uncontrollably at the richness, and I breathed deeply, desperate to swallow it down. The meat, softly stewed, brought back memories from before the war, of my mother's birthday meals – beef with

German ale. Guiltily, though, I had to leave a third of the portion. With nothing else to occupy me, I laid my wet hair on the sumptuous pillow, drinking in the laundry soap smell, and fell into an immediate sleep.

Light from a small window above the bed signalled daytime, and I moved my shoulder slowly, as I had done every day in previous months. My wooden bed rack had caused painful sores on my shoulders, and getting up demanded restraint to avoid opening up the skin and inviting infection. Only when I felt my skin sunk into soft cotton did I remember where I was. Even then it took several moments to convince my waking brain that I wasn't lost in a fantasy.

The noise of a house in full motion crept through the walls and I tiptoed to the bathroom, feeling the inevitable grapple inside me between starvation and distension. Christa was heading into my room as I arrived back, wearing a slightly startled look, as if she had lost me momentarily. As if I could escape.

'Morning, Fräulein,' she said, addressing me like a true guest. I had warmed to her already, mainly for treating me like a human being, and because she had brought me more food. Her flaxen hair was pulled tight into a bun, making her high cheekbones rise and her green eyes sparkle.

'I'm sorry, I couldn't quite finish the dinner,' I said, as she eyed the leftovers. 'I'm not so use—'

'Of course,' she said with a smile. The staff clearly had their suspicions, whatever they had been told. It took me a good while to absorb the eggs and bread on my plate, yolks the colour of the giant sunflowers swaying in my mother's garden. Memories, carefully kept in check while at the camp, were swimming back. I forced the protein into my already overloaded system and Christa was at the door as I pushed in the last mouthful.

She led me upstairs to a large lounge, skirted on three sides by wide picture windows, a view of the forest in one, mountains in the opposite. It was roomy enough for several leather sofas in an austere German design, with sideboards of dark wood and ugly, showy trinkets. The inevitable portrait of the Führer loomed over the huge fireplace, which provided a gentle lick rather than a roar.

A woman was sitting in one of the bulky armchairs and stood as I arrived. Tall, slim and elegant, her blonde hair swept in a wave, clear blue eyes, and a pout of ruby red lipstick. Groomed and very German. Not obviously pregnant either.

'Fräulein Hoff, welcome to my house.' There was only a hint of a smile; from the very outset this was clearly an arrangement, and not one she was overly happy with either.

'My name is Magda Goebbels, and I have been asked by a very good friend to find someone with your knowledge to help her.'

At the mere mention of her name, I realised why I had been treated so well. Frau Goebbels was the epitome of German womanhood, married to the Minister for Propaganda and mother to seven perfect Aryan specimens – an obvious model for those zealous posters. Since the Führer had no wife, she was often at his side in the newsreels and pictures, in the time before I was taken. She was the perfect Nazi, albeit a woman, tagged 'Germany's First Lady' by the columnists.

She went on matter-of-factly. 'I know of your reputation, your working knowledge, and your . . . situation.' I noted there was always a pause when the threat to my family was mentioned. Was it shame, or a minor embarrassment? For people so unashamed about the cruelty they inflicted, Nazis appeared almost shy about calling it blackmail.

She carried on, unabashed: 'I know that since your work has been so varied, you clearly care deeply for women and babies in any situation. I can only trust that you will do the same for my friend who has need.' She paused, inviting a reply.

'I will always endeavour to bring the best outcome for any woman,' I said, leaving my own, deliberate pause. 'Whoever they are.' I did, in essence, mean it. The rules of my training as a midwife didn't discriminate between rich or poor, good or bad, criminal or good citizen; all babies were born equal at that split second and all deserved the chance of life. It was the moments, months and years afterwards that fractured them into an unequal world.

She caught my meaning, clasping her hands in front of her, nails perfectly manicured.

'Good. You will spend today getting prepared, and then travel to meet your new client tomorrow.' She said the word 'client' as if I was a private professional about to take on a task of my choosing. I wondered then how much, and how deeply, they felt the lies. Or if they really believed their own propaganda? *Truly* believed it?

I said nothing, refusing to qualify her offer even with a 'thank you'. She wouldn't let it go.

'You should be clear that this is a good opportunity for you, Fräulein Hoff. Not many would be trusted with such an important task. We feel you will be a midwife first, what-ever your own politics.'

They were taking a gamble, but they were probably right. I was no angel in life, but I took my duties seriously. Mothers were pregnant to have healthy babies, and babies were meant to survive, for the most part. That was the golden rule.

I turned to go, seeing a shape ghost past the doorway.

'Joseph?' she called from behind me. 'Joseph, come and meet the midwife we have engaged.'

A small, dark-suited man clipped towards me with a slight limp, stopped and pulled his heels together in that automated way. This was no Aryan, but his face was often in the papers my father had pored over in the days before we became the disappeared. Joseph Goebbels – one of Hitler's trusted inner circle, master of the truth twist, gilding lies and hoodwinking good, honest Germans. Wasn't it Goebbels who had declared: 'The mission of women is to be beautiful and to bring children into the world'? I remember my sister, Ilse, and I laughing at the words, but now that I looked at his wife, I understood why he imagined it possible.

'Fräulein Hoff, pleased to meet you.' He gave that half smile Third Reich officers clearly practised in training, designed to err on the edge of threat, his little spiny teeth just visible. He was rakishly thin, dark hair slicked back, cheeks sunken; if Himmler – Hitler's right-hand man – was painted as the rat in the Reich's higher circle, then Joseph Goebbels was the perfect weasel. For his wife, the attraction must have been more than skin deep. I felt an immediate shiver that he even knew my name.

He faced his wife. 'The arrangements, they are all in order?'

'Yes, Joseph,' she replied with clear irritation.

33

'Then I bid you good day. I hope you are well looked after, Fräulein Hoff.'

He walked out, his wife's red lips thin and her gaze fixed on his back. She may have been beautiful and a copious breeder, but I had the feeling Frau Goebbels was more than a pretty face.

The interview over, Christa appeared in the doorway to lower me back to the servants' quarters. The 'getting ready' consisted of making me presentable for my mystery client, something of a task in just one day. Christa was sent with carbolic, tackling the lice eggs embedded on the shafts of my thin hair. She worked cheerfully, talking affectionately about her family near Cologne, and although she skated over the hardships of war, it was evident that real, working German families were suffering too. Her brother was already a casualty, blinded and returned from the Eastern Front, leaving her father struggling on the family farm without a younger man's muscle. She hinted only briefly at his disdain for the Reich.

She had been a nursing auxiliary before the conflict, in a home for elderly women. Part of the care, said Christa, was in teasing their thinning locks into something of a style, far better than any medicine. After the last of the lice were evicted from my own head, she worked miracles with her scissors and the hot iron, appearing to double the volume of my weakened strands, skilfully hiding my scabbed scalp. I barely recognised myself in the mirror, having not glimpsed my own face for what seemed like years. I had aged notice-ably – lines around my eyes, gaunt cheeks, and tiny red veins pushing out in patches on my skull bones – but Christa's efforts lessened the shock. Much like my body below, I chose not to dwell on the reflection.

Christa brought several suits and skirts, plain and practical, gleaned from the wardrobes of previous governesses or house managers; I mused only briefly on how many had left under a cloud of death. In the camp, we scavenged greedily on the corpses for useful clothes without a second thought. 'The dead don't shiver,' we said, as justification for our guilt. It was accepted as survival. So that now, I didn't flinch as I pulled on rough stockings, which morphed into silk, and buttoned a blouse that wouldn't cause my skin to itch with renewed insect-life. They hung on me loosely, but Christa nipped and tucked, spiriting the clothes away and returning them within hours for a neater fit.

Towards the end of the day, an unexpected visitor appeared at my door. Christa noted me tensing at the sight of his small black carrying case, balding head and thick glasses. She spoke quickly, as if to reassure me he wasn't a caricature of Dr Death: 'Fräulein Hoff, this is Dr Simz. Madam has asked that he attend you before your trip tomorrow.'

Dr Simz had a dual role of both physician and dentist, checking over my body from top to toe, giving me balm for the most obvious of skin sores, pronouncing my lungs 'a little wheezy' but not infected, and my teeth in surprisingly good condition. He didn't balk at the sight of my ribcage or sorry breasts, working methodically to check I was no threat to my proposed client. His positive mutterings told me I was ready. I would do.

I slept uneasily that night, despite the sumptuous bedding. I thought of Rosa, cold and vulnerable, of all the women in the maternity hut, my own hut too, and of Margot, eight months into pregnancy, barely recognisable as a mother-to-be. Her bulge was tiny, but it had sucked every particle of nutrition from her needy body nevertheless. On the day, she would be stripped of energy and life and baby in one fell swoop, and Rosa left to deal with the physical debris, as well as Margot's deep, vacuous keening, rising above the hut as she grieved the life and loss of her baby. And here I was, sleeping in near luxury. 'Unfair' didn't begin to describe the lottery by which we lived, died, or merely existed.

I took my last meal in that house with Christa, who had been almost my only real contact since arriving. In such a short time, we had struck up a small friendship; I recognised in her some spirit that was here simply to live, for her family, and yet she revealed in those young, green eyes that she wasn't one of them. It was survival, of a different kind to my own, but survival nonetheless. Maybe there were more of us than we imagined, just doing our best.

But was it enough? Was it right?

4

Climbing

The large saloon engine gave off clouds in the crisp air as Christa waved me goodbye. 'Be careful,' she said, giving my hand a meaningful squeeze. 'Look out for me – I'm sometimes sent up to the big house on errands.'

'I will, and thank you, Christa. Thank you so much.' I was genuinely sad to leave her, feeling we might have been better friends given time. We drove about a mile past large, lodge-style houses before the road started upwards, banked on either side by tall evergreens, climbing higher and higher up a stone coil of good road. The air changed, a tinge of blue clarity even inside the car, and it began to feel very mountainous. We passed through several checkpoints, and I had a distinct feeling that I would not be descending for some time to come.

After a quarter of an hour of slow climb, the car's engines beginning to grumble like a troublesome uncle, the trees fanned out and the view became clear – we were, it seemed, scaling a virtual mountain. Even with a light mist, it was spectacular, a feathery white collar to the rock mass, giving way below to a chequerboard of farmland, only dotted here and there with small clumps of dwellings. Like a child, I pressed my nose to the window – if we climbed any higher I felt we might be like Jack ascending the beanstalk, slipping through candy clouds.

In minutes, the top came into view, a concrete lip that looked as if it were teetering over the side of the granite peak, like the tree house my father had built in our garden, fun but always slightly tenuous. Just as I thought the road couldn't get any steeper, it suddenly evened out and became a flat plain, and we drove through guarded black gates and onto a wide path. The view from below had been misleading; the mountain had a flattened area – by man or nature I couldn't easily tell – and the house complex was large and sprawling, set into the side of the natural rock and not at the peak, as it first appeared. The main house was a mix of old stone and wood, chalet-style, two storeys but with an iceberg promise of more below. It was a tiny village on top of the world, small gardens and wide balconies surrounding the main house, with outbuildings here and there. Uniformed soldiers were dotted at various points, knights at the ready.

I was led upstairs onto the wide porch, breathing in air so dramatically different from the camp smog that I thought I must be on a different planet, my lungs wheezing on the purity. The light up here made me think there was life, after all; in all those dark days, this world had existed in parallel, outside of hell. It was almost too much to comprehend.

The door opened to a woman's harsh, thin face, topped with a jet black cap of hair, bearing a reluctant smile.

'Welcome Fräulein Hoff,' she said. 'I am Frau Grunders, the housekeeper.' This last statement was said with reverence, but I managed only a 'Hello' and 'Thank you.' Her prickly greeting mirrored the cacti and spiked greenery dotted in the hallway, set in rows of colourful, ceramic pots. She bristled as her ebony, austere shoes clipped on the wooden flooring, leading me through a high, vaulted hallway, and down to the servants' quarters. I was shown into a small parlour, which could have been called either cluttered or cosy.

'Please take a seat and wait here,' she said, and closed the door.

Minutes later an officer in grey SS uniform entered, stooping through the doorway to avoid his lofty height making contact with the gable.

'Morning Fräulein, I am Captain Stenz.' He clicked his heels and sat awkwardly, although his face was open. 'I will be your official contact here. My information is that you have been told only a little of your duties.' A deep well of blue irises looked at me directly.

'I have, Captain, yes. I was only told that my skills as a midwife would be needed.'

He paused, eyes scanning the floor, as if revealing any more was physically painful. Silently, he peeled off black leather gloves, finger by finger.

'The situation is delicate,' he said finally. 'We are relying not only on your practical skills but on your professional confidentiality . . . and integrity.'

I only nodded, eager for him to go on.

'There is a lady residing in this house who is currently pregnant – four to five months we believe. For a number of reasons she cannot attend a hospital for care. She will be your sole charge.'

'Am I allowed to know her name, if I am to be her constant carer?'

He sighed at the inevitability of opening a secret but dangerous box, and placed his leather gloves on the small table between us, as if he were really laying down a gauntlet.

5

New Beginning

'Her name is Fräulein Eva Braun.' With those words Captain Stenz sat back in his chair, aware that a volatile cat had been let out of the bag. I had never been a follower of the magazine gossip columns but my younger sister, Ilse, keenly crawled over the fashion pages, following the rounds of Berlin's social parties. 'Look at this, Anke,' she'd often say. 'Don't you think she's just *gorgeous*? Shall I have my hair like that?' Thanks to Ilse, I had heard Eva Braun's name – as the sister to one of Hitler's inner circle, a wholesome German girl, from a good family, blonde and blue-eyed, someone Hitler could and would be associated with. It was never stated that they were close, or even romantically involved – the Führer was married to Germany, after all. In the propaganda newsreels engineered to show his human side – the Führer 'at play' – she was sometimes in the background, filming with a camera, alongside her sister, Gretl.

Now, my mind spiralled. Up until then, I thought I had been engaged to look after the wife of a Nazi dignitary, or even the illegitimate child of the Reich's inner circle. But now, something far more sinister ran like electricity through my brain, so incredible it seemed beyond reason.

Could it be that Adolf Hitler, the Führer, the Commander of the Third Reich, and possibly all of Europe, in time, was the father of Eva Braun's baby? And what would that mean to his standing as the Father of Germany – to be shared with a population who he claimed as his children? To those of us who had experienced Hitler's version of cleansing, who had witnessed first-hand what he was capable of inflicting on human beings, any offspring with a semblance of his thinking was a frightening prospect. A son and heir to both name and genetics was too much to fathom.

I struggled to react, to absorb such news. Captain Stenz only looked at me with those deep blue eyes, as seconds ticked slowly by. Searching, enquiring.

'Fräulein Hoff?'

'Yes?'

'Are you quite well?' He said it with a note of true concern, and then a hint of a smile. 'We can't have you falling ill, not on your first day, can we?'

'No, no,' I said. 'It's just . . . the change of circumstance, so quickly. It's hard to take in.'

I wanted to test his reactions by referring to my other life, to see if he masked them in the same automatic way as the others, empathy sucked from his psyche. His eyes dropped, and he moved to pick up his gloves.

'Yes,' he said flatly. So, a complete Nazi – one of them. Inevitable. But then, the quickest flick of his blond lashes towards me, a rich, blue spark. In that second I caught some doubt, some recognition. And he caught me catching it. Over the past two years I had barely looked at any man without feeling hatred or disgust, since most were guards infected with a profound disdain for humanity. Yet the man before me caused an unexpected reaction deep inside; a tweak low into my being. Did I recognise it as attraction? I rebuked myself for such shallow and immediate feelings.

He needed to leave soon – a car was waiting – so we covered my duties swiftly. I would remain at the Berghof for the duration of the pregnancy, and for at least four to six weeks afterwards, helping my charge to adjust to motherhood. The baby would be born at home, but transport and a doctor would be available at all times should I need them, and would reside in the complex for a month or so before the birth. A small room would be set aside for anaesthetics, ready to be transformed into an operating theatre if necessary.

It was elaborate and excessive, and clearly they were keen to avoid a trip to the hospital, however private, at all costs – the true nature of the Reich's propaganda machine was laid bare. Appearances were a good portion of this war, and I was to be known as a companion to all but the inner circle. This baby must remain hidden until it was prudent to reveal to the world, under the Führer's terms. I almost felt sorry for Eva Braun already.

'I have arranged all the equipment necessary,' Captain Stenz went on, in officer-speak. 'Should you need anything else, please contact my office. While I am absent, you can refer to my under-secretary, Sergeant Meier. He will see to your day-to-day needs, and report to me directly. We expect you to keep regular and detailed notes of all care.'

'I understand,' I said. All too well. I would be reported

on, scrutinised under a microscope, from now until the birth. Charged with bringing a live Aryan specimen into the world. *The* Aryan. The responsibility of life had never fazed me, in all my years working with mothers and babies, but this life . . . this poor, unsuspecting child might prove to be something different. No less, no more precious than any I'd seen, but with the potential to create unrelenting shock waves throughout Europe and the world. Throughout history. I almost craved to be back in the camps, among my own kind, where I could make a difference, save lives, instead of merely pandering to rich Nazi handmaidens. Then, hot with shame at even wishing such degradation on any living being, even myself, I reminded myself I'd been lucky to walk out.

The abrupt heels of Captain Stenz brought me back.

'I will say good day then, Fräulein,' he said, bowing his head briefly, then adding, 'Um, Fräulein Braun, she knows nothing of your . . .'

'History?' I helped him.

'Yes – history,' he said with a mixture of embarrassment and relief, a slight curl to his lip.

He was one, I decided then, who had coveted his mother, climbed on her lap for bedtime hugs and kisses, been real, individual, accepted and returned love. I looked into his turquoise eyes and wondered what the Reich had done to him.

6

Adjustment

After the Captain left, I was alone for some time among the clutter of the housekeeper's personal world, the room obviously doubling as her office and private sitting room, the obligatory Führer icon placed altar-like above an unlit fireplace. My stomach growled noisily, having soon become accustomed to food again, and I realised it was nearing lunchtime. I waited, since no one had issued any other instruction, and I realised how quickly I had fallen into a servile role. In the camp, it had become second nature to obey the guards as the basic rule of survival, but then to find methods of defiance in between our 'yes, sir; no, sir' reactions. We, none of us, ever thought of ourselves as second-class citizens, merely captives of the weapons wielded against us. Each and every day it was a fight to remind ourselves of it, but we saw it as vital, a way to avoid sinking into the mire.

Eventually, Frau Grunders entered, bringing a tray of bread, cheese and meats with her, a small glass of beer on the side.

I hadn't seen or tasted ale in over two years, and the rays of midday light created a globe of nectar in her hands. I could hardly concentrate for wanting my lips to touch the chalice and breathe in the heady hops. I had never been a connoisseur of beer, but my father would have a glass at night while listening to the wireless, and he'd let me have a sip every evening as a child, to make me 'grow big and strong'. *He* was that smell, was in that glass, ready and waiting.

The housekeeper crackled as she moved, irritation sparking from her thin limbs and her crown of plaited hair as she put the tray to one side. Her mouse-like features set in a wrinkle before she spoke.

'You will reside in one of the small annexes next to the main house,' she began, indicating I was neither servant nor equal. 'Unless Fräulein Braun requests that you be nearer, in which case we can arrange a cot in her room. Your meals will be in the servants' dining room, unless Fräulein Braun wishes you to eat with her. If you need anything else, please come to me.'

I was unperturbed by her attempt at ranking; servant or not, it was about staying alive, and maintaining my own personal measure of dignity. Still, I understood that for Frau Grunders, her own self-respect lay in creating order in this strange little planet on the crest of the world, a tidy top to the chaos. With one beady eye on that beer glass, I had no reaction except a 'Thank you,' and she turned to leave.

'Fräulein Braun will see you for tea at three o'clock in the drawing room,' she said on parting. The beer was the nectar it promised to be, sweet and bitter in unison, and I choked pitifully on the third mouthful, partly through greed, but largely because I couldn't stop the tears cascading down my cheeks, or fighting their way noisily up and through my throat.

In the camp, I had resisted dwelling on the horrors my family might be facing: whether my father's asthma was slowly killing him; whether my mother's arthritis had become crippling in the cold; if Franz had been shot as he stood, for that flash of dissidence his hot temper was capable of; if Ilse's innocence was making her a target for the hungry guards. Now, amid the quiet, the comfort, the relative normality of where I sat, it cascaded from me, sobbing for the life that I, and the world, would never have again.

I felt dry as I forced down some of the bread and cheese, still not cured of camp conditioning that dictated where there was food, it must be eaten, right then and there. I gazed longingly at Frau Grunders' bookshelves for a time, unable to move with a stretched belly and a wave of overwhelming fatigue. I yearned to finger the pages of some other world, a historical drama perhaps, to take me out of where I was. But the next thing I knew there was a gentle knocking on the door, and I opened my eyes to a young maid in her full skirt and pinafore of red and green, telling me it was past two o'clock, and enquiring whether I wanted to go to my room before meeting Fräulein Braun.

We moved on the same level from Frau Grunders' room, through a servants' parlour, out of a side door and onto a short gravel incline, bringing us to a small row of three wooden chalets, built on a slope so that they looked up towards the top of the house on one side, and down towards a sloping garden on the other. Mine was the middle door, with a tiny porch and patio, just big enough for a small table and chair outside the window. It was like a tiny holiday home, a place to relish freedom and the view.

The clothes Christa had adjusted were laid out on the bed; a toiletry set, fresh stockings and underwear on the drawers opposite. Next door, in the small bathroom, soap, shampoo and fresh towels were set neatly. Also laid out was a working midwife's kit – a wooden, trumpet-like Pinard to listen to a baby's heartbeat, a blood pressure monitor, a stethoscope, and a urine testing kit. All brand new. Guilt ran through me like lightning. What else was I expected to sacrifice for this luxury? Not just my skills, surely? Over the last two years I had faced my demons over death; I had strived to avoid it with any careless slips, but resigned, in a way, to its inevitability in all this fury. My biggest fear was in being made to choose, trading something of myself for my own beating heart, of living without soul.

In the camp, it was an easy black and white decision. It was them and us, and when favours were exchanged it was for life and death. It wasn't unheard of for the fitter women to barter their bodies with the guards in exchange for food to keep their children or each other alive; an acceptable contract since we already felt detached from our sexuality – it was simply functioning anatomy. But information that might lead to fellow captives being dragged towards a torturous death – that was another matter. It happened, of course, when cultures were pitted against each other, but I had trusted the women around me implicitly. We would die rather than sell our sense of being.

The maid would return for me just before three, she said. I resented the time alone when she left, when I would have

48

to think. I deeply envied those with the ability to empty their minds for some peace, to enter a blank arena with doors leading to more and more emptiness. Peace? Merely the prospect, either universal or personal, seemed utterly remote.

I found a blanket in one of the drawers and sat on the porch, basking in a winter sun slowly tipping across my face, warm and comforting. The gardens were quiet, no uniformed guards in sight, so either they were discreet, or not on full alert. I wondered if the Führer was present, and if being near to the centre of evil felt any different – whether I might sense its strength if he were near. What I would do if I came face to face with the engineer of Germany's moral demise?

Berlin, March 1941

It was inevitable, and the one that nobody wanted: the baby of our fears.

'Sister?' Dahlia's voice was already unsteady as she found me tidying the sluice.

'Yes, what is it?' My back still to her.

'The baby in Room 3. It's, erm—'

I spun around. 'It's what? The baby's born, breathing?'

'Yes, it's born, and alive, but . . .'

Her blue eyes were wide, bottom lip trembling like a child's.

'There's something not quite . . . his legs are . . .'

'Spit it out, Dahlia.'

'. . . deformed.' She said it as if the word alone was treason.

'Oh.' My mind churned instantly. 'Is it very obvious, at just a glance?'

'Yes,' she said.

'Anything else?'

'No, he looks perfectly fine otherwise – a gorgeous little boy. Alert, he handles well.'

'Has the mother noticed? Said anything to you?'

'Not yet, he's still swaddled. I noticed it at delivery, and again when I weighed him. I'm not imagining it, Sister.'

We both stood for a minute, searching in ourselves for the answer, hoping another would hurtle through the door and provide a ready solution. It was me who spoke first, eyes directly on her.

'Dahlia, you know what we've been told. What do you feel you should do?'

With such knowledge I was already complicit in any decision, but if we covered this up, would I regret it? Would it be me as the ward lead who got a visit from the hospital administrator, and the Gestapo? Or would we both bear a secret and keep it within each other? Sad to say that in war, in among the Nazis' pure breed of distrust, even your colleagues were unknowns.

'I'm frightened of not saying anything,' Dahlia said, visibly shaking now, 'but he shouldn't be . . . he shouldn't be taken from his mother. They will separate them, won't they?'

'I think there's a good chance. Almost certainly.'

Dahlia's eyes welled with tears.

'Are you saying you want my help?' I spelled it out. 'Because I'll help if you're sure. But you have to be certain.'

We locked eyes for several seconds. 'Yes, I'm sure,' she said at last.

I thought swiftly of the practicalities of making a baby officially exist but disappear in unison. 'Dahlia, you finish the paperwork and start her discharge quickly. I'll delay the paediatrician, and we'll order a taxi as soon as possible.'

Adrenalin – always my most trusted ally – flooded my brain

and muscles, allowing me the confidence to stride into the woman's room. I painted on a congratulatory smile, and in my best diplomatic tones I told her it would be in her best interests to leave as soon as possible, to forsake her seven days of hospital lying-in, to quit Berlin and to move to her parents' house, where her father was dangerously ill and not expected to last the night. Wasn't that the case? It was, wasn't it?

She was initially stunned, but soon understood why, as we unwrapped the swaddling and she saw with her own eyes the baby who would be no athlete, but no doubt loving and kind and very possibly a great mind. I hinted heavily at his future in the true Reich, and she cried, but only as she dressed hurriedly to go home. We were taking a large gamble on her loyalties to the Führer, but I had seen enough of mothers to know all but a few would lay down their lives for their child's survival and a chance to keep them close. Looking at her stroking his less than perfect limbs, I wagered she was one of them.

Dahlia and I took turns in guarding the door, while I forged the signature of the paediatrician on shift. He saw so many babies, and his scrawl was so poor, it would be easy enough to convince him of another normal baby if the paperwork was ever questioned.

Dahlia's face was a mask of white, and I had to remind her to smile as we shuffled the woman out of the birth room, as if leaving only hours after the birth was an everyday scenario. The baby was swaddled tightly, with only his eyes and nose visible to the world. The corridor was clear, and we moved slowly towards the labour ward entrance, the woman taking the pigeon steps of a newly birthed mother. Dahlia assured me a taxi was waiting, engine running.

'Are you not transferring to the ward, Sister? Is everything all

right?' Matron Reinhardt's distinctive tones ripped through the air, stern and commanding. I swore she could silence the clipping of her soles at will.

I spun on my heels, but gave Dahlia a gentle tug on her shoulder, which meant: 'Stay put, don't move.'

My face fixed itself. 'Sadly, family illness means we need to discharge this mother early, Matron. A grandfather who is keen to see the little one, as the doctors think his time is limited.'

The woman turned her head, nodding agreement, lips pursed.

Matron stepped towards us, her face unmoved. She looked quickly at the woman, turned up the corners of her mouth slightly and said: 'My congratulations, and my sympathies.'

Then to me: 'Is the baby fit for discharge, Sister, properly checked?'

I thought I heard a slight squeak escape from Dahlia's direction, but it could have been the baby, in protest at being held so tightly.

My beautiful friend adrenalin came to my rescue again, pushing courage into vessels where I needed it most. I smiled broadly, and in my best officious tones, stated: 'Of course, Matron. Fit and healthy and a confident mother with the feeding.'

She took a step forward again and aimed a long, thin finger towards the blankets around the baby's face. Matron — who rarely touched a baby, but who directed, admired and encouraged from afar — pulled at the woollen weave and said: 'Quite the handsome fellow, isn't he? I hope time is on your side, my dear.' She aimed a sympathetic smile at the mother. 'Perhaps you'd better hurry, if you have a journey ahead of you.'

Dahlia's face tumbled with relief, and the woman was pulled in her slipstream towards the exit. I stood with Matron and watched them go, waiting for the third degree, and her inevitable request to look at the file in my hand, to crawl over the paperwork and the fiction within. She of all people would see through my lie. A bell for one of the delivery rooms rang, and I stood unmoved.

'Better see who wants your help now,' Matron said, gesturing towards the room, and stepped in the opposite direction.

We never spoke of that baby or referred to him again.

7

Eva

I must have drifted on the edge of real sleep for some time, because the maid woke me gently: Fräulein Braun was waiting. I had just enough time to check my appearance in the bathroom mirror (when was the last time I had done that?) before heading back to the main house. The corridors were eerily empty, with only shadows of bodies moving here and there. I was led into the main drawing room, vast and airy with a jade tinge, where she was waiting, dwarfed by the oversized, dark furniture. Somewhere in the background a small bird twittered, a flash of yellow in a hanging cage.

Fräulein Eva Braun stood up as I came in, offering a hand and a smile; she was average height but athletic-looking, a healthy sheen to her face and broad lips, with a touch of colour and scant make-up. Her hair was strawberry blonde, crimped and worn free, and she had on a plain, green suit – the skirt of which was strained below the waistband, its jacket barely hiding an unmistakable roundness. My eyes immediately settled on her abdomen, sizing up the gestation, while her hand instinctively went to her bump, a reaction signalling she was already attached to her baby and naturally protective. Lord knows this poor creature would need all the help it could get, a mother's love being its best ally.

'Fräulein Hoff,' she said in a surprisingly small voice. 'I am very happy to meet you. Please, sit down.'

Almost instantly, I felt that Eva Braun, mistress of Hitler or not, was no Magda Goebbels. She struck me as the girl next door, easily someone who might have worked in any of the large department stores in Berlin before the war, ready to help with a bottle of cologne in her hand. She had a potential and a smile that would have opened many a door. Maybe that's what had charmed the most powerful man in Europe? Except I wasn't sure if I should hate her for it.

She asked the maid for some tea, and we were soon alone. I sat without offering words, simply because I had nothing to say. There was a brief silence, split only by a crackle from the grate, and she turned squarely to face me.

'I gather you have been told that I am expecting a baby . . .' The words came out furtively, with a flick of her gaze, as if the dark, wooden walls were on alert.

'I have.'

'And that you were requested specifically to become my midwife. I hope that is acceptable to you.'

Possibly, she was unaware I had no real choice, of the emotional leverage involved, but still I said nothing.

'You probably won't know that several of my family's friends have been cared for in Berlin during their pregnancies,' she went on, 'and your skills are highly thought of.'

Again, I only nodded.

'You are also aware that, due to . . . circumstances, the

birth of my baby—' again she palmed her belly '—will be here. I want someone I can trust, who has the skills to deliver my baby safely. And discreetly. My mother was lucky enough to have the care of a good midwife several times, and I would very much like that too.'

She sat back, relieved, as if such a speech had winded her. Still, I didn't know what to offer in reassurance. What I did know was that Eva Braun appeared, on the surface at least, an innocent. By design or sheer naivety it was hard to tell, but I couldn't believe she had set out to sleep with a monster, let alone to carry his bastard child. The Nazi way was the family way; 'Kitchen, children, church' was their motto and good German wives were named as soldiers in the home, bizarrely rewarded with real medals for copious breeding. Eva Braun had broken with protocol. Her position was now untenable, her body and life no longer her own, at least while she carried the Führer's baby – and I had to assume it was his blood, given my treatment since leaving the camp. She looked neither like a soldier nor the accomplice of evil.

Rather than feign a false delight, I focused on the pregnancy – how far along she was, when the due date would be, what types of checks she had already gone through. She had seen a doctor to confirm the pregnancy, but no one since. The dates of her menstrual cycle suggested the baby was due in early June.

'But I'm feeling the baby move now, every day.' She smiled, almost like a child pleasing its teacher, the hand paddling again.

'Well, that's a very good sign,' I replied. 'A moving baby is generally a happy baby. Perhaps, if you would like, I could gather my equipment and do a check, just to see if everything is progressing normally?'

'Oh, yes! I'd like that. Thank you.' She exuded the glow of a thousand pregnant women before her.

Confusion draped again like a thick fog, twisting the moral threads in my brain. I was supposed to feel dislike towards this woman, hatred even. She had danced with the devil, created, and was now nurturing, his child. And yet she appeared like any woman with a proud bump and dreams of cradling her newborn. I wished there and then I was back in the camp, with Rosa by my side, where the world was ugly, but at least black and white. Where I knew who to seethe against, and who the enemy was.

I collected the new equipment from my room, and Fräulein Braun led me through a maze of corridors towards a bedroom. It was mid-size, comfortable but not ornate, family pictures on the mantel – holiday snaps of healthy Germans enjoying the outdoors. In all, there were three doors to the room: one we had come through, another leading to a small bathroom, and, on the opposite side, one linking to a second bedroom. I glimpsed a double bed through a crack in the doorway, a heavy brocade covering. She caught me looking and closed it quietly. And then it hit me. Was that *his* room? The leader of all of Germany, engineer of my misery, *all* misery at this point? Instantly, I wanted to find an exit from this surreal normality, but Fräulein Braun – my client – was already standing by her own bed, waiting.

'Do you want me to lie down, Fräulein Hoff?' Her face was full of expectation, of hope.

There were times in my career when I hated the automatic

elements of midwifery. Early on, some of the labour wards in the poorer district hospitals had seemed like cattle farms – one abdomen, one baby after another. But now, I was thankful to my training, piloting my way through the check. With her skirt lowered, Eva Braun was any other woman, a stretching sphere to be assessed, eager to hear her baby was fit and healthy.

I pressed gently into the extra flesh she was carrying, kneading downwards until I hit a hardness around her navel. 'That's the top of your womb,' I explained, and she gave a small squeak of acknowledgement. I pressed the Pinard into her skin and laid my ear against its flat surface, screening out the sounds of the house and homing in on the beating heart of this baby. She remained stock still and patient throughout – and I finally caught the edge of its fast flutter, only just audible, but the unmistakable rate of a galloping horse.

'That's lovely,' I said, bringing myself upright, 'a good hundred and forty beats per minute, very healthy.'

Again, her face lit up like a child's. 'Can you really hear it?' she said, as if Christmas had come early.

'The baby's still quite small,' I said, 'so it's very faint, but I can hear it, yes. And everything feels normal. It seems to be progressing well.'

She stroked the bump again and smiled broadly, muttering something to the baby under her breath.

We talked about how often she might want a check, when we would start planning the birth, if she might take one last trip to see her parents – a good day's drive away. I realised I would be redundant for much of my time at the Berghof, amid this luxury, and the intense guilt rose up again.

As I turned to go, she called behind me: 'Thank you, Fräulein Hoff. I do appreciate you coming to care for me.'

And I believe she meant it, innocent or not. I didn't know whether to be gracious for my life chance, or angry at her naivety. A thought flashed, 'a child within a child,' and I forced a smile in response, while every sinew in me twirled and knotted.

8

A New Confinement

I ate breakfast the next morning in the servants' quarters. I was introduced as Fräulein Braun's companion, yet no one asked where I had come from, or about my life during or before the war; everyone's history, it seemed, had been washed away by the turmoil.

We had agreed I would see Fräulein Braun briefly each morning after breakfast, and once a week for a full check. In between, I would see her only if she needed me or had questions – this was all made clear in my first meeting with Sergeant Meier, who proudly introduced himself as I returned to my room.

'And I needn't make it clear you cannot leave the complex without Fräulein Braun,' he added, 'or her express permission – in writing.'

He gave a reluctant smile, his small, neat moustache rippling, wire-rimmed glasses sitting astride a short, pointed nose, topped by oiled, cropped hair. His creeping arrogance and the way he wore his sombre SS jacket made me shiver;

I had seen a hundred SS guards wielding heavy coshes, lined up before a thousand powerless women. Before the war, this man had been small and insignificant. Conflict had granted him gravitas, and he basked in it.

'Given where I have come from, Sergeant, I'm under no illusions about my place here,' I said. 'I'm still a prisoner, engaged in slave labour, however you want to dress it.'

'Very comfortable slave labour, Fräulein,' he said without skipping a beat. 'Just remember that. And your family. Good day.'

The rest of January and into February passed slowly. The house was quiet, and I could only assume its chief resident was conducting the war from elsewhere. Fräulein Braun and I soon settled into a routine: I would go to her room after breakfast, enquire about her night, how the baby was moving, and if she wanted me to listen to the baby's heartbeat. Once or twice a week I performed a full check, with her blood pressure and urine. She was healthy and there were no obvious problems.

The weather was bitterly cold, but on clear days the views were spectacular across the wide valleys below the house, and I was itching to venture further afield. Strangely, though, I never once thought of talking my way past the guards and out into the world. At times, it didn't feel like a prison; I was treated with respect by Fräulein Braun, engaged in conversation with the other servants, and was tolerated by Frau Grunders. It was the constant spectre of my family's future that kept me in check. If there was the tiniest chance that my compliance would allow even one of them to survive, it was a small price to pay.

I spent hours wrapped in my blanket in the corner of the wide, stone terrace attached to the main house, drinking in the winter sun and reading. On still days, the space was dotted with tables and striped sun umbrellas, giving it the feeling of a hidden and exclusive resort hotel. Fräulein Grunders had granted me blissful access to her bookshelves, and I was hungrily eating my way through volumes of German and English classics – Austen and Goethe, Dickens and Thomas Mann. The skies buzzed with small aircraft, possibly fighters, but up here, surrounded by the purest air, there was no hint of a war raging across the world; our cotton clouds bore no resemblance to the gun smoke below.

The war, in fact, seemed a lifetime away. Aside from the young jackboots who patrolled the complex, smoking in their breaks, there was no hint of anything untoward in the world at all. They were bored and eager to chat, wearing the guns slung across their shoulders like elaborate trinkets. In the camp, we'd had scant news from the outside world – only when a new inmate had been brought in did we learn which borders had fallen, or what new countries had been occupied. There were no newspapers, nothing by which we could judge our place in the great scheme. I presumed it was intentional, since our ignorance contributed to the regime of fear, to their ability to leverage our lives, and that of our families. Anything to isolate our humanity.

High on up in the Bavarian hills, we also seemed to be in a news black spot. I sometimes glimpsed a newspaper on Sergeant Meier's desk and harboured a ravenous hunger for the print on its pages. But I also knew it was pure propaganda – as the daughter of a politics professor I had been taught to have a healthy disrespect for the media. 'In the pocket of the politicos,' was one of my father's more familiar groans. 'Always read between the lines, Anke. Accept nothing on face value.' Any Nazi newspaper these days – slavishly controlled by Goebbels – was more fiction than fact.

In the servants' hall, there was a small radio set, one of the Reich's People Receivers, but it was rarely switched on, and conversation was limited to enquiring about immediate family who weren't away in the war, or the plentiful meal in front of us. In fact, everything about the Berghof made it seem as though the war was an elaborate figment of our imaginations: the quality of the furnishings, the luxuries of soap, shampoo and even shoe polish, which were refreshed in my room regularly.

Inevitably, my waist started to fill out, my ribs gaining a fleshy coating, so that I could no longer tap on them like a xylophone and produce an echo. In the mirror, I noted a subtle change in my face, a gradual colouring coming into more rounded cheeks, and my hair became thicker, acquiring a slight sheen. I looked almost healthy. It was the old Anke I saw, but not one I recognised. My outer and inner selves were at strange odds with each other.

On one or two occasions that month, I was allowed to go further afield. Fräulein Braun usually took a walk after breakfast with her terriers, Negus and Stasi – I often saw her heading through the perimeter fence and along a path linking another hilltop area. One morning, after our usual meeting, she asked if I would like to go with her. When I said I didn't have a coat, she looked slightly taken aback, and fished in her wardrobe for one that might fit me.

'There, that should keep you nice and warm,' she said,

beaming, and for a split second the atmosphere was almost sisterly, as if we'd been swapping gossip for hours, teasing each other's hair into the latest style.

Eva donned her sunglasses against the bright, white sun beating out to warm the icy air. Our breaths left brief trails as we headed down the frosty path, followed at a discreet distance by an armed guard, with the dogs gambolling on ahead. Conversation was stilted at first, given that there were few topics on which we could share, and many off limits. In the circles she mixed, she had picked up a certain amount of tact in chattering diplomatically, almost about nothing. We talked about some of our favourite films, our school days, and she told me a little about her family, whom she clearly missed. Her sister, Gretl, was often at the Berghof, since she was engaged to a senior officer in the SS, but she rarely saw her older sister, Ilse. When I revealed I had a sister of the same name, she smiled and seemed genuinely pleased we had a small thing in common. She stopped short of asking where my own Ilse was, and how she fared.

'So, tell me about when you were working in Berlin, and the babies you delivered,' she said, eager to know. 'I often think it must be a lovely job. I think, if things had been different, I might have been drawn into nursing, or something like that.' That was as far she came to alluding to the war and its catastrophic effect on the entire world below us, and not for the first time it made me question her true knowledge, or her willingness to ask.

I told her some of the positive stories about birth, of the quirkier events, but nothing of the downsides, the times when it could go wrong, and the emergencies we might have to deal with. The bitter part of me might have hinted at those, but it was an unspoken rule among midwives that we didn't dwell on the negative side. After all, what was the point? Pregnant women were set on a journey, through the winding hours of labour and into motherhood, with no option of taking a shortcut. Why would I reveal it was potentially fraught with danger, reaffirming the old German view of childbirth as infected with jeopardy? As midwives, we knew intense fear could stop a labour in its tracks, with resulting consequences. We needed mothers to welcome it into their bodies, as much as anyone could invite pain and discomfort. Over endless hours of watching and waiting with women in labour, I was a firm believer that anxiety was our enemy, a generous dose of humour being the best medicine.

It took us half an hour to reach a turning point, a little clearing cut into the trees with a rectangular building on one end, part brick and part wood, becoming circular at the other end. Windows looked out onto the expanse below, across the border and into Austria. The dogs barked our arrival.

'Quiet, you rascals!' Eva chided them playfully.

The building was one main room, with the circular ante-room visible through an open door. Comfortable chairs were dotted around the walls and the wood floors covered with expensive rugs.

'We call this the Teehaus,' said Fräulein Braun, as the dogs flopped onto their embroidered cushions. She was pleased to be playing the hostess. 'Isn't it lovely?'

She beamed as she offered me tea from a little stove, pre-lit and set for her trip – making her regular morning walks anything but arduous – and talked as she filled the cups.

'We come here and take tea on some afternoons. On a clear day you can see for ten miles or so. The view is breath-taking.' She didn't look at me but the 'we' was heavily weighted for my benefit.

'It's lovely,' I said, as if I was in some kind of fairy tale myself.

'Goodness!' she said suddenly, as we finished our tea. 'Time to head back. Frau Grunders will be calling for lunch and wondering where we are.'

I mused on what might be calling her away – to my knowledge, she hadn't left the house in weeks. I'd overheard some of the maids gossiping about how full the Berghof used to be with a constant stream of guests. The social whirl, however, had stopped abruptly, no doubt at the Goebbels' bidding. Eva flashed a naughty child's grin, inviting me to be complicit in her mild mockery of the housekeeper, and I smiled back as a reflex. Unwittingly, Frau Grunders had helped us forge a small alliance.

9

Contact

A week later, Eva asked me to walk with her again. The day was crisp, but the air heavier with mist and her mood was dampened, though she made an effort to keep the conversation flowing.

'So, do you think you will ever have children, Fräulein Hoff? I mean, your position – seeing what you do – it hasn't put you off?'

I was slightly taken aback at her frankness, as we hadn't broached anything so personal before. She might have known from my files that I was only a year younger than she, and still capable of having a baby, assuming camp life hadn't rotted my insides – I hadn't had a monthly cycle in over a year.

'I hope one day to have a baby,' I said. 'I'm certainly not put off, or frightened, of it. Far from it. I think – I hope – I would relish it, welcome the experience. My work has taught me to have great faith in women. Mother Nature seems to get it right most times.'

'I hope she'll be kind to me,' Eva Braun countered in a wistful voice. 'I really do.'

I couldn't tell if she was talking of the birth, the baby or both; the pressure on her to produce a consummate heir must have been sitting heavily even then. Nothing less than perfection would be tolerated.

'And of course, the reward for a hard labour is always the baby,' I said to lighten the mood, but as the words emerged, I thought instantly of the mothers who hadn't been allowed to keep their prize, and I was ashamed of coating this dirty business with an acceptable sheen. How could I have forgotten so quickly? So easily? I was hit squarely by a swell of contrition and I coloured with the shame.

Eva Braun, however, heard only the gloss. 'Oh! I'm so glad to hear that. My mother talked of childbirth being so positive, "powerful" she once said. I hope I feel that way when the time comes.'

'And your family, are they excited?'

The pause in her step told me I'd gone too far, but Eva's Reich standing did not turn on me. Instead, she pulled up her shoulders and assumed the facade.

'Gretl is very excited. In fact, she's coming in a few days, so you'll get to meet her. I'm hoping she'll be there at the birth.'

Her false chirpiness spoke volumes. The shroud of secrecy meant only her closest relatives would know – parents and siblings – and if they were enthusiastic Nazis, they would be proud beyond words. But if they were going through the motions of Third Reich belief, as I knew many families in Berlin had been, well versed in etiquette as a survival technique, they would fear for their daughter as well as themselves. I had heard some of the servants talking about Eva as if she weren't worthy of her place at the Berghof, questioning what or who her family were – I put that down to envy and jealousy, since almost all seemed loyal supporters of their master. I wondered then if her parents regretted their daughter's place in the inner circle.

Fräulein Braun cut short our walk, saying she urgently needed to write some letters before lunch.

'I expect you do, too?' she said.

I toyed with letting it go, but the lack of contact with my family rankled, especially since news of their wellbeing had appeared to be part of the agreement. And yet Sergeant Meier was always terribly busy whenever I tried asking him.

'I'm afraid I'm not allowed letters, either in or out,' I said flatly.

'Oh . . . I hadn't realised. I'm sorry.' She flushed red, embarrassed, and turned in to the house.

After a minute or so, I went in through the servants' entrance, and made my way to Frau Grunders' parlour to choose a new book. There was the usual kitchen bustle but her room was quiet. Through the ceiling I heard voices, agitated and urgent. I caught only the edge of some words, muffled sounds – Fräulein Braun's voice and the distinctive whine of Sergeant Meier.

'I will have to . . . only the Captain can say . . .' The words faded in and out.

'I would be grateful . . . as soon as . . .'

I cocked my ear to tune further in to the sound, intently curious. I had never seen them in the same room before, and Sergeant Meier's office and Eva's room were on opposite sides of the house.

'I will arrange . . .'

'Thank you . . .'

A chair scraped overhead, that unmistakable click of heels and then silence.

I was returning to my room when Sergeant Meier caught up with me.

'Ah! Fräulein Hoff.'

'Morning, Sergeant Meier, and how are you?' My amusement over the weeks had been in appearing as sweet and courteous to this odious man as I could bear to – my reward being his visible, sweaty discomfort.

'I'm perfectly well, Fräulein. I have some news for you.'

'Yes? My family?' I was quick to presume.

'Not yet, but I hope soon. It has been decided that you may write some letters, to your family if you wish. Or your friends.'

'Oh,' I said. 'That comes as a surprise. I thought my work here wasn't to be spoken of.' I smiled innocently.

'There will be no mention of your work, of course,' he said, forehead glistening. 'Just that you are well. You could talk about the weather, or how well the war is going, but no details. Each letter will, of course, be reviewed by myself.'

'I wouldn't expect any less, Sergeant Meier. How many letters am I permitted to write, and what should I write on?'

Sergeant Meier had already driven home that the small ledger and some loose paper I had been given were to be used only for my clinical reports on Fräulein Braun. Keeping a diary was not permitted.

'No more than two per week, and I will arrange for you

74

to have ample paper and envelopes,' he said, a tiny bead of perspiration snaking towards one eyebrow. 'If you put the letters into my office, I will see that they are forwarded, and any replies are given to you. And I will expect your monthly report on my desk soon – Captain Stenz will be visiting to collect your copy.'

I virtually ran all the way to my room, stepped inside the door and hugged myself, a broad smile turning into a laugh. A letter! The prospect of some news in return was so exciting. I realised then how isolated I had felt in recent weeks, with no friends to confide in or physical contact with anyone. Clearly, Eva Braun had engineered this change, either as a genuine act of friendship, some pity on her part, or as a way to engage my favour. The truth was, I didn't care. I wasn't too proud to accept her help if it meant I could know my family were alive. And if they were dead I wanted to know, I really did. To stop the hoping, the endless, unknown void.

The paper and envelopes duly arrived in my room that same afternoon – sheets of thick, grainy parchment, each stamped with the eagle icon of the Third Reich. I sat down to write to my parents, a letter each since it was almost certain they weren't together, likely in different camps. What on earth to write? How to describe my state of mind – that constant, fizzing thread of anxiety that jolts you out of sleep at three a.m., to stare at the ceiling for hours on end, when you wonder what on earth you are doing, and how you might survive? How to convey meaning in a message in which even the words have bars?

I concentrated on making the tone of my news positive, relaying that I was at least out of danger – for now. When our lives in Berlin had become ever more precarious, my father and I had created a loose code between us. We'd settled on two words to signal our wellbeing; any mention of 'sunshine' meant we were safe, in relative terms, but greying 'clouds' or a 'flat horizon' signalled the opposite.

I wrote that I was fine, eating well – very true at that point – and that the sunshine was making me feel upbeat. 'The horizon is sometimes quite bright, Papa,' I rambled on, desperate to convey something he could interpret, not quite safe yet not in imminent danger. The rest was padded out with, 'I hope you and Mother are well, I think of you and Franz and Ilse every day.' If my father's mind remained sharp, he would find a way of reading between the lines. And I had to rely on his faith, to know that, despite the notepaper, I had not become a zealous Nazi. I had not turned.

I was wrapped in a blanket on my porch and fighting against the dying light when I heard footsteps. Engrossed in my novel, I didn't look up.

'Goethe? I'm impressed.'

'Captain Stenz,' I said in greeting. 'Do you need to see me? Would you like me to come into the house?'

'No, no,' he said, taking off his cap, 'I don't want to disturb you. But I would like a brief talk. May I?' He gestured at the second chair. His tone suggested I wasn't due for any rebuke, and his manner seemed relaxed as he sat.

'Of course.' I was glad of the company and yes, I was actually pleased to see him. Was it merely because he wasn't Sergeant Meier? The Captain wore the same uniform, and yet my reaction to the man inside was entirely different.

He sat, turning his gaze and squinting as the sun slipped

behind snow-capped mountains to the right of our view. I watched his eyes glaze over for a few seconds, then heard a sigh slip from between his lips, before the noise pulled him to attention.

'So, how are you getting on? Are you being treated well, and do you have everything you need?'

'Yes, I am well looked after,' I assured him. 'I have everything I need to do my job.' I watched him catch my meaning.

'Fräulein Braun tells me she is very happy with the arrangement, and says she is feeling well, so we can be grateful for that.'

'Yes,' I said. 'She's in good health. In fact, I feel rather underemployed. It's not what I'm used to.' We both seemed aware of exchanging niceties that said very little.

'I wouldn't be too concerned about that,' he said, smiling. 'Your value will be in the later stages, I have no doubt. It's an important job.'

His eyes turned again to the horizon. The sun was dropping rapidly behind the peaks, white against the orange blaze. I fingered the pages of my book, looking at his blond hair cut neatly into the nape of his black collar, but which might have turned to curls if left to grow. From the neck up he looked like a boy from the country, and not a man who carried power in the threads of iron-grey below.

I wondered why he didn't just up and leave, since he clearly had nothing else to say. It was me who sliced the silence, preventing his sudden departure.

'Captain Stenz, can I ask you something?'

His fair head swivelled and he looked faintly alarmed. 'You can ask, although I can't promise to answer.' Suddenly, he was SS again.

'Well, I understand that secrecy is a safety issue with Fräulein Braun, given what I believe the bloodline to be—' he flashed a look but didn't contradict '—yet no one aside from a small number of people has acknowledged this baby. No one seems to be welcoming this news. The Third Reich believes in families, in large families. And I have worked at a Lebensborn before – before all of this. I know unmarried mothers are tolerated when it comes to helping . . . the cause.' The words caught in my throat. 'So I don't understand this show of fake ignorance. This baby will be born, and then it will be difficult to hide. Shouldn't they be happy as a couple? Wouldn't it boost morale for the war if the country knew?'

He took a deep breath, and clasped his gloved fingers together. 'It's complicated, Fräulein Hoff, and I don't pretend to be an expert in public relations – we have a department for that.' He gave a resigned smile. 'You give me too much credit – I am simply an engineer and a messenger, nothing more.'

'So what *are* you an expert in?'

'Excuse me?'

'I mean, what did you do, before the war?' Finally, I was engaged in a discourse that didn't feel submissive or dangerous.

'I was a student of architecture. I had to give up my studies.'

'Had to?'

'It was expected,' he said.

'And will you go back to them? After, I mean?'

'That depends.'

'On what?'

'On whether I live through the war,' he said, dropping his smile. 'And whether there is a world left to rebuild.' He stood up, almost wary he might have let his guard slip. 'I must go. If I could have your reports, Fräulein Hoff?'

'Certainly,' and I brought them from inside the door.

'Goodbye, until next time,' he said, and clicked his heels, stopping short of the salute. He replaced it with a nod of his head, although his eyes held mine. I watched his long shadow disappear towards the house, and felt suddenly very lonely.

10

Visitors

The following days saw a dramatic change in the calm of the Berghof. At breakfast the next morning there was a palpable tension, and the kitchen was unusually noisy and busy, the kitchen porter unloading a large delivery from the town. Frau Grunders drank her morning tea in gulps, rushing out and barking at the under-maids as she went. I heard them grumbling about 'More work than we're paid for, just for his majesty's pleasure,' but scurrying nonetheless.

I guessed what might be happening, and a sickening ache rippled among my innards. During the past weeks, I had thought little of the master of the house as a real entity – the war felt so far away, and he was out of sight, out of mind. And that suited me. I hadn't wanted to consider coming into real contact, what I would say or do, or how I would behave. Outward dissent would be stupid, fatal even, yet anything less would also make me feel like a traitor – to my family, and our friends before the war, all those women suffering in the camp, all those babies whose birth and death days fell on the same date.

The excitement in the household was reflected in Fräulein Braun. She was agitated, enthusiastic and unusually flighty – she had clearly been reviewing her wardrobe before I arrived, and was teasing her hair out to a more natural style, moving like a child unable to contain her excitement. She was keen for me to listen to the heartbeat, but impatient to postpone the other checks.

'I feel fine – can we do that tomorrow?' she said.

I tried smiling, as if I understood her eagerness to be with her loved one, but my sentiment was entirely selfish; the less time I spent in the house the better for me. As I was leaving Frau Grunders stopped me, suggesting I take meals in my room over the next week 'as we'll all be very busy'. To me, it signalled the connivance over Eva's baby was complete. Excepting Eva, the entire Berghof was in denial about the pregnancy. How did Herr Hitler feel, I pondered, about fatherhood to one human as well as an entire nation? I could only assume he didn't share the same excitement as the baby's mother. And what would that mean for the child's future, and Eva's?

He arrived later that afternoon, the throaty rumble of engines drawing me onto my porch. An army truck led the cavalcade of cars sweeping up the drive, spitting gravel as they swooped in. The truck held regular troops, who fanned out around the perimeter fence, guns cocked and ready. The first cars spilled out several army officers in green, followed by SS officers in their contrasting slate jackets, perfect ebony boots reflecting the afternoon glare. It was the fifth or sixth car that ground to a halt, and sat idling while the officers formed a semi-circle around. The cluster stopped me from seeing him emerge, but I could tell by the wave of deference that he was out of the car and standing. I didn't spy the blond, capped head of Captain Stenz among them, and part of me was glad I couldn't see him bowing and scraping. My stomach churned, mouth empty of saliva, and I wanted to peel my eyes away, but somehow I couldn't. It was hard to take in, that a few hundred yards away was a man who held so much of the world in his palm, and whose fingers could fold over and crush it, on a whim. Not just me or my family, but anyone he wanted, anywhere. Not for the first time I pitied Eva Braun, for all her blind love and faith.

She was, by this point, at the top of the small flight of stairs leading up to the porch. Hair loose and face almost scrubbed free of make-up, she wore a traditional blue dress gathered at the bust, which had the effect of hiding her bump. Unusually, Negus and Stasi weren't at her feet, as she had already told me they didn't get on with Blondi, the Führer's own beloved Alsatian; Blondi's size and status took precedence at the Berghof. The look of expectation on her face, of a child wanting to please, was almost pitiful.

He walked slowly up the stairs and planted a friendly kiss on her cheek; hardly the embrace of long-lost lovers eager to be alone. They turned and went inside together, and the uniformed entourage followed – I spied the hollowed features of Herr Goebbels in the group – while the troops encircled the house. The fortress was complete.

For the first time since my arrival at the Berghof, I had a desperate urge to run as fast as my legs would carry me away from this infected oasis. That feeling of uneasiness, which had smouldered in the pit of my belly since arrival, was now stoked to an inferno and I wanted so much to escape, even if it meant a life of uncertain danger. But I didn't. Fear of reprisal kept me sitting, rooted to my chair, doing as I was told. And, not for the first time, I hated myself for it.

After eating in my room, I sat out late on my porch, reading at first and then just watching as the light died. The house itself became more illuminated, and sounds of male laughter drifted out into the mountain air. Down there, across the world, thousands – millions – of people were sobbing, screaming and dying, and all I could hear was amusement. I went to bed and rammed the pillow against my ears, desperate to shut out all the wrong in this mad arena called life.

11

The First Lady

Eva sent word the next morning to see her at eleven a.m. on the terrace – relief washed over me that I may not need to enter the house at all; the Führer was hosting an important war conference, and the Berghof would be full of the green and grey for some time.

The day was glorious, a rich sun climbing in the sky as I skirted the house. Its brightness blotted out a good deal of the increasing green below, only the cobalt of several lakes breaking through. Fortunately, the terrace appeared almost empty, aside from Eva sitting under a large sun umbrella, sipping tea. Facing her, with neat blonde crown visible to me, was another woman. I assumed it was her sister, Gretl, who had come to the Berghof with her fiancé. They appeared deep in conversation as I approached.

'Morning, Fräulein Braun,' I ventured.

'Ah, Fräulein Hoff, good morning,' she said. 'Thank you for delaying our meeting. You've met Frau—' and as I rounded the chair I saw it was the head of Magda Goebbels, her blonde style faultless in its design, her face with limited make-up but the familiar ruby lips. She made a small attempt at a smile but stopped short of making it friendly.

'Yes. Yes, Frau Goebbels and I have met.' I was taken aback and it showed.

'Please, sit down, Fräulein Hoff,' said Frau Goebbels, taking immediate control and looking comfortable with it. 'We – I – have a favour to ask.'

I smiled, still mildly amused that they could think of anything as a favour, as if a request meant I had a right to refuse.

'First of all, I want to thank for your care of Fräulein Braun so far – she has been most complimentary about your skills.' She took a long drag on her cigarette. Eva merely looked uncomfortable, as if she was a child being spoken for, while I felt like a favoured slave – it was a knack that Frau Goebbels had perfected. Her eyes met with yours for a split second, but she drew them away just as swiftly, giving the impression you were worthy of her attention, but not of maintaining it.

She went on. 'But since she is in such good health, and does not need your services daily, I wonder if we might borrow you for a few days?'

What was I expected to say – 'Let me think about it'? I said what they wanted to hear. 'If Fräulein Braun is agreeable, then I will go where I can be most helpful.'

This time Magda Goebbels smiled fully, stubbing out her cigarette. She turned her attention on me, as if delivering orders.

'A cousin of mine is preparing to have her baby. She has reached her due date and beyond, but she is being . . . well

. . . in all honesty, I think she is being rather difficult, and refusing to leave the house to go into hospital. However, I am not her mother, and therefore the only influence I can bring upon her is to offer what help I can.'

I found it odd that she had thought of me, but I was equally irritated at being the hired help. From somewhere inside, a small chink of courage rose out of the annoyance.

'Frau Goebbels, with all due respect, I am happy to help any woman, but I am not the type of midwife to force anyone into treatment they don't want or need.'

Her wide eyes were on mine in seconds, fixed and fiery. Then, the familiar break away.

'No, no obviously,' she acquiesced. 'We simply wanted an experienced midwife to attend her at home. I'm hoping a week at the most. Is that reasonable, Eva?' She swivelled towards her host. It was obvious this had not been sanctioned by the Reich, and was a favour on Eva's part.

'Of course, perfectly fine,' she nodded like an obedient puppy.

The house was an hour away, and I was to leave early the next morning. Standing there, I calculated my current worth to Frau Goebbels had created a little bargaining power.

'I will need someone with me to assist at the birth,' I said. 'Someone I can rely on.'

'I daresay there will be a willing housemaid, or reliable servant,' Frau Goebbels said dismissively, turning her gaze away.

'I would like Christa to come with me,' I said with conviction. 'She's very resourceful, and I feel she won't panic.'

'Christa? *My* Christa? But you hardly know her,' Frau Goebbels reasoned.

'But I trust her to help me when I ask,' I said.

Perhaps she was bored with any potential confrontation, because Magda Goebbels agreed to my request – she would release Christa. Maybe she didn't view it as a concession, a small triumph on my part, but I did. I went back to my room, relieved that I had been released from this house of war games, and that I would meet up again with the only person within miles I might one day call a friend. Or indeed, an ally.

I arranged to meet Fräulein Braun later that afternoon for an ante-natal check, given I might not see her for a week. Part of me also wanted to gauge her mood at this strange, unsettling time – we hadn't exchanged more than a few words since the Führer had come to the Berghof. In the house there had been low whispers on the fierce words coming from the Führer's apartment – his and Eva's. I pretended to be absorbed but my ears were fixed on the maid's tittle-tattle of tears and pleadings seeping from Eva's room.

'Lord forgive me, but what he called her was cruel,' the maid said. 'I wouldn't want to be in her shoes, not even to be mistress of this place.' The details were lost as they turned and walked away, but the meaning was clear. In their own domestic war, Eva's baby had made her weaker instead of stronger.

That afternoon, Eva's door was ajar and she was at her dressing table, grimacing at her own reflection. She looked weary. There were muddy puddles under her eyes, and her normally fair, vibrant skin seemed dry and rough. No wonder she was disapproving of what she saw.

'If you don't mind me saying, Fräulein Braun, you look tired. Is the baby keeping you awake?'

'A little,' she said. 'An aunt of mine always said babies come alive at night, and this one seems to be no exception. Is that right?'

'Yes, they don't have any conception of day and night for a long while. Perhaps once you lie still the baby remembers it needs to move. Are you managing to nap during the day?'

'Not right now, not while . . .' she hesitated and chose her words '. . . not while the house is so busy.'

Still, we hadn't managed to move beyond the spectre of Adolf Hitler. It was clear they were intimately involved – she was the only female who consistently had a virtual free rein at the Berghof, aside from Magda Goebbels – and Frau Goebbels' barely suppressed jealousy was enough to signal the affair between Eva and Adolf. She was pregnant, and yet she couldn't quite acknowledge out loud that he was the father. From what I had seen, the SS hierarchy barely acknowledged her worth, and yet she seemed glued to the place that was his creation, that contained a piece of his heart. Always supposing he had one.

We went through the motions of a check, and I listened to the fast rump, tump of her baby's heart. This was when Eva's face softened and became girl-like again. I was conscious of my face screwing up in concentration as I began, but I could feel it relax as the sounds came into my own ear, and her face too would spread in joy as I nodded that all was well.

'I won't be too far away, and if the baby hasn't arrived within a week, I'll request the chauffeur brings me back up, at least for a check,' I told her.

'Thank you,' she said, with genuine gratitude. 'That's kind of you to think ahead. But I will be fine.'

In truth, I did feel sorry for her – she seemed so alone. Even her sister, Gretl, hadn't appeared for this mountain war summit. The response that such a feeling stirred within me was hard to process. Eva Braun consorted with Adolf Hitler, willingly. She appeared to love him. How much sympathy was she worthy of – and how much was she making a very dangerous bed to lie on? In between all of this was the baby, a new life with a heart that was – for now – empty of all sin.

Berlin, February 1942

The pot was still warm from Mama's oven as I hugged it close to my chest, and walked towards the checkpoint. A bored-looking sentry stood halfway down the Friedrichstrasse and shuffled his feet as I approached. He made some attempt to look masterly by plucking at his gun holster and pulling back his shoulders. He was all of twenty-one, twenty-two at a stretch. Someone's baby boy.

'Good evening,' I said, with a wide smile.

'Evening, Fräulein. You know you are approaching the Jewish section?' He glanced quickly at the arm of my coat, in case he had missed seeing the yellow star patched onto the sleeve.

Without blonde, typically Aryan features or the heavy stature of some German women, it's true that my looks were ambiguous and sometimes drew suspicion. I found it strange that people's reactions were either put on hold or tempered by where they thought I belonged. I was me; I was Anke – the same person in front of them. Sad to say that in war there was little guesswork; Jews no less proud of their religion were forced to display it to the world, the crudely stitched yellow star to be used not as a talisman of luck or pride, but as a cosh to beat them with.

'I'm going to visit my aunt,' I said, producing my hospital identity card.

'She hasn't moved out yet?' the soldier quizzed. 'There are plenty of apartments over on the west side, where the Jews have moved out. She could get a nice place there, very posh I'm told.'

'She's old and, well, you know what old people are like,' I laughed. 'She's very stubborn and won't be persuaded, and the least I can do is visit her with some dinner.'

'Sounds as stubborn as my grandmother. And what's in the bag?' He gestured with the butt of his rifle to the large satchel on my shoulder.

'Oh,' I said, as if the bag was an afterthought. 'Typically, one of her leg ulcers is playing up and, as the nurse in the family, it falls to me to sort it out.'

His face crinkled. It was a certainty that any mention of ulcers would stop a detailed search. He looked briefly into the bag, as if the contents themselves might be suppurating, and waved me on.

'Good evening to you,' I trilled over my shoulder.

'Good evening, Fräulein. Don't forget about the curfew.' I felt the guards' eyes follow me down the street and into the unknown quarter of humanity, and then laughter as their attention moved elsewhere. Relief quivered through me.

In the city, there was no official ghetto as such, but Jewish families had been ordered out of their west side homes and businesses early on in the war, and herded into a small enclave in the north-east corner of the city, an area neatly marked out by the burnt-out synagogues of Kristallnacht. Thanks to a huge voluntary exodus of

92

Jewish families since the grip of Nazism had taken hold, the Jewish population in Berlin wasn't as high as in some German cities. Those with great foresight had moved entire countries to escape persecution. Others had fled Berlin after the fires of Kristallnacht but were still within reach of the net.

In the past months we had heard of large transportations of Berlin Jews sent to live in newly created ghettos across the border in Poland, fenced and hemmed in, overcrowding and disease living side by side. It wasn't common knowledge, but those with links to black market trade or letters filtered back the grim details. In just a few short years, the bright yellow star had become muted, and Berlin's rainbow of cultures had smudged to a dull spectrum.

I walked up the Kaiser Wilhelm Strasse with as much confidence as I could muster and – gauging that no uniforms or unknown men lurked who might be Gestapo – turned left and into the heart of the Jewish quarter. Minna's one eye appeared through a slit in the door.

'It's me: Anke,' I whispered.

She opened and ushered me in, taking the pot and leading up to the first floor, where our clinic was waiting.

As with the past months, the room was a mixture of old and young, the sick and the simply weary, who no longer had the right to access German welfare, and were forced to squeeze into an already overcrowded living area for some help. Ever efficient, Minna had sorted the line into those with the most pressing need first. As a nursing assistant up to the point when her skills suddenly became unnecessary to the Reich, she was a master of organisation. The pot went immediately onto a table in the impromptu kitchen, where the stew would be dished out to the hungriest children.

I emptied the satchel and began organising the workstation. A bowl of clean water was waiting, alongside a tiny tablet of soap and *a towel; it never ceased to amaze me that in such crowding and potential for dirt, the linen was always spotless. A pot of water was already boiling the scissors and instruments we might need for today's variety of ailments, Minna's mother at the helm.*

I had brought whatever I could ghost away from the hospital in the pockets of my uniform, which were mercifully deep. Each day for the past year, I had been careful not to overfill them, to take just one of everything so the store cupboard never looked raided: sterile dressings, antiseptic creams, needles and surgical thread, bandages and any amount of medicines not locked in the official cabinet. I was stealthy in my thievery.

Did I ever think of it as stealing? Never. The Reich had abandoned its own people, good families who had worked hard through their lives, paid their taxes and deserved more than this filthy betrayal. It would be instant dismissal — and worse — if I were ever caught, but my own moral compass never wavered. Besides, folklore through history was littered with others happy to redistribute wealth. I was just one in a long line and, I suspected, one of many in this war too.

Without wasting a moment, Minna guided the first patient to one of the two chairs, and we worked through the list of twenty or more. I took on the wounds that needed stitching, with Minna in charge of wound dressing, eking out the bandages to make them last longer. We spoke little to each other, working industriously. There were always one or two dog bites to disinfect and stitch, mainly in young men who had chanced a night raid on an allotment and been almost caught by the dogs, if not their guards. In winter, the ground hard with frost, they were forced to breach the walls of factories or warehouses, sprinting for their lives.

The rest were chest infections, children mostly, their little ribs standing proud as I listened to their flimsy chests and the dusty wheeze within, a bare membrane of skin between the world and their own brittle skeleton. Minna took time grinding the precious antibiotic tablets into a fine powder, blending with water, and we spooned the mixture into the children's mouths as if they were baby birds in the nest – one or two, depending how deep the rattle of their breath.

At the very end came the old and the infirm, some of whom we could treat, others who simply needed a place to go and a friendly ear. Minna and I dispensed a good balm of sympathy and empathy, peering at sore toes and mysterious bruises, nodding together and pronouncing them well enough to go home. There was no other choice, but the act of taking the time to look was often medicine enough.

As we finished, Minna's mother was there with a cup of fresh tea. I'd never seen her without a kettle in her hand, thin beads of sweat just above her heavy brows, and a friendly smile despite the sad turn her life had taken, her husband lost in the violence of Kristallnacht.

'Have you time to see Nadia?' Minna said. 'She's just a few weeks off. I'm not sure the baby's turned yet.'

I glanced at my watch. 'If we're quick. The curfew is strict, and if I'm stopped my name will be taken.'

She handed me a coat belonging to her sister, the yellow star already stitched on its sleeve. We walked in the gloom to a similar house two streets away. Minna seemed unaffected by hers, but I felt that yellow pulse like a beacon on my arm, fiery with meaning and the deep injustice of my own countrymen. Weren't stars meant to shine brightly? This one, it seemed, could only lead to darkness.

Nadia was on the second floor, in the far corner of a small room with her mattress curtained off by an old bed sheet. It was something nearing luxury, though, since only one family occupied this room, and she shared it with her mother, father and two younger brothers. Nadia was tight-lipped about the baby's father, but the family's suspicions leaned towards a German soldier, one who thought his superiority gave him the right to invade her innocence. It was only her family's love that had overcome the shame and anger in equal measure.

She sat up as I ducked under the curtain, clearly pleased to see me. Her belly rippled at the effort, causing her to laugh and wince at the same time.

'Is this baby still doing gymnastics?' I said.

'It never stops. I hope it's full of life — but perhaps not quite so active when it comes out!'

Nadia's face was animated but pale; she was likely to be anaemic. I handed her mother a few iron tablets, and told her to make them last at least a week, with as much nettle soup as they could manage.

'So, shall we see how this baby is doing?' I dipped my head to hear the heartbeat, conscious that under my fingers the baby's head was still nestled below Nadia's ribs and not deep into her pelvis. In the past four weeks it hadn't showed any signs of wanting to spin round.

'The baby sounds lovely, pumping away,' I said with a broad smile. She beamed back, delighted at growing such a bounteous baby. With Nadia's blood pressure and urine normal, I said I would call again the next week, since we'd estimated a due date somewhere in the next three weeks.

'Is the position a problem?' Minna asked as we descended the stairs.

'It's difficult to tell,' I said. 'It doesn't feel like a big baby, and plenty are born breech but it is a more difficult journey through.

They either come smoothly, or there's a problem that soon becomes an emergency. There's no middle ground with breech babies.'

'You know she won't go to the hospital?' Minna said.

I feared as much. The Jewish Hospital was the only health centre open to Jews now, but it was also a collection point for the first transport to the ghettos out of Berlin. Word – and deep suspicion – had already circulated.

'You know Nadia's uncle was on the first transport out?' Minna said, eyes bright in the gloom.

'Yes. And I can't say I blame her. But it would be better if she was at least nearer to the hospital. Can you talk to her?'

'I'll try.'

I made the curfew just in time, the same young lads at the sentry post.

'Did she enjoy the stew, your aunt?'

'She can't get enough of that fake fish,' I laughed, embroidering the lie. 'You'd think it was a gourmet dish, the way she wolfs it down.'

'Well, there's no accounting for taste,' one bantered. 'Goodnight, Fräulein.'

I turned and walked, not a saunter, but neither was I too quick, and I could feel their bored eyes upon me, weighing up the question as they stamped their toes against the cold.

'Would you?' one of them would say.

'No, not for me, too dark, too much of a Jew's look about her.'

'Yeah, perhaps you're right. You got a cigarette?'

12

Employment

I left early the next morning, as the sun's rays began their crawl up the mountain. Doubtless, the ever-efficient Sergeant Meier would alert Frau Grunders I had not absconded. The Berghof chauffeur, Daniel, was waiting, and as I moved into the car, Captain Stenz's own black sedan drew up and he stepped out. On seeing me, he adopted a quizzical look.

'Are you going somewhere, Fräulein Hoff?' He stooped to peer through my open window. With Daniel by my side, his voice wasn't confrontational, only curious. And perhaps tinged with a little regret?

'Um, yes, I'm to help out a relative of Frau Goebbels. Fräulein Braun has given her consent.'

'I don't doubt it,' he said with wry smile, and then looking up. 'Drive carefully, Daniel – we need Fräulein Hoff back safe and sound.'

He pulled his long fingers from the car door, and they hovered somewhere around his pockets. As we drove off I cast a glance backwards – one of the Captain's hands twitched and rose slightly in a semi-wave. I couldn't help but be perplexed – and yet curl my lips into a smile.

Beyond the gates, I felt a physical weight lift from the crown of my head, as if it had been clamped in a vice for weeks on end. Until then, I hadn't appreciated the level of oppression; for all its beauty and isolation, the Berghof was an effective jail, and not just for me.

We spiralled steadily down the road, and Daniel began to talk. He was an amiable man, middle-aged and content, grateful it seemed for the stability he had been given in this wartime of horrors. His son was in the Wehrmacht, and he hinted at the scars war had inflicted. I wondered how much this unreal world on the mountain could mask what was happening, although in the last month or so, I had been as oblivious as any. We drove through the town of Berchtesgaden and I eyed the shops covetously. It had been at least two years since I had browsed in a boutique, bought groceries, or even handled money for that matter. Just the chance to sit in a cafe and watch the world go by seemed like an unobtainable luxury.

We moved through the well-to-do neighbourhood of the Berchtesgaden middle classes, comfortable behind thick fences of yew and pine. Christa was waiting as we swept up the Goebbels' driveway and I was relieved an audience with the mistress wasn't required. She hopped into the car eagerly and we made our escape.

'Christa!' I hugged her like a long-lost friend.

'Fräulein Hoff, you look well!' She beamed. 'I'm so pleased to see you again. And they are clearly taking care of you.'

She sat back and surveyed my form, which had filled out since I had seen her last. It wasn't only my cheeks that had grown in the past months – my body had none of the natural curves it'd had in Berlin, but the rich food and lack of exercise and work meant I no longer looked a complete waif.

'I know. I'm spending too much time sitting and not enough time doing,' I said.

'I thought there might be some change,' she said, nodding towards the large bag sitting beside her. 'I've been clearing out some more clothes, and I've brought needles and thread – I thought we might have some waiting time to adjust a few things for you.'

We settled on benign conversation – I was desperate to know about the direction of the war, but Daniel's allegiances were unknown, and like most chauffeurs I had encountered, he appeared to have acute hearing. We drove on through open countryside, seeing little evidence of troops or conflict, only the odd army truck here and there. Life seemed virtually unchanged down here too.

Eventually, we came to a small village, turned off the main road running through it, and then into a short drive. The house was less grand than the Goebbels', but still substantial, solid and detached, and banked on all three sides by a large, well-kept garden, which was in turn bordered by well-established trees. Two children were playing in the garden, along with a young woman, not obviously pregnant.

A maid met us at the door and showed us to a room on the ground floor, then up to the bedroom of the mistress. I was surprised – no one had told me she was unwell and bed-bound, and I began to wonder what scenario I would be faced with. Frau Schmidt had been crying, that much was obvious. Her eyes were reddened bruises, sunken and dried out, and she barely lifted her head as we came into the room. The curtains were drawn and the air heavy with sorrow.

It took only a few words to discover her distress; Sonia Schmidt was grieving. On the expected day of her baby's birth, she had received the telegram all loved ones dread – her husband of ten years killed in North Africa. Bravely, and with honours, but nonetheless dead. Faced with the prospect of him not only missing the arrival, but now the rest of the baby's life as well, her body had shut down and labour was postponed. Her family had urged her into hospital, feeling sure the doctors could easily induce a third baby. But she was virtually catatonic, almost unable to function, and they had also withdrawn, mistaking her genuine sadness for difficult behaviour.

'The children don't know yet,' she sobbed, 'and I don't know how I can tell them their papa will never be home. What will I tell this baby?'

I felt nothing for her general predicament – her life seemed more than comfortable – but what she was enduring there and then would have been painful for any woman, any human, whatever her husband might have been capable of.

The baby's heartbeat was normal, it was moving well and deeply engaged in the pelvis. Sonia was also tightening; her abdomen hardened like an egg on the merest touch, but she was simply in denial. The physical side of childbirth was a powerful force, but at times a woman's psychology – her sheer will – could override even Mother Nature for a time. This mother simply didn't want to hold her baby, not yet. Its mere presence, a creation of its father, would remind her so acutely of the loss.

I helped her into the bath, remade her bed with clean

sheets, and told her we would simply wait for this baby. There was no hurry: it was healthy and robust, a nice size, and she needed to feel well before she wanted to labour. I did nothing but give her permission to grieve, and then have a baby when she chose.

'Are you sure?' She looked at me through a mist of disbelief. 'There's nothing you need to do?'

'Not right now. I'm sure your baby will come when you are both ready.'

It took just two days. The wait felt much like a holiday; the weather was chilly but I wrapped myself in the coat Christa had brought for me, and we both walked and talked. There was no visible army presence save for a guard at the gate, and as we moved further from the house, Christa revealed a little of what she knew: information gleaned from talk in the Goebbels' house, the shops in Berchtesgaden and the letters she received from her father.

The war was going badly for Germany – the Allies had attacked Italy and were in a strong position, Stalingrad was now in Russian hands, and parts of Germany had been bombed in sustained attacks by British fighters, with huge losses on the ground and in the air. Leipzig had been virtually flattened and Berlin had been targeted many times. I felt so ignorant of what was happening in the real world and angry at our cocooned position up on high. I wondered how much of this was being discussed at the Berghof among the German high command, and how long it could remain a protected fortress. No wonder Fräulein Braun felt ignored. Hitler had an entire war on his mind, a war that we – Germany – might be losing.

At the Schmidt house, the maids kept the two of us fed and comfortable, but their time was taken up with the children and the young governess. Christa's adept hands fitted me out with several new dresses, and we revelled in the freedom of being able to talk, the ears of the Goebbels and the Berghof loyalists far away. We even dared to talk of life after the war, what we might do as women in perhaps a stronger position, who we might marry, and what our children could look like. Christa was so full of life – when the war began she'd been about to leave her job and become a student of fashion. Yet we both seemed to sense it would depend on our timing – when to climb down and away from that mountain and to safety.

We laughed a lot but there was an edge to each topic we broached. I felt the cobwebs clearing towards a real discussion. And then, as we walked, her sweet features became unusually serious.

'And what will you do about the baby?'

'The baby? It'll come soon, I think,' I said.

'No, I mean *the* baby. Fräulein Braun's baby.'

I stopped walking and turned squarely to face her. 'What do you mean, what will I *do*?'

Suddenly, Christa seemed old beyond her years. Her face hardened and her eyes flashed. 'I mean, Anke, that you have a certain amount of power over what goes on. Don't think you don't. Have you never wondered how your actions might influence events way beyond the Berghof, way beyond Fräulein Braun?'

I didn't want to admit it, but I had. In all those hours of unemployment, my mind had wandered into uncomfortable corners of possibilities. Every fibre of my professional being would move heaven and earth to save any mother or baby, even after what had gone before. But I knew the gravity of this pregnancy, what having an heir would mean to the Reich. Could I contemplate sabotage, as a midwife? I liked to think not, but in truth it had crossed my mind, and there was only one alternative to a happy mother and baby. No baby.

'I . . . I suppose I have, briefly, but I don't think, when it came to it . . . no. It would be suicide for one thing, for me, and certain death to my family. Christa, all of this, I'm doing it for them, you know, for any chance they might have. Besides, I don't even think Adolf Hitler cares about this baby. Any action I could take might not affect him at all.'

I felt winded, and walked on again, anything but stand and face the heavy atmosphere between us. Christa moved silently alongside me.

'I think you're wrong,' she said finally. 'What happens at the Berghof could have a big effect. It's just that what I hear, at the house—'

'At the Goebbels'? What do they say?' I snapped back. My distrust of Magda was already well entrenched.

'They fight like cat and dog over it,' Christa said. 'Hitler might not want to be a father, but Goebbels is desperate for that baby, to use it as a morale booster, as a way of turning the war, towards a "new hope" he says. But the mistress, she wants it to be kept secret forever, for Eva to be like some Rapunzel in the sky.'

I had seen Christa full of fun and smiles, mischief even, but I had never seen her so animated, so hardened. Her eyes were fiery dots, red with passion.

'But why does she want the baby hidden?'

'Jealousy,' said Christa squarely. 'She has seven fine examples of Germanic blood, but they are not Adolf Hitler's children. She would have done almost anything to be his woman, if she hadn't already been married. And he knows it, the master. Joseph Goebbels knows it.'

'And so why did she bring me here, to care for Eva?'

'It wasn't Magda, but her husband. She wanted Eva sent to Austria, out of sight, but Goebbels insisted on bringing in the best. He wants to keep it discreet, to keep her out of hospital until he reveals the baby in his own good time.'

'And you've heard all of this? It's not just tittle-tattle?'

'With my own ears,' Christa said. 'They don't hold back, and the walls, they're not that thick. Frau Goebbels may look like the perfect German wife, but she can wield the power within that house.'

I was silent in absorbing Christa's revelations. I thought of Eva, of her stupid naivety, but also of her yearning to hold her baby. The fact that it was *his* baby shouldn't come into it. Or should it?

'I just don't think I could do anything other than care for her in the best way I know,' I said finally. 'It's the baby who holds all the cards now. If the baby survives, or not, it won't be because I played God or anything else. I'm a midwife; I don't have that right. No one does.'

Christa looked at me, her silence needling, as if she knew. That she could tell. It was her eyes that said: *Don't you?*

'I hate this war, Christa, I really hate what it's done to Germany, to Germans, and everyone else – the pain it's caused. And yes, that man – that loathsome man – is responsible. But I can't be held to account for the direction of this whole war. It won't be turned by a birth – something so small.'

'Can you be sure about that?' Christa's eyes flashed again.

'Where has this come from, Christa? I've never seen you like this. Why are you suddenly so angry?'

'It's my brother,' she said. Her voice was barely audible, the liquid fire of a volcano breaking free.

'Yes, I know, he was blinded in the war. It's tragic and—'

'He's dead.' Her words sank like stone into the air. 'Two weeks ago, he hanged himself in the barn – he couldn't face a life depending on my father. It was Papa who found him, who had to cut down his own son, and then bury him. Bruno would have been twenty-five next month.'

'I'm so sorry,' I said. 'I didn't know. Why haven't you said? You gave no hint, you seemed so, so . . . normal.'

'Because this is war, Anke. I don't want to think of myself as suffering more than anyone else, but it has to stop. It *has* to.' Her granite gaze gave way to pear-drop tears and she looked small and vulnerable again. I pulled her towards me and she sobbed her pain into the coat she had so kindly fixed for me.

'Oh Lord, Christa, where will it end?' I said into her glossy hair. 'When will it end?'

13

Life and Death

After our second restful night in the house, I checked on Sonia. She had spent time with her children, dressing in the afternoon and coming downstairs for tea. She was moving with impromptu squeaks and groans and her eyes were dark and troubled, but she was holding herself together for the family, despite her increasing discomfort.

'How long do you think, Anke? How long before I can birth this baby and tell my children?' she pleaded during our check, desperate to purge herself of the double burden within her.

'I don't know, but my guess is not too long,' I said. 'You look different now and your body is ready. Your mind simply has to let go.'

'I'm trying,' she said, 'I really am.'

'Just don't try too hard and it will happen.'

The maid woke me at midnight. Sonia was pacing in her bedroom, flushed and agitated. This was labour, although I left Christa to sleep until her hands were really needed. The baby's heartbeat was good, and Sonia was having to stop and breathe every three to four minutes, so likely to be in the first, or dilating, stage of labour. In between, she smiled for the first time since we had met.

'This is it, I know it is,' she panted. 'This is like before, with the other tw—' and she went into another contraction, blowing hard to climb the mountain peak of sixty seconds before respite again.

I sat rubbing Sonia's back, murmuring reassurance in the half light. During my time at homebirths in the Berlin suburbs I had learnt to work in near darkness, in contrast to the brightness of the maternity ward, where we could see everything yet not feel the progress. Here, I was in my comfort zone. In the gloom, I stared at the opulence shining through, the expensive furniture, and thoughts of my last birth in the camp hung heavily. Of Irena, and her baby born onto dirty paper instead of the thick, carefully woven blanket waiting for this baby. And yet stripped of all but her nightgown, Sonia could have been Irena or any other woman I had known; uncomfortable, scared and needing reassurance. And equally strong.

It was only thirty minutes or so before the pitch in the room changed. A momentous contraction caused Sonia to drop down on the floor and crawl like a heavy-bellied cat towards a corner. As she reached the peak, her body let out a distinctive bray, which seemed to surprise even her. For me, though, it was the familiar call to birth. I signalled the maid to wake Christa, and asked for the hot water to be brought upstairs. Christa was with me in minutes, eager and with no hint of anxiety. She busied herself in the corner, quietly laying out any equipment we might need, and then sitting and watching – another who would make a great midwife.

Sonia quickly appeared to be in transition, that half world between the need to hold on and the body's desire to purge itself of everything grown in the intense months of pregnancy. With each contraction now, she breathed, bayed and howled her way through, in between swaying and muttering to her dead husband: 'It's coming, Gerd, it's coming, darling. It's nearly here for you . . .'

I mouthed reassurances, but she wasn't hearing much beyond her own noise.

Christa sensed her cue, silently taking her place at Sonia's head end, her fingers clasped at greedily by Sonia, whose eyes were closed in deep focus. I stayed at the bottom end, feeling she wasn't too far from pushing this baby. Her waters broke in the next contraction, but instead of a clear gush, it was a thick, grainy brown soup – signs of meconium, the baby's first bowel movement. The pregnancy was overdue, but it was also a signal of distress, the baby's 'fight or flight' mechanism for survival. If we were in or near to a hospital, midwives would normally call in a paediatrician, but we were thirty minutes from the hospital, a local doctor our only other back-up. As a midwife, I was unfazed by meconium – it was a natural reaction and caused problems only if the baby inhaled the dirty fluid on its journey out. Most emerged kicking and screaming with no treatment needed, other than a good bath.

It was impossible to check the baby's heartbeat given Sonia was kneeling on all fours. She was pushing with the next

111

contraction, and her skin began to stretch and mould in the normal way, with a little tuft of hair soon pouting through. She was in that nether world, calling her husband's name constantly, while Christa tried to calm her anxiety, stroking her hand and talking next to her. My main concern was in slowing down the progress of the head – third babies often emerged with one huge push, as the mother couldn't hold on any longer.

'Sonia, just breathe for me,' I tried over her constant rambling. 'Small pushes, take it slow.'

In the next minute, she let out a whelp as the baby's crown breeched and slipped through the skin in one sudden leap forward, bringing her back into the here and now. Suddenly, the room was silent.

'That's wonderful,' I told her, moving to get sheets under her for the final arrival. 'The baby's head is born, you're nearly there.'

In most births, there's a minute or two's pause when nothing much happens, the baby's bluish face peering and pouting, its neck clamped in the mother's opening, sometimes fluttering eyelids and making a small bid to cry, but not yet a person in the world, the umbilical cord still being the lifeline for oxygen. With most mothers, confirming the head born was a way of rousing one last effort to birth the shoulders, in the moment when they were ready to give up. But in hindsight, it was the wrong message for Sonia, a woman who was almost afraid of meeting her baby. *She* may have wanted to meet her last-born, but her in-depth fear, her psyche, did not.

We waited, in the silence. One minute crept into two and still no contraction. The prickle on my neck increased as the baby's face turned a mottled purple.

112

'Sonia, just tell me when you feel a contraction,' I said, trying to temper a rising concern.

'It's not coming,' she said, now lucid and aware. 'What's happening?'

'Just give me a push, a good one, really low,' I told her.

Her body attempted to bear down, but the effort was pathetic compared to the mammoth, unrelenting efforts a few minutes before.

'I can't,' she moaned. 'It's just not there.'

In a split second I was up at Christa's side, whispering urgently. 'We need to get her upright,' I said, the flash in my eyes doubtless evident even in the half light.

Christa understood immediately, and we both hauled Sonia from her knees, and into a squat, her dead weight of fatigue making us breathe heavily, me guiding to protect the baby's head.

'Christa, can you hold her?' It was a big request given Christa's small frame, but a natural shot of adrenalin had injected untold strength in her limbs.

'Don't worry about me,' she said.

As she cradled Sonia from the back, I scooted around the front. The baby's head was hovering only inches from the blankets on the floor, and I didn't like to guess at its colour, let alone look. It needed to be born – now.

Sonia's head was lolling, back in her half world.

'Sonia! Look at me!' I was direct and she snapped up, wide-eyed. 'I need you to give one *really* big push. Please, Sonia. For me, for the baby.'

One look at my face and the urgency was apparent – her own features contorted and she bore down without the aid of a contraction. The baby's shoulders moved a little as I put a hand on each side of its head and pulled down with firm traction, but it sprang back as she ran out of breath and the effort stopped. I knew instantly what the problem was: shoulder dystocia, the baby's shoulders wedged behind the pubic bone of the pelvis. No amount of pushing or pulling would move this baby until they were free. It was among the midwife's worst nightmares, since the baby had to come out, and there was no reversing and delivering by caesarean, even in a hospital. We had to free this baby, or it would die half born.

'Christa – on her back, *now*!' She caught my tone and instantly lowered Sonia onto the floor. I forced Sonia's legs up and backwards towards her head, as far as they would go, all moves designed to dislodge the baby's shoulders. Sonia was moaning, slipping in and out of reality but thankfully not resisting our forced gymnastics.

'Over here,' I said to Christa, urgent but restrained. I took her left hand and placed the heel just above Sonia's pubic bone, with the right hand on the top of Sonia's still proud but flaccid bump.

'Now rub firmly on her belly, in circles,' I said. 'When I say, push backwards towards her belly button and down with your other hand. And, Christa?'

'Yes?' Her eyes were saucers.

'Push hard.'

I came back to the baby's head, hanging limply without much sign of life. Christa was rubbing furiously and Sonia's increased groan told me a contraction was brewing.

'Sonia,' I said loudly. 'Sonia! You need to push, give me a *huge* push.'

Somehow, through her confusion, she did. I placed my

right hand inside her vagina and found the front of the baby's right shoulder, ready to screw the baby round. In unison, we pushed and pulled – the light caught the sinews on Christa's arm as she bore back and down, the effort from Sonia I could feel as the baby's shoulders tried to move forward, and my own muscles stung as I rotated the shoulders. After what seemed like an age, yet was only a few seconds, the shoulder popped free, descended suddenly and I swiftly grabbed under the baby's arm, literally hauling both shoulders through, followed by the torso and legs. Sonia whelped again and Christa exhaled loudly in relief.

The baby was a good size, but completely flaccid, a blue head and white body that was never a welcome sight for any midwife. Oxygen had been severely limited in the last five minutes and he wasn't breathing. He looked lifeless, and I was glad Sonia's eyes were cast towards the ceiling; no mother should see this. Again Christa – brilliant Christa – was there in seconds with my stethoscope and a towel. While she vigorously rubbed life into the baby, I listened for the heart rate. Thankfully, we had one, but it was weak and slow, under sixty beats per minute – we needed to physically move more oxygen around the baby.

I did it in the only way I knew how. I rolled a small sheet, wedged it under the baby's neck so he faced skyward and checked there wasn't a plug of meconium in his throat. I couldn't see any debris, so I closed my own mouth over his tiny nose and lips. They were cold and unwelcoming. Keeping my own adrenalin in check, I blew what life I could into that baby, slowly and steadily. I faced his chest and watched for the rise, a tiny sign that air was entering his ribcage.

On the second or third blow I saw the magical lift of his

skin, and then drew away, placing two fingers over his chest and pumping quickly on his soft sternum – one, two, three, another blow, one, two, three. Repeating it three or four times, maybe more, Christa sitting beside me and muttering 'Come on, baby; come on, baby' over and over.

After another age, I felt him jerk and kick back a breath at me – he gasped, coughed some more and began mewing, soft at first, and then louder. It reminded me of the air raid siren back in Berlin getting into full swing. The whine turned into a cry, and his body flushed from white to blue, and then a reassuring pink. I picked him up and checked his tone, still a little floppy but improving with every breath. Within a minute he was howling his displeasure at the two women manhandling him.

Christa's face said it all. Her broad beam showed relief and joy, but her eyes reflected the terror of the past minutes. The baby's healthy cry brought Sonia round and we placed the baby next to her, tucking his naked body under her nightdress. She looked at his face, congested and purple from his birth efforts, and her mouth first smiled and then crimped, followed by tears – of joy or sorrow, I couldn't tell.

'Oh, baby,' she said. 'There you are.' Then at us: 'Is it a boy or girl?'

'A boy,' I said, slightly afraid it was the wrong answer.

'Oh, a boy.' She smiled. 'I hoped so. A boy for Gerd. A boy for my man.'

She was a mass of emotions, good and bad, but in that minute she was grateful that life had followed death.

It took us more than two hours to clean up and settle Sonia in her bed, the baby suckling contentedly at her breast and showing no effects of such a traumatic entrance. The maid volunteered to stay with her, and Christa and I retreated to the kitchen.

I've always maintained the first cup of tea after birth is the best for any mother, no matter the quality of the brew, but it's the same for midwives too. We held on to our cups across the table, and Christa couldn't suppress her grin.

'You're hooked, aren't you?' I laughed.

'How do you that again and again?' she said. 'It's so intense!'

'Well, it's not always so dramatic,' I said. 'But you do get used to the high and lows. In fact, you get to depend on them. I do know some midwives who are quite happy to do all the routine care, but avoid birth. For me, it's the pinnacle; it's what I feed off. Birth is like a drug.'

Swiftly, the camp images came into view. 'Well, in the old days, before the war,' I qualified.

'And now?'

'Well, let's just say I've seen too many tragedies to think of those as enjoyable.'

We both pondered the silence, hearing the household beginning to wake up, but I didn't want to dampen Christa's effervescence – she had just witnessed her first momentous birth, one she would never forget. She looked alive.

'But I have to admit, that does go down as one of the most demanding, if only for a few short minutes,' I said. It was Christa's cue for a barrage of questions – why I did what, and when, the what-ifs and the consequences. By the time we crawled into our beds, I was exhausted, yet bathed in the balm of satisfaction I hadn't felt since the early stages of the war, a salve to enjoy since this mother and baby were destined to stay together.

We stayed a further three days at Frau Schmidt's house, making sure the baby was feeding well, and supporting Sonia in her recovery. She was sore from the birth and moved slowly, while her mood seesawed between a contented, happy mother to the grieving widow she was. The children doted on their new brother, innocently telling their mother how much Papa would love the new baby – named 'Gerd' – when he came home. Sonia's face creased but she wasn't ready to deal with their grief just yet.

Christa and I waved goodbye to a fractured household, although Sonia's gratitude made us feel we had done something to paste some of the cracks together, for a short time at least. I began to wonder that she was related to Magda Goebbels at all, since she was warm and emotive, with very little reserve. She was married to a Nazi officer, but she had a human side nonetheless.

14

Renewed Ascent

The journey back caused mixed emotions in both of us. Christa was clearly unhappy in the Goebbels' household, more so since her brother's death, and desperate to be nearer to her father. However, her wage was needed to send home and positions like hers were not easy to find with a war raging. Inside the car near the Goebbels' porch, we hugged goodbye, unwilling to let go of our strengthened bond.

'I'll try to engineer a trip up to you,' she said, pre-empting my thoughts again. 'I'm sure I can manage something. Take care, Anke. Just keep safe.'

The air down below was muted and foggy, but as we climbed through the mist, up and out into sunshine, there was that feeling again – the Berghof existed on another plane, a world beyond the beanstalk. The knot in my stomach, which had been noticeably relaxed at the Schmidt house, now started to tighten and twist. Seeing Eva didn't concern me – I had neither missed her nor was unhappy about seeing her – but I hoped beyond everything that *he* was gone.

Several cars were in front of the house, their drivers smoking and hovering, engines idling. People of note were leaving soon. I took my small bag and headed over to my chalet, my mind occupied with nothing beyond a bath and checking in with Eva. My eyes must have been fixed on the ground, because it was only at the last minute that I flicked them up towards the mountain caps and found myself in a trap.

He was directly in my view, walking towards me, head also down, stature unmistakable. The sight of a German shepherd at his side confirmed what I feared. I could neither dart towards my room, nor turn and walk the other way without the aversion being obvious. Perhaps sensing another person, he looked up a second after I did, his distinctive features bearing slight confusion though not alarm. I, of course, recognised the Führer instantly, though his expression showed some kind of acknowledgement.

I stopped in my tracks, unsure what to do. I had always thought of myself as a person unaffected by status, celebrity or false gravitas, and yet I was dumbfounded. Our eyes met, his dark and unyielding; mine undoubtedly like those of a startled fox. And that knot in my stomach, it was yanked hard, like a dog on a leash. Time stood still, for a second or two, until he broke the static air and nodded, as a way of saying, 'Good day,' clicked his tongue at the dog and took his eyes back to the ground, moving on.

And that was my encounter with the Führer, not a syllable uttered – no fear exuded, no monster on show, no devilish glint in his eye. A man who showed common courtesy, to someone he had never met before.

For some time, I lay on my bed, heart racing, conjuring

all the things I had wanted to say to him – about my family, the camp, the suffering, the tortured women, the dead babies, more suffering – but didn't. Above all, I thought about how my life was more like a warped fairy tale than anything of reality, then sensed a profound relief as I heard the engines retreat, one by one, into the distance.

Inside the Berghof, it was as if the fervour of Christmas had come and gone; rooms reflected a heavy void, servants moved deftly and the kitchen noises reverted to a steady industry rather than the perpetual fury of the previous days. Frau Grunders was nowhere to be seen, and I ate lunch almost alone. Later, I reported to Sergeant Meier, barely suppressing the temptation to offer a mock salute. He seemed underwhelmed to see me.

'Ah, Fräulein Hoff, you're back.' His left eye twitched irritably, and I wondered how lost he felt not being in the glow of the Führer's presence.

'It seems I am. Is there any news I need to know before I meet Fräulein Braun again?'

'I think she's been rather preoccupied with the company to be thinking of your visits,' he said with a note of triumph. 'I know she's retired to her room currently, and has asked whether she can see you tomorrow.' His smugness pulled up the bristles of his moustache, revealing unattractive, yellowing teeth.

'As she wishes,' I said without missing a beat. 'Good day, Sergeant Meier.'

So, more wasted hours in which to ponder. Over the years, I'd told impatient women time and again that pregnancy is a waiting game – I could hear myself repeating it endlessly – but it had never seemed that way to me, with a constant stream of births and women needing care. And yet waiting for one baby to be grown, cultivated and nurtured was painstaking and endless. Like a lifetime.

I wasn't sure of what mood I would find Eva in the next morning – vibrant at seeing her lover for more than just a few days, or melancholy at his leaving. She was all smiles as I arrived – 'Oh, Anke, how lovely to see you!' – but the facade soon fell and she drifted into a sadness and deflation. Yes, the baby was moving fine, and yes, she felt healthy, sleep sometimes elusive. There was a change in the bump during the last week or so, and she had clearly eaten well during the Führer's stay; there were still three months to go but the baby had grown, along with the flesh around it. She was watching my face intently, translating my expression, as I laid on hands to read her abdomen.

'Is everything as it should be? You look . . . perplexed.'

I put on a smile. 'No, everything's fine, Fräulein Braun. It's only that I sometimes get carried away in trying to map the baby's position. It's quite early days but I think the baby is head down. It might not stay that way – the baby is still capable of somersaults, but it's a good sign it can go into your pelvis.'

'Clever baby,' she said, and gave it her familiar palming touch.

I turned to go. 'Will you require a check tomorrow?'

'Yes, thank you.' I turned towards the door, and heard her voice again, this time weak and needy. 'Anke?'

'Yes?' She looked small and vulnerable, peering at me.

'The baby. It will be . . . all right, won't it? What you can feel, is . . . normal?'

It was as if simply uttering the words could jinx the baby. I'd needed to reassure countless women of the same thing – whether it was their first, second or fifth baby, German women, rich or poor, educated or not, believed in a strange, cultivated myth that mere whims about a baby's condition, even unpleasant thoughts, could influence their health and create disabilities. Without a window on the womb, it was a reliance on Mother Nature's benevolence that was forced upon us, and increasingly we didn't like the surprises she occasionally threw into the mix. The Third Reich had accelerated that fear a thousand fold. I knew exactly what Eva Braun was driving at.

'Everything I feel and hear leads me to believe your baby is fit and healthy,' I told her. And it was the truth, at that moment. As a midwife, I had learnt early on you could not give absolute promises. One winter night I'd worked a home-birth with an old-school midwife on the outskirts of Berlin. I was ready to take the lead, she said, and she would stay in the background.

The woman in labour was normally anxious, but seemed reassured when, each time I listened to the heartbeat, I told her: 'The baby is fine, everything will be all right.' I felt a wave of satisfaction at my ability to calm her. Up until the baby emerged lifeless, a chalky white girl who had choked on her own cord, the lifeline pumping breath until those late stages. Through her tears, the woman looked at me in disbelief. She didn't say a word, but she didn't need to. I had promised what I couldn't give, and it was a lesson hard learned.

'You tell them "The baby *sounds* fine," which is the truth at that moment,' the midwife explained after, with kind but wise words. 'Mother Nature is bigger than any of us, and only she knows.' So Eva Braun's baby *appeared* fine and *seemed* well, but my words were well chosen.

'Thank you,' said Eva, clutching at the hope. 'Oh, and, Anke?'

'Yes?'

'Please call me Eva. I think we are beyond niceties now.'

15

Waiting

Nature moved at a faster pace than our lives over the next month. Spring flowers were in bud and the air distinctly warmer; the snow on the peaks opposite receded towards the tops, as if someone were unravelling a woollen hat from the bottom, keeping just the tips warm. Eva was well, so I spent daytimes on the main terrace in the sunshine, stalking the sun towards my own little terrace in the afternoon, shifting my chair around until finally the low, mandarin rays disappeared completely and I was forced to go inside or pull out my blanket and a light.

I ate my way through the books on Frau Grunders' shelves, the housekeeper near silent when I went to raid her parlour. She was almost in mourning since the Führer's departure, as if her own son had left for the front. The whole house, it seemed, was in a state of depression.

Eva's health was stable but her mood was unusually labile. At times she was upbeat and childlike in her enthusiasm for life and the pregnancy, twittering about baby clothes, and upcoming visits from her sister, who always seemed to cancel at the last moment. 'She's so busy, what with planning the wedding,' Eva said, making excuses for her 'devoted' sibling. On other days she was noticeably down, barely acknowledging me or the baby, and seemed to haul her increasing girth around as if it were an inconvenient suitcase.

The maids could predict her manner from the flow of letters; in the early days of the war, Hitler had written to Eva almost every day he was away. Her mood, and her treatment of the staff, was genial and pleasant when his affection on paper flowed. On days without a letter – and those were becoming increasingly common as the war and the pregnancy wore on – they tiptoed into her room, wary of her bark and bite, sometimes sent packing with a sting of words and a thud of the woodwork.

I continued writing my obligatory letters to my parents, Franz, and Ilse, even though it became harder to phrase the same sentiments again and again. Each week, I took my offerings to Sergeant Meier, who merely nodded as I laid them on his desk, and who always shook his head without expression when I asked him if there were any returns.

To pass the time, I began making a wish list of practical items for Captain Stenz, should he ever appear again. I was strangely concerned he had been ghosted away to another part of the war and its fiery arena, fatally exposed. I surprised myself by how much time I spent looking towards the gates and hoping it was his car crunching on the gravel path. Despite the dark shade of his uniform, the menace of the skull bone insignia pinned to his collar, I did look on him as human, almost as a friend.

Berlin, February 1942

The snow was flurrying as I wound my scarf tightly at the hospital entrance. It was only three in the afternoon, but the sky was already a ceiling of dark sludge, little tornados of flakes whipping in the air. Despite the weather, I planned to walk home after a busy shift, then sink into a hot bath, a good book and sleep — in that order.

He approached as I headed down the steps, the wide brim of his hat pulled low over his face. I started for a moment — he could easily have been Gestapo, with his belted mackintosh and black brogues.

'Fräulein Hoff?'

'Yes?' I carried on walking, determined he wouldn't catch the alarm in my face.

'Minna sent me.'

'Minna? Do I know her?' I kept my head bent down, as any hesitation was a true giveaway.

'She says the bottom is falling out of the market, and you need to come quickly.'

My head snapped upwards, flakes settling on my nose. This was the code we had set for Nadia going into labour; it was too risky for me to be on-call for all the births in the ghetto, but if there were no women in the neighbourhood who felt confident with a breech, I'd said I would come. If Minna had sent for me, she needed my help.

I stopped. 'All right, how soon?'

'She said to bring you immediately.'

'It'll take us a while on foot, just as long if we take the tram halfway.'

'I've got a car, and passes,' he said. 'This way.'

I hesitated. It was one thing walking alongside this stranger, another getting into a car with him. He caught my wariness.

'It's all right,' he said, 'I'm not Gestapo, I promise.'

'But you are German?' There were blond flecks under his hat, and his features were undoubtedly Aryan.

'As are you.' He smiled, white teeth and a genuine warmth. His breath puffed into the icy, grey air. 'I'm just trying to help, like you. Do what I can.'

'And your name?'

'No names,' he said. 'It's safer.'

Even in this fog of distrust, there was a point where you had to believe in some things, in people, and my gut told me I should follow. I had no choice if what he said was true. Nadia could be in strong labour. Strong and quick.

Whatever passes he possessed worked like magic, and we sailed through the checkpoints with few questions. The car reached the perimeters of the Jewish quarter, where we parked and walked the rest of the way.

'Take my arm, Fräulein,' he said as we headed into the flurry, bigger and more consistent flakes falling now. The sight of us

128

would be more convincing from afar, a couple walking home through the snow to warmth and safety, skirting the Jewish quarter, arm in arm.

We walked on, feigning an innocent conversation and slipping into the ghetto under a snow cloak. At Nadia's door, he rapped four times, paused, and rapped twice again. A face I recognised as Minna's brother appeared, and I sidled in.

'Good luck, Fräulein,' the man said, and turned back into the white storm. I felt a pinch of sorrow at seeing him go.

The room had been cleared of everyone but Minna and Nadia's mother. 'Sorry to call like this,' Minna said with true regret. 'The old woman who'd volunteered was found dead this morning.'

A kettle was on the boil and the bed sheet had been pulled back. The room was warm enough, every contribution from the house having made it into the woodpile. Nadia was on the mattress, on all fours, head in her hands and her bottom in the air, clad in her knickers, swaying as a perfect pendulum.

I had my Pinard to listen to the baby, but nothing more, although we had stockpiled sterile gloves in the house, and the inevitable towels, clean and folded, were waiting. I sat on my haunches beside Nadia as she went into a contraction, watching the twist of her pelvis as her groans rose to a crescendo, blowing fiercely into her hands. I resisted touching, even to offer massage on her back, as it was important with any breech to let mothers wriggle and writhe in reaction to the baby's internal corkscrewing.

Contraction over, I came on a level with her head, her black fringe wet and stringy.

'Hey, Nadia, you're doing so well. This baby really wants to come.'

'I think so.' She smiled weakly.

129

'Can I listen to the baby? You might need to move a little — is that possible?'

She flopped onto her side, and I came down and found the heartbeat, still at the top of her abdomen.

'Baby sounds fine,' I said. 'No problems.'

'What will you do?' she said, beads of sweat falling into her eyes, anxiety rising in their blackness.

'Me? Nothing, just watch and wait.'

She seemed surprised I wasn't armed with some mechanical tool to extract her baby, but she was also young enough not to have been at any births amongst her community.

'What should I do?' she asked.

'Exactly what you've been doing, Nadia. Let your baby come through. Don't resist, just open yourself to whatever feelings you have inside.'

She nodded, childlike. But for one so young, she seemed to understand what I'd said, as if those pressures were already brewing. Instantly, she hoisted herself back onto her knees as another contraction took hold, and the groan turned into the slightest of moos. By her pitch, I estimated it wouldn't be too long.

Minna held out a welcome cup of tea, while she and I retreated to the back of the room as Nadia's mother took her place at her daughter's side, rubbing her shoulders, murmuring encouragement and telling her she would be a mother soon, and to hold on, keep going. The snow fell onto the dirty panes, and the room grew darker still as the powder weaved a white blind to the world outside. We sipped and waited, while the men smoked downstairs, their anxious mutterings pushing through the floorboards, no laughter or macho chiding until the baby's cry was free.

Nadia's pitch rose and fell over the next hour, and I listened to her and the baby at intervals. Eventually, the slightest of squeaks

130

broke through the peak of a contraction, followed by a split-second grunt, and she descended the mountain of pain again.

'I can't do it!' she cried into the air.

Just as I'd hoped, two pieces of the jigsaw in place. I put down my tea, and moved to her side.

'Nadia, maybe it's time to take off your knickers. It's safe. It's just us.'

She nodded into her hands and her mother peeled off the flimsy material, wet with a patch of fluid – likely from the waters – centred with a healthy mucousy blood streak. Piece number three.

The next contraction slotted in number four; at the crest, a groan broke free of her mouth, and a bear-like growl coiled from within this innocent girl, a top-to-toe effort of purging as her buttocks parted, and the purple line above her sacrum rose to signal the baby moving down.

'Mama! Anke! Help me!' Her distress was muffled as she thrashed her head but couldn't move it from the mattress.

'Nadia, this is all fine, all normal,' I whispered, my mouth close to her ear. 'I think you're ready to push your baby, but will you let me feel inside, just to make sure?'

She nodded again. Minna was there instantly with water and gloves. Ideally I wanted Nadia to roll over onto her back, but once there, she might not move again, and her position now was best for the baby's journey. I slipped my fingers, first one then two into her moist opening, slippery from the body's own birth jelly, and they stopped sharply at the baby, a hard and stretched buttock filling the entire space and acting exactly like a head. The same sensation had caught me out more than once, so my expectations were still for a bottom first. I circled the bony parts, and felt no cervix, important as we had no idea how big or small this baby might be. If a small rim of cervix remained, the rump might slip through but

131

the bulbous head could be trapped inside, a dangerous – almost always fatal – scenario with scrawny babies.

I withdrew and turned to Minna, smiling and nodding. She flashed relief to Nadia's mother, and the whole room let out a communal breath. Minna stoked the fire to busy her hands, and put more water on for tea. I retreated towards the edge of the mattress, as Nadia felt the full force of her body's commands.

The baby's buttocks soon showed themselves, with a telltale crease. Nadia shunted back and forth on her knees uneasily, as if she was working a washboard at the other end, a true sign of her reactions, deep into her own self, crying out to us but not expecting a reaction. There was no chance to listen to the baby now, with the speed of the labour and the position. I had to hold my own breath and trust in the baby's.

I beckoned Minna closer, as Nadia's mother couldn't bear her own daughter in pain and stood by the kettle, hugging herself.

'When will it come? When?' Nadia pleaded.

'Soon, Nadia, soon. I can see your baby. It's very close.'

Minna began humming softly, something I'd heard in a previous labour, and the air lifted a little, until a contraction took hold and Nadia's loud cry cloaked over it. In one seamless move she pushed herself back, onto her feet and haunches, and Minna caught and cradled her before she fell backwards. The baby launched forward, the rump fully through, and the legs folded upwards, tiny feet only just held inside Nadia's strained skin. Facing me, I couldn't help but see the swollen but unmistakable genitalia of a boy's bluish plums.

'Beautiful!' I told her. 'Nadia, just keep going when your body tells you. You're nearly there.' The labour was going much more smoothly than I'd expected, but sweat still pricked at my neck. I did nothing but hold a gloved hand under the buttock, ready to catch if the baby released suddenly. Nadia panted a lion's breath, ready for the next roar into the world.

The next contraction was a mighty one. She let fly with her voice upwards, and downwards with courage. By the light of the nearest candle I watched in awe as Nadia pumped her body up and down, her legs muscles taut and wet — the baby's feet plopped out one by one, then the arms in quick succession, left and right, and the baby's chin appeared at the opening, as this young but all-knowing mother lowered herself to land the baby onto the mattress. He sat, folded at his midriff, as if wearing his own mother like a little hat. Behind Nadia, Minna's wide eyes were fixed on mine for clues, and she saw me visibly relax in that split second — if the chin was through, I could be sure the head wasn't trapped. Minna's own strength kept Nadia upright and floating, and the whole room existed in a state of suspension.

As we waited for another contraction, the baby gasped and bucked his legs, as if desperate to suck in air, but I pulled back my voice. I wanted to say, 'Just give a push, Nadia,' sweat dripping from me now. It was a crucial time for the breech, still not fully born, the cord being trapped and flattened against the mother's tight skin. I wanted this baby out — now — but I knew in my mind the time had to be right.

It was less than a minute but felt like ten. Finally, Nadia opened her eyes, looked at me as if she had caught sight of the devil, and bayed her baby into the world. Released, he flopped forward and rolled onto his side, sparking himself into life before I had a chance to reach him with a towel. The little man was the loudest, but the women in the room joined in with their own joyful noise — theirs with a welcome tone, mine of sheer relief. Seconds later, we heard a whoop below the boards, as the news filtered down to the men.

There was more tea, interspersed with birthing and checking the placenta, washing and clearing, as the newest resident of this tiny room suckled eagerly at his mother's breast. Nadia's face was flushed, a halo of wet hair around her head, beaming with pride and relief. The baby, thankfully, was dark, with tiny, nub nose, no sign of any Aryan features as yet. Nature had mercifully given him the looks of his mother, acceptance into the family being his best chance of survival.

Almost two hours after the birth I signalled to Minna I was ready to go. After dark, and with the snow now settling, one of the men usually walked me to the perimeter, where a well-hidden entrance into the ghetto pushed me out into the Berlin beyond, so that if I was stopped by a patrol, it was usually only curiosity and not an inquisition I had to deal with. I could easily claim being lost in the afternoon's weather and the darkness.

Minna went downstairs to search for one of Nadia's brothers. I heard a distant rap on the door two floors below, and imagined the news was already out – families would come calling with whatever gifts they could spare. But a thunderous ascent on the wooden stairs sparked sudden alarm, and before I had time to bar the door to any unwelcome guests it was flung open.

The men who waltzed confidently into the room didn't just look like Gestapo. They were Gestapo.

16

Plans

April saw a late bloom in events at the Berghof. I was reading on my porch when I recognised the lean frame of Captain Stenz walking towards me. I felt a brief tingle of . . . was it excitement? Or simply relief at the prospect of real conversation? It was the first time I had seen him since the war summit, and it felt like an age.

'Captain Stenz,' I said, trying to mask an overenthusiastic greeting.

'Fräulein Hoff.' He smiled. 'I assumed I would find you here. You are well?'

'As expected.'

His eyes, the turquoise shade of my memory, glinted in the light. 'I've just had a brief meeting with Fräulein Braun, and it seems there are no problems. The relatives of the Goebbels are also very grateful for your expertise.'

'I did what I would do for any woman, and, to be honest Captain Stenz, it was a change to get away, and to be a midwife again. I know I've said it before but I feel very underemployed here – quite useless.'

He sat down, took off his cap and flattened his blond strands with a lean hand, fixing his pupils on mine. 'But just having you here – your experience – is vital for keeping everything in—' he pondered his words carefully '—in balance.' He smiled again, a little crinkle appearing in the corners of his cheeks where I hadn't noticed it before. 'Don't underestimate it, Fräulein Hoff. Your contribution. It certainly makes my life, my work, a lot easier.'

I was never glad to make this loathsome war any smoother for the Nazi Party, but he did make me feel worthy again. Equally, I hated myself for needing it.

Mindful of the recent emergency at the Schmidt household, I was keen to discuss details of the birth – the timing of bringing in equipment, and the pain relief I knew Eva was anxious to have on standby. Captain Stenz took copious notes in his black leather book, his script classical and ornate, fitting for an architectural student.

'And the medical staff, when do you think they should arrive and take up their post?' he said.

It was a question I hadn't wanted to address. But Eva would never be allowed to birth halfway up a mountain without medical support, and since I didn't relish an emergency and a bumpy ride down, with consequences for her or the baby, I had to accept their presence. Given my recent reputation, though, I tested my bargaining power.

'From about thirty-six weeks would be standard,' I said, 'but I want to stress that they are to remain outside of the birth room at all times, unless invited in. Really, my preference would be outside the building.'

'Surely, Fräulein Hoff, there is a benefit in having everything on hand, just in case?' He wore that familiar look of confusion about birth I had seen in countless faces.

I sat back and smiled. 'It's hard to explain,' I said, 'especially when I'm talking to someone from your background.'

'What do you mean?' He was sharp. Defensive.

'Well, I don't know much about architecture, but I assume that when you plan a building, you plan for it to stay upright first and foremost, and you build solid foundations, as a good basis?'

'Yeees.' He softened at the analogy, though clearly unsure where my argument was heading.

'And you feel sure that your building will be safe and secure because you've put all that in place, based on the laws of physics, of science?'

'Yes.' Still sceptical. He sank back a little further into the chair, perhaps sensing I was playing.

'Well, I work in exactly the same way, except my foundations are rooted within people – experience, intuition, training, protocols. Midwifery is an art much more than it's a science.' I leaned back, satisfied I had explained myself.

'But what about the nasty surprises, Fräulein Hoff? What about the fact that babies are humans and that human behaviour cannot always be predicted. After all, look at this wa—' He stopped abruptly, before we led ourselves into a truly moral battlefield. It was a recurring theme in debates where I defended my unshakable belief in birth.

'And can you tell me, Captain Stenz, that when the last brick is placed on top of your building, you know with absolute certainty – one hundred per cent certainty, mind you – that it won't topple?'

'Well, nothing in this life is a hundred per cent, but—'

I leapt in. 'So what makes you fix that last brick on? If you're not absolutely certain, beyond a shadow of doubt?'

'I suppose there's a small amount of faith . . .' and he smiled as he said it, conceding defeat. Checkmate. 'But it's faith in the science,' he qualified quickly.

'It's faith nonetheless,' I said. 'In my job, I'm allowed to have a lot of it. And where the faith runs thin, where nature goes sideways, then you have training and protocol.'

'And surely that means equipment, medical staff, back-up plans?' He was confused again.

'Yes, sometimes, but we don't assume it will go wrong. Labouring mothers may look, at times, as if the process is awry, as if they are out of control. But they are not. It's the labour talking, the journey progressing. And that's always temporary.'

I sat forward, enjoying the argument. 'That's my one and only surety, Captain Stenz. That pregnancy and labour always end. The bits in between, that's what keeps us on our toes. That's what I love.'

He looked genuinely amused. 'Well, Fräulein Hoff, if what you say is true then we are in good hands, although I don't pretend to understand.' He got up, and I was suddenly deflated at his going. 'It doesn't fit with the military way of the Reich, of order, or rules—'

'I'm not sure you do either,' I interrupted.

He smiled, mouth closed. 'Perhaps. But I must go and—' he held up his book of lists '—work on your demands.' He grinned as he turned.

'Ah, one more thing, Fräulein Hoff,' he said, swivelling back. 'Were you reassured by the letters from your family?'

138

'Letters? What letters?' My heart rate shot up twenty beats.

He coloured, and his mouth set firmly. 'I believe some letters have arrived for you. Please excuse me for a moment. Wait here.'

Without explanation, Captain Stenz strode quickly towards the main house, while my heart bounded in my throat. In minutes, he returned, his neck flushed a cherry red above his tight collar. His hand shot out and presented a small bundle of envelopes – I counted four edges quickly.

'My sincere apologies, Fräulein Hoff,' he said. 'I can only think that Sergeant Meier's memory was not what it should have been. You can be assured that any future correspondence will be forwarded to you as soon as possible.'

I plucked at the bundle, like a small child snatching a new toy, and immediately pulled them in to my breast, wanting to rip them open there and then and drink in the sentiments. I stopped myself, in time to halt my rudeness and acknowledge his efforts. His body was rigid and starched, I imagined from an angry encounter with his deputy.

'Thank you,' I said. 'You don't know how much this means. Really.'

He dropped his head, but stopped short of clicking his heels – he seemed less inclined to do it in my presence.

'Well, good day, Fräulein. Have a good afternoon.'

'Good day, Captain Stenz,' I said, but I was already turning towards my room. I needed to be contained, to breathe in everything they said, to be in my own world.

My hands were shaking as I spread the four envelopes out on the bed, cheap paper fashioned into makeshift packages. Two were in my father's distinctive hand, although a little more spidery than I remembered, two in my mother's, solid and upright lettering. There was nothing, however, from Franz or Ilse and I didn't allow myself to guess at the reason.

Tentatively, I brought each letter out from the envelope and scanned the date. The first, from my father, was dated five weeks before, and the last, from Mama, two weeks ago. As of then, she was alive! I lay back on the bed, hoping the mattress would absorb the nervous pulse of my body, although it did nothing to quell the shake in my hands. The letters were only a page each, as if a maximum number of words had been dictated. My eyes swam, making the ink a scrawl. Papa began:

My darling Anke,
You can't imagine how relieved and delighted I was to
receive your letter — so unexpected. You sound well, in fair
health. I am with some lovely comrades, and we are
keeping up our spirits together.

You would not believe how practical I have become,
working all day at my bench — I almost feel like I have a
proper job, darling girl, just like you! My chest is holding
up, even through the winter, so there is every reason to be
cheerful. We can see the sunshine from our workplace, but it
would be nice to glimpse a consistent horizon every so
often too. Maybe one day.

I think of you, my gorgeous one, of all of you, and hope
one day we can be reunited — if not at home, then all
together. Please, be well, be good.

I hope to hear from you again.
All my love, Papa

140

I read it through several times, scanning for hidden messages. He was in a men's camp — he only used the word 'comrade' in the male sense — and there was no mention of my mother, so they were not together and — I had to assume — hadn't been for some time. Clearly, he was in a labour camp doing some type of factory work, which quietened my nerves a little. Our agreed code — talk of smooth or rocky horizons — told me he was surviving, and he was pleading for me to 'be good', to follow the rules, to *stay alive*. Most of all, Papa's tone was reassuring; his old tenacity about politics had transferred itself into survival. He hadn't given up.

The next letter, date-wise, was from Mama. She relayed the same sort of messages, of being in a packed hut of women *with many new sisters*, but her tone smacked of being alone, without her family, until she wrote: *Ilse is well and sends her love. I still have to chide her about trying to protect her wheezing chest but you know your sister! We are both working hard, but managing to rest also.*

So Ilse was alive, and they were together! It seemed almost a miracle, but then when I thought about the night we were all taken, they would have been together. Men and women were automatically separated, but not necessarily female relatives. It had been common in my camp to see mothers and daughters spooned into each other on the bed racks, feeding off each other's heat, those children old enough to work, teenagers usually, with bodies like chiselled stone from the heavy lifting of machinery around the factory.

While Papa had chosen his words carefully to avoid the censor, Mama's naturally emotive style had attracted a few black marks. I held the tissue-like paper up to the light in the hope of seeing through, but the Reich's black stain was foolproof to the naked eye.

The second letter from each said almost the same; like me they struggled to say anything new, and when they signed off a second time, there was a masked plea for news. *I hope you are all well and smiling through*, wrote Papa. *Perhaps we will all be together again someday*, said Mama. They were ravenous for news of each other, and of Franz. It was my task, in the new letters I could write, to be their conduit.

I felt buoyed, though not entirely free of the smouldering belly glow. I had imagined I would explode with emotion, but I found myself not sobbing, only a steady rivulet of tears trickling, settling into each ear. I let it pool, and when I woke briefly, it had made a little salt crust around each lobe. The room was dim, and it reminded me we were all still in darkness.

It was the hacking that brought me to my senses, a steady rhythm of alternate dry and wet coughs, heavy phlegm rolling around some poor unfortunate's lungs. I walked nearer to the bed, my hospital shoes clipping in time to the noise behind the screens – clip, clop, cough, clip, clop, cough. I looked down and noticed several spots of blood on my snowy white apron. That will never do, I thought concisely. Matron will be very cross.

I pulled the screen to one side. 'And how are we today, Herr Hoff?' I said, feeling for the lank wrist of the man lying on the bed. His grey hair was wild, beard long and unkempt, and his striped pyjamas peppered with spots of blood across his bony ribs and mottled flesh. 'Oh, our spots match,' I mused, while counting his languid pulse.

'Surviving, Nurse Hoff,' he managed, chest peaking with each

laboured breath, the wheeze of bellows working hard to function. 'I mustn't complain.'

'That's the spirit, Herr Hoff,' I trilled, and turned to go. 'Just make sure you stay alive a little longer. There's a war on, you know.'

His spindly fingers caught the edge of my apron as I swivelled, another ball of spittle pushing up in his throat. 'Please stay,' he rasped, suppressing the rattle of death. 'Stay with me.' His fingers crawled into the air, probing for contact.

Another voice rose above the curtain, urgent and pleading, 'Nurse! Nurse!' I stepped smartly into the ward, white rays of sunlight bleaching the chalky walls, adjusting my eyes for the figure calling. The contrast was dramatic: a halo of light, in the middle of which was a head, bleating like a lamb in need.

'Anke, Anke,' it said, a gowned body melting into the glare, straw-coloured legs connecting with the floor. I clipped towards the form, its gaze focused on the scrubbed, pristine tiles. A slick of red was snaking its way towards my black, austere shoes, meandering like a reptile tasting the air. 'Oh no, not more blood,' I sighed to myself. 'This really won't do.'

I followed the source of the ruby river, towards bare feet, and upwards, a tiny pulse noticeable on the ankle as it continued to trickle steadily from inside the gown. Two hands emerged from the halo, bloodied across the fingers and palms, like a naughty child who had spread its hands into a paint pot. 'Anke, Anke,' the monotone cry continued. It was only then I looked up, into and through the ivory mist and saw it was Eva's face, her eyes fixed on mine. 'The baby, the baby,' she said, one, two, three times over, looking down mournfully at the uneven pool of blood. 'What about the baby?'

Behind the curtain, the air dirtied with a phlegmy cough, and *a voice travelled over the screen. 'Nurse Hoff, come back, please stay.' My shoes swivelled on the viscous claret, one ear tuned in to either plea, pulled towards the dying needs of the old man, and drawn in the opposite direction by the pathetic bleats of Eva's distress. Which one needed me most? I felt my own anxiety pulse and I clutched a hand to my chest as my heart literally tore in two.*

I woke, and this time it was sweat, not tears, coating my face, heavy gasps keeping pace with my racing heart. The room was light, a morning brightness, with a fresh taint to the air, and I lay for some time, relieved it was daytime and consciously slowing my breath. Nightmares were not common for me – in the camp some women were plagued by a continuous newsreel of horror in their sleep – but I had had only a few, and surprisingly none since leaving the camp.

As I washed away the salt stains, the dream images hung like a faint negative of a photograph, never quite showing themselves properly. Those letters had triggered something inside, but I was somehow comforted. I possessed the right emotions. I could still feel as me. Human.

17

A Slice of Life

There was little talk in the servants' dining room the next morning and, once more, I ate virtually alone. Sergeant Meier intercepted me on the way to Eva's room – he had his own little game whereby he stepped out and startled me.

'Morning, Sergeant Meier. Can I say you look a little tired? Are you well?'

Automatically, he palmed his waxen face and the moustache bristled. Mission accomplished.

'I am perfectly well,' he said. 'I came to tell you that Fräulein Braun has asked you attend her later. She is feeling a little under the weather and is sleeping.'

'Well, perhaps I should see her now, if she's unwell?'

'I think it would be better if—'

'I think that's my decision, Sergeant, since I am the health professional.'

He started at my attempt to pull rank but stood firm. 'She has given me strict instructions to be left alone. You can see her after you return from your trip.'

'Trip?' The thought of a sudden exit created a small panic, but he had at least spoken of a return. Strange how the mountain top seesawed between a prison and a safe haven.

'Fräulein Braun was planning a shopping trip to Berchtesgaden, to purchase supplies for the baby. She is anxious not to delay and has asked that you go instead. She has written out details, but says for you to use your experience if you feel it's not complete.'

He handed me a piece of paper, thick and expensive, and I glimpsed eight to ten items listed.

'And who am I to go with?' I balked at the idea of Sergeant Meier as a shopping companion, trailing my every move and making awkward small talk.

'I am happy to accompany Fräulein Hoff this morning.' Captain Stenz approached from behind. 'I have a meeting in the afternoon; I can drive on from Berchtesgaden. Sergeant Meier, I'm sure you can arrange for a driver to collect Fräulein Hoff later?'

The oily head dipped, heels clicked, and Sergeant Meier was gone.

Unusually, I was bemused and stood silently.

'Shall we?' Captain Stenz gestured towards the hallway. 'Do you have anything you need to collect from your room?'

I half laughed. 'You mean, like a bag, Captain Stenz? What on earth would I put in it?' I didn't mean to be inflammatory, especially towards him, but it was a natural reaction to my smouldering anger, the in-built subversion of an inmate. His deadpan expression was neither irritated nor amused, a sign of his well-honed diplomacy.

146

'I was thinking more of a jacket, but if you don't need one, then perhaps we should we go?'

His car was well used and comfortable, the odour of ageing leather and his own scent, a light cologne I couldn't identify yet.

'Thank you, Rainer,' he called to the driver, and we moved off. I looked at Eva's list, her recollections of the conversations we'd had while walking to and from the Teehaus – nightdresses and muslins, napkins and blankets. She had scribbled on the bottom in pencil – perhaps as an afterthought – *rattle*.

'I'm quite relieved Fräulein Braun wasn't able to travel today,' the Captain said as we drove, and I felt my heart skip sideways. We locked eyes, his blue pools dipping swiftly. 'Well, Herr Goebbels is very keen she is not seen in public, however much her . . . *condition* can be disguised.' Only then was his expression awkward.

We drove to the centre of town, stepping out into a bright, spring day, a smell of domestic industry in the air and a steady bustle of people who gave neither the car nor his uniform a second look.

'Do you know the town well, Captain?' I asked, casting around for the shops we might need.

'Not well, no,' he said. 'We may need to follow our noses.' He smiled, the playful one again, and he'd visibly relaxed on getting out of the car. Was I wrong, or did his uniform of mere material act like a straitjacket to the real man inside?

I walked towards the town square, a fountain marking the middle, feeling we could fan out into the side streets of shops if needed. The town was typical Bavaria, with gabled and shuttered houses sporting newly planted baskets, giving

147

colour shots against the black and white timbers. Crystal-cut mountains peeked between the buildings, with a clear blue sky as their backdrop. Much like the Berghof, here it was hard to even imagine there was a war on. Only the numerous swastikas, their hard and sharp edges set against the floral display, reminded us this was Reich country, infinitely proud of their local boy.

'Perhaps we should head for the nearest draper's, and then ask about the best stores for baby clothes?' I suggested.

'If that's what an expectant couple would do, then I bow to your knowledge, Fräulein Hoff.' His expression was pure mischief.

Amid the sumptuous display of the draper's, the rotund shopkeeper beamed broadly, talking about the 'arrival' and how his own wife had used this particular cloth for napkins, and were we hoping for a boy or a girl? I glimpsed a further flick of amusement in Captain Stenz's eyes.

'Oh, no,' I said quickly, 'it's not for me, it's . . . for my sister. She's not terribly well.'

'Oh, I'm sorry to hear that,' the man said. 'But you know she will be pleased with the quality of the goods.' Behind me, Captain Stenz's silence only reinforced the lie, and he pulled out a sheaf of notes to pay. He took the package under his arm, rather than having it delivered. Without sight of Eva in the past few months, the town wouldn't have been aware of the pregnancy. Loose lips wouldn't be tolerated at the house, and its residents understood all too well the dangers of gossiping. The Goebbels' cloak of secrecy appeared to have been drawn tightly.

At a nearby shop selling children's clothing, I almost

enjoyed myself picking out several outfits and nightdresses, snowy white and angel-like. The irony wasn't lost on me, nor the swell of guilt at such luxury and decadence, when I knew camp women were still peeling rags off the filthy floor as a means of keeping their babies warm. Alive. I could only justify it as surviving. Could I – should I – have refused to go? A small act of defiance, but one that reminded them, the enemy, of where my feelings stood? Instead, I had complied, and – if I was truly honest – was enjoying the experience of being out, some kind of liberty beyond the barbs of the Berghof. Yet the shame always burned hot, a fire pit licking at my insides.

As Captain Stenz was settling the bill, my eyes wandered over the well-stocked shelves towards a wooden rattle. I fingered the smooth, beautifully carved handle – hours of human life gone into this trinket, so far from the ugly, cold machinery of guns, of the camp workbenches, of the rough wooden cosh.

I recalled Ira the carpenter knocking tentatively on the door of our hut one day – he was allowed into the women's section for repairs – and handing me three versions of the rattle I now held in my hand, simple and coarse, but imbued with his talent and selflessness. I saw him sitting in his own darkened hut, straining his old, watery eyes as he whittled away for the pleasure of others. I didn't reveal each baby would never live long enough to hold the simple toy, more likely dead before they even smiled. Their value was as a keepsake for their mothers, a tangible reminder of a baby whose tiny palms might have one day gripped the wood. Memories, when so brief, would fade in time, but the toy would prevail.

'Fräulein Hoff, are you all right?' Captain Stenz was beside me as a fat tear rolled down my face.

'Pardon? Oh, yes, just remembering something.' I wiped it smartly away and gave him a weak smile.

'Do you want to purchase this?' He gestured at the rattle.

'Er, no, I don't think so. Fräulein Braun is better off choosing these things.'

There was an awkward silence as I half turned to rid myself of the other tear he hadn't seen, and he shuffled his feet.

'Perhaps if we've finished in the shops, we could go for some refreshment? A cup of coffee?'

I stared in silent disbelief. Did he say go to a cafe? Together?

'Well, if you had rather get back . . .?'

'No, no! I just didn't expect . . . that's all.'

He smiled – the diplomatic one, just lips spread and no teeth on show. 'I think it perfectly fitting that I take my companion for a drink,' he said. 'I am a captain, after all, and there are some benefits to rank.' Now, he was playing with me.

'And do many prisoners get treated this way?'

'You are an employee of the Berghof, Fräulein Hoff, and as such, it's perfectly fitting.'

'Well, perhaps employee is a little extreme, but thank you. And please, call me Anke. I think after shopping for napkins, for *our* baby, we are at least beyond niceties.'

He laughed, and I felt more relaxed than I had in I don't know how long. The breeze blew through the sunny streets, and for a moment, I forgot there was a war on.

Captain Stenz led us confidently to a cafe on the square, traditional and ornate, with chairs and tables outside. He sat under an umbrella, took off his cap and gloves. To anyone else, his back was straight and his demeanour fitting of an SS officer, but I was close enough to see his muscles melt into the chair, to hear that small release of breath.

'Coffee?' he said. 'I do know enough of Berchtesgaden to know they have real coffee here, no fakery.'

Real coffee. The last cup I'd had, with strong, thick fluid topped off with real milk – when was that? In Berlin, with Papa, as war broke out? When the bitterness of the coffee had matched our mood. Since then, rationing had brought the infamous Ersatzkaffee, cups of which my father screwed his mouth at and raged against the war, the Reich and the world. 'Coffee made of acorns!' he vented at poor Mama. 'Now I know we've all gone mad!' To Germans, good coffee meant stability, exchange, friendship, the world in its rightful place. The ground fakery of Ersatzkaffee signalled the universe was spinning out of control – insipid, weak and disingenuous.

'A cup of coffee would be *wonderful*.' Once again, he caught my meaning. He ordered – the waitress flirting with his uniform – and we sat looking at the scene in the square, people milling about, just getting on with their lives. The turquoise in his eyes looked richer under the umbrella, as he stared into the distance, and he looked at peace. But I was too curious for any lengthy silence.

'Am I allowed to know your name, Captain Stenz?'

'Oh – it's Dieter.' He said it like he'd almost forgotten it himself.

'I have an uncle Dieter, right here in Bavaria,' I said, 'although he's a farmer.' I laughed to myself. 'I can't imagine him in a uniform at all. Or even in a suit, for that matter.'

'Is that your father's brother?'

'Yes. Although you wouldn't guess it – they're nothing alike. Uncle Dieter is never happier than when he's with his ladies, his beloved herd. And my father wouldn't do well knee-deep in muck, only books. But strangely, they get on.'

'Is he married, your uncle?'

'Only to the herd,' I said. 'And your father, what does he do?'

'He's an engineer – aircraft. I grew up under engines. Until I was a teenager I thought all fathers smelt of engine oil.' The light in his eyes smacked of true affection.

'And yet you chose buildings?'

'Yes, but I think it's all about construction, putting things together. I stripped back so many motors I could see the value of good foundations. Besides, my brother became the engineer, a better one than I would have made.'

His lips settled together, half smiling in memory.

'Is he serving?'

'In the Luftwaffe, something high up in engine design, I believe. I'm thankful he's too important to be a flyer.'

I felt we were on even ground, the exchange not stiff or pricked by embarrassment. My curiosity was further piqued. 'Is that where the expectation came? To follow suit, I mean?'

He turned and looked at me squarely, eyes boring into mine, as if he couldn't believe I had dared to be so open. And yet there was no anger. 'Something like that,' he said, and swiped the blue stare elsewhere.

The waitress saved any awkward silence by arriving with the coffee. The smell knocked me sideways – deep and rich, taste and promise rising as the deep mocha broke the surface of lightly frothed milk – evoking images and memories of real life before the war. Normal. Safe. I sat looking at its beauty for at least a minute, watching tiny bubbles fracture as the breeze caught the top.

'Is that suitable?' he said, already sipping at his own cup.

'Yes, yes, fine,' I said. 'It's just been a long time. I'm savouring it.' Then I smiled, so that he knew I was making light, and not wallowing in sadness. 'My father would never forgive me if I didn't enjoy the full experience.'

The first sip fulfilled every promise, bitter and thick, skating over my taste buds and down into my throat like heavy silk, and I think I sighed audibly. The Captain turned and smiled again at the noise. For all its food luxuries, the coffee at the Berghof couldn't hold a candle to this; Frau Grunders didn't drink coffee and the servant supplies were naturally second rate.

We talked a little of our childhood – his near Stuttgart– and he quizzed me about Berlin, our recollections sticking to safe ground: before the war, school and teenage years. Except at that moment I didn't mind talking about my life there, I wasn't too angry or bitter about my family to speak of them. Even if my father was living without liberty, under the threat of death possibly, and Captain Stenz's own may have been contributing to the war effort still. If we were talking of my parents, of Franz, and Ilse, they were at least alive to me, in this world. I felt there was some hope as long as their personalities were coloured, part of the landscape, instead of shadowy and pallid, almost past tense.

Dieter didn't appear to be in any hurry, and he ordered a second coffee. I had just drained the last, precious mouthful when the driver appeared, red-faced and breathless. Captain Stenz tensed and the grey jacket stiffened.

'Rainer, what is it?'

'Pardon the intrusion, Captain, but Fräulein Hoff is needed back at the Berghof – immediately.'

It was my turn to brace then. It could only mean one thing. Eva.

'Is she unwell?' I could hardly expect him to know if she was in early labour. At thirty-two weeks, this could be a problem.

'My instructions are to fetch you immediately. Daniel has been dispatched to bring a doctor, but he may be some time.'

'We'll leave now.' Captain Stenz was the officious SS officer again. He pulled out some bills and left them on the table, following Rainer, their long limbs needing to slow for me to keep pace.

My mind was racing with possibilities. Why hadn't I insisted on seeing her this morning? Why had I bowed to that man Sergeant Meier? I might have picked up on something. If the baby came now, we would struggle to have the right help in time. We would be making the best of a bad situation, and that wasn't good enough for the Reich.

18

Calming the Fire

Rainer drove at speed, forcing the raspy engine, but the journey seemed painfully slow and it was forty minutes before I stepped out of the car and ran up the steps. Frau Grunders herself opened the door, with my small bag of equipment in her arms, her steely gaze fixed.

Eva was in her room, her head just visible over the blankets. Glistening with sweat, she was hot to touch and the colour of the beetroot soup served up by the kitchen. Her lids drooped, fighting to stay open.

'Eva, Eva,' I said softly, then louder, 'can you hear me?'

She roused a little, moaning, and finally opened her eyes, blinking several times before she appeared to recognise me.

'Anke? I'm glad to see you. I don't feel well. Tell me the baby's all right.' Her speech was slow and laboured, and she was drifting in and out of consciousness. Frau Grunders was hovering outside the door, and I asked for some cold towels and help in moving Eva. She clipped away smartly, and the senior maid appeared almost instantly.

Together, Lena and I peeled back the blankets and moved Eva onto her side. Though her skin radiated the heat of hot coals, she was shivering as if in an ice bath, whining for the blankets to be put back. Her pulse was racing at a hundred and twenty beats a minute, veins fighting to push blood around her infected body. There was no doubt it was a fever – the cause unknown, although I had my suspicions.

Under duress, we helped Eva to the bathroom, where I coaxed a urine sample from her as she sat, heavy-lidded and semi-aware. Back in the bedroom, the windows were thrown open and Lena applied the cold towels to Eva's head and chest while I got to work on the dresser, putting a flame to the sample. It was heavy with protein – a urine infection as I'd suspected, common to pregnant women and easily treated in the early stages, but more of a danger if it took hold. The intense irritation if it reached her kidneys could cause her uterus to spasm, and bring on a premature labour. At thirty-two weeks and without specialist care, the baby would have little chance of survival.

Eva was still moaning softly, showing less angst but now clutching her belly while her brow crimped. I hoped the contraction of her facial muscles wasn't mimicking anything lower down. 'The baby,' she kept saying, 'save the baby, Anke.'

Automatically, she was still as I put my Pinard on her belly, lying close enough to feel the waves of heat come off her skin. The baby's heartbeat was strong and even, a good rate, but I sensed a slight rise on my ear while it lay flat on the wooden trumpet, the mesh of belly muscles pulling together. She was tightening.

'The baby sounds fine, Eva, good and strong. We just have to cool you down.'

She moaned, signalling some understanding. She didn't need to know about the tightening. If it was strong enough, she would tell me.

I told Lena to keep cooling with the towels and spooning iced water into Eva's mouth, and went in search of news. Halfway down the hall, Captain Stenz appeared, his face fraught with worry for the first time since I'd known him.

'How is the Fräulein?' His voice was thick with anxiety.

I explained about the infection and the need for a doctor immediately. 'But we have to ensure they are carrying antibiotics, and the means to administer them quickly. Has the doctor already left the hospital?'

'I'll ring ahead and check. I'll send the fastest rider as a back-up. Do you think the baby is in danger?'

'Not at the moment, but if she starts to labour properly, then yes. The next few hours will tell, but we can't risk moving her right now.'

'I'll get word to the doctor.' As I turned, he caught my arm. 'Anke?'

'Yes?'

'I'm glad it's you. Up here, with her. With everything you know.'

'Let's just see about that,' I said. 'We need luck on our side too.'

19

Watchful Waiting

I sat with Eva constantly after that, scanning her face as she moved uneasily in and out of sleep, instinctively palming her abdomen while her face crimped in discomfort. Her bump was warm to the touch and at times, hard and unyielding, retreating after sixty seconds or so to a soft shell under my hand. I couldn't help it, but the image of a dragon's egg swam into my thoughts, illustrations from my dog-eared fairy-tale book, a favourite story my mother read to me at bedtime. And yet in all my years as a midwife I hadn't thought of it once, likened any birth or baby to that fiery image. Until now.

Eva's tightenings moved closer together, from one every fifteen minutes to every ten, then averaging at seven or eight, spiralling dangerously towards labour. As with any woman, it was difficult to gauge the level of pain, but I watched Eva's mouth and eyes intently with each contraction, watching for the contortion in her features. So far, the pain dial was static. Nature's little gift of luck perhaps? Her skin remained pasty, but had lost the violent flush of earlier, only a faint salt line settling around her hair.

It was then that I noticed it, while rearranging the thin nightshirt – a disturbance in her skin low into her neck. At first glance I thought it was a water splash, and moved to wipe it away, but soon realised it was part of her, fixed. The skin was raised like an old burn, flecks of star-like pink around a small, circular crevice, a tiny volcanic crater. Almost as if she had been burned by a pointed object or – and my imagination stretched wildly here – stabbed, or even shot? In her semi-consciousness, I couldn't help skimming my finger pads over the area, and Eva squirmed irritably, forcing me to snap my hand away, like a child caught in the cookie pot.

The minutes ticked by noisily on the mantel clock until, at last, the spitting gravel outside signalled an arrival. The doctor was a middle-aged local medic who had specialised in obstetrics in his hospital days, and he readily agreed to the antibiotics. We worked together setting up an intravenous line into Eva's arm and a catheter into her bladder, to monitor her urine.

With the drugs snaking into Eva's veins, Lena took over the vigilance for half an hour to give me a break, and I walked towards the offices. The doctor was perched nervously on a leather chair in front of the desk as I appeared. He and Captain Stenz looked at me with anxious enquiry.

'She's sleeping now, no change for the worse,' I said quickly. 'Certainly, in the last half hour the tightenings have subsided, and the Fräulein doesn't appear to be in pain. Her temperature is down. It's looking positive.'

Two pairs of shoulders relaxed visibly.

'Dr Heisler tells me the antibiotics should work quickly, and we will know a lot more about Fräulein Braun's condition by the morning,' Captain Stenz added.

'I think so too,' I agreed. 'But just to be on the safe side, I'll spend the night in her room, and report to you both at breakfast.'

The doctor shifted again, perspiration pricking his brow. 'I can arrange transport to the local hospital as soon as possible, this evening if needed. And a private room, of course. Complete privacy.'

Captain Stenz looked at me, his features inviting an opinion.

'Well, I agree the doctor should review her condition in the morning,' I said. 'But if the Fräulein's urine is clear, and her condition improves, I can't see any reason not to nurse her at home, as planned.'

'Doctor?' Captain Stenz was playing diplomat again, but his expectations were clear.

Dr Heisler plucked at his words carefully. 'Naturally, I would err on the side of caution, but again I would be happy to consult on the Fräulein at home, if the general consensus is to remain here.'

'Thank you, Doctor, your expertise is very much appreciated,' said Captain Stenz, bringing the game of words to a close.

I was suddenly irritated. Why couldn't they simply say what they meant? Why dress every exchange in etiquette and niceties, when everyone present knew the true meaning was dirty and ugly, a sinister threat to the only thing you could truly own in this war – your life? The doctor would go away, not crowing or boasting about his fortune in treating the Führer's mistress, but looking over his shoulder daily, praying nightly that she and her baby survived, and that he wouldn't open his door late one night to the Gestapo looking for retribution. That was the Germany we lived in.

More than anything, I couldn't figure out why I was so irked at Captain Stenz for being part of it. After all, he was SS, one of the chosen, one of Hitler's boys. Stupid woman, stupid Anke. Why had I been so blinkered, why had I opened a little of myself to someone who could never be anyone other than my overseer or my captor? After years of creating a shell to protect myself since the war began, I had let my guard slip a little for him. Exposed an already wounded heart. And yet I expected more from him, from the exchanges between us so far; since our first meeting I had not seen him as the black crow of Nazism. Now I wondered: was he merely very good at putting on a front, masked by that jacket? If so, was it a front for me, or the Nazi regime? The feeling rankled, like an itch I had no hope of scratching.

Berlin, February 1942

Snow was still falling thickly, but the car was at least warmed by our bodies, two of them in the back either side of me, a driver in the front. They said very little under the brims of their hats, staring straight ahead. I took a measured guess at exactly where we were going. The imposing building at number 8 Prinz-Albrecht Strasse was the same bricks and mortar as when it had acted as an art gallery in the early 1930s, but it had since adopted a dark cloak. It was no secret that thousands had been sucked in through the ornate doorways, or worse still the back entrances, absorbed into its bowels. Gestapo headquarters was no place for a fun visit.

In the car, I was shaking uncontrollably, every artery pulsing and a sick, rolling pit in my stomach. Perhaps because of my job I was able to contain it to a violent twitch in the little finger of my left hand, keeping it clenched and cupped in my other hand, while I thought of my family and all the things I hadn't said to them. When was the last time I told Mama I loved her? Spent a day with Ilse? Even had a conversation with Franz? The war had flooded us all, and now it was about to engulf me, perhaps forever.

We drew up to the elegant front entrance; the Gestapo had many deep secrets, but their questioning of dissidents wasn't one of them. They were unashamed about the cull of opponents to the Reich. The large, marbled foyer and corridors were dimly lit – we passed through several long, door-lined walkways before walking up stone steps, several floors until my calves were aching from the climb. Here, the building was much less ornate – it was scruffy and generally unkempt. Eventually, we stopped at a faceless door, with the number 9 on the tatty, scratched wood. My escort opened it and said: 'In here.'

The room was dark and freezing cold, with bare boards and a small window up in the top of the wall, out of my reach. It had been left open, on purpose, I imagined. I rubbed at my arms instinctively. I'd changed out of my uniform into a light blouse before I left the hospital; my cardigan and coat were at Nadia's, and they – the collection squad – hadn't allowed me to snatch at either of them before I was escorted out. Cold itself was an effective torture method, I reasoned. That word kept flashing in front of my eyes, and try as I might, I couldn't push it back down – an ugly, black and oily stain of meaning that made my whole body shake with dread.

There was a bed, with a bare mattress at least. But nothing more, no water jug or bowl, no chamber pot. I was suddenly aware of being very thirsty and needing to empty my bladder at the same time. The sweat from Nadia's birth had dried on me and I could smell a sour odour rising from my body. That bath I had promised myself now seemed a distant fantasy. If I didn't reach a toilet soon I might be forced to relieve myself in the corner of the room, and then live with the stench. Perhaps that was what they wanted, part of the ritual? Break you with your own disgust.

I felt a sudden wave of tiredness and curled on the bed, staring at the faint glow from the settling snow, which cast a square on the ceiling. I strained my ears for sounds of Berlin – cars, trams, laughter or rising conversation that would convince me the world outside was normal, and not frozen solid. But up here, it seemed the Gestapo had a monopoly on noise as well. I hugged myself into a ball, feeling totally and utterly alone.

After my early morning shift and Nadia's birth, exhaustion must have washed over the fear, because I woke to two men coming into the room.

'Fräulein, get up – quickly.'

It was still dark, and I could just make out their shapes from the light in the corridor. I sat up and pushed on my shoes, while they shuffled impatiently. We wound through more corridors, down several floors, and back into the former art gallery, facing another looming doorway.

It was warmer in this room at least, with a single-bulb electric light, but no window. I was guided to a chair tucked into a bare wooden table, with an empty chair opposite. I would be joined. But by whom? And what would they do? Rumours of creative Gestapo torture constantly circulated in Berlin, and it was difficult to know what was fact or fiction or simply cultivated fear. All seemed despicably inhumane.

They left me for I don't know how long, since my watch had been taken from me. I rationalised this was part of the plan – to suspend a mind in limbo, where I couldn't place my own fatigue, thirst or hunger. And I was all of these things, since I'd missed supper, and the last drink I'd had was tea from Minna. I thought of her terrified, grief-stricken face as their noisy boots had invaded the safe space we had created, mouthing 'Sorry' as I looked back. I had no doubt she did not betray news of the birth – her sorrow was in placing me in harm's way.

I kept myself from the horrors of looking forward by casting backwards: counting the numbers of babies I had seen into the world, the homebirths I'd enjoyed – something in the world that would be left behind if I was spat out of this building in a box. A legacy my parents could be proud of. Oh Lord, Mama and Papa – they would be worried sick!

He walked in, clicked his heels together, flopped a file on the desk and sat directly opposite. Opening the file, he flipped over a few pages and looked up, with a weak smile. It was half friendly, not the dirty smirk I'd expected.

'Fräulein,' he said formally. He was blond, but with a reddish streak to his hair, and a small wiry moustache, wider and thinner than the Führer's, giving him more of a film star air. His eyes were a bright, watery blue and he looked, in his brown suit, like a humanised fox.

I sat in silence and something told me not to show my desperation. To try at least.

Hands flat on the table, he began. 'Do you know where you are?'

'At the Gestapo headquarters.'

'Do you know why you are here?' He leafed through the pages, and I glimpsed my hospital mug shot.

'I imagine it's because I was helping a woman give birth. In the Jewish quarter.' Surprisingly, there was no quiver to my voice. Keep soft, Anke, I reminded myself – don't antagonise.

'Is this something you make a habit of?' His tone was of a headmaster dealing with a mildly irritating pupil.

'Not a habit.'

'But you have done this before?'

'What does my file say?'

He smiled, enjoying the game, perhaps because he knew he couldn't lose. 'It says you like to help Jews.'

'I like to help people. People who need help. It's true that some of them are Jewish.' Careful, Anke – temper the fury, be smart.

He took out a packet of cigarettes from his pocket and offered me one. I smoked only occasionally but I was sorely tempted, except I thought it would highlight my thirst. I shook my head. He lit one himself, blew out a plume of smoke towards the light bulb and sat back.

'It seems your whole family – your German family, Fräulein – are unsure where their loyalties lie. To the Reich, or your Jewish friends.'

I started at the mention of my family. Surely they had been watching just me, tracking my movements in the ghetto – where someone had betrayed us? At worst, spying on me at the hospital. But not at home?

'This is nothing to do with my family,' I said sharply, desperation evident.

'I beg to differ,' he replied. Now he was rooting out his trump card, a cunning slant to his eyes. 'Quite apart from your father's association with two prominent Jewish community leaders, there are your mother's visits to several Jewish households, to bring food.'

This was a surprise to me; I knew they had been in touch with several families – Papa's former colleagues at the university – but neither ever spoke of real contact.

'Perhaps they were hungry,' I said.

'Perhaps so.' Before, we had been bantering, now his voice was cut glass. 'But perhaps there are German families also in need. It has been noted on—' here he peered at the written notes '—three occasions that your family has failed to leave out the required *contribution on one-pot Sunday, and twice have not contributed funds to the German Welfare Fund.'*

It was true. I knew Mama hated the order that required each family to provide a pot of food for collection each week, distributed supposedly to German families in need, but widely known to be appropriated by troops already well fed.

'I'm sure it was an oversight,' I defended. 'She's sometimes forgetful.'

'Hmm, maybe so. But tell me, Fräulein, are you also forgetful when you omitted to report on—' he made another show of looking through the notes '—three occasions when infants have been born with handicaps in your hospital? In direct opposition to the directive that you received — very clearly — from your superiors. I can quote the date if you like.'

I looked blank. There was no denying it. I had twice colluded with other midwives to spare babies the separation and an unknown future. Once, with an obviously blind child, his smoky, opaque eyes thick with cataracts, I had acted totally alone. Sitting here, remembering that baby's blank, unseeing gaze, which nonetheless had looked like a plea, I didn't regret my actions — only where they had taken me.

'What will you do with me?' I said flatly. 'Can I at least contact my family? They'll be worried sick.'

'Your family are well, and in good hands, I'm assured,' he said casually.

'What do you mean, in good hands? They have nothing to do with my actions, with what I've done.' My voice betrayed panic.

He closed the file and laid his hands on it, the blue of his eyes sparkling with . . . was that enjoyment? Excitement?

'Given your experience, Fräulein, and your profession, I am surprised at your naivety,' he said calmly. 'Don't imagine that such actions against the Reich will go unpunished.'

He saw the look of sheer terror flash across my face, enjoyed teasing it out.

'Ah, don't worry, Fräulein Hoff, there will be no physical reprimands – I'm confident you have nothing of worth to tell us. We know everything about you. But your presence in Berlin is, let's say, a disturbance to the strength of the Reich. Loyalty is key. And we cannot rely on your family to assert that loyalty.' He went on, 'Have you heard of the Decree Against Public Enemies – or national pests, as we like to call them?' He really was smiling now, at his own Nazi brand of humour. 'Well, you are one of that band – a pest. And what do we do with pests?'

'Squash them, I imagine.'

'Oh, nothing so inhumane, Fräulein.' He shuffled the papers in conclusion. 'But we do need to stop them infecting others with their poison. We put them in a jar – it's an effective barrier and sometimes the poison drains away.'

'Punish me, but not my family,' I said, in a last-bid effort as he stood up.

'I'm afraid it's not my decision, Fräulein. You have sown your own seeds, and what's that saying? You reap what you sow.' This time his eyes and the line of his mouth exuded a smug superiority. Easy work for him tonight. A simple task with a thrill to boot. 'Goodnight, Fräulein.'

They let me stew for a good while, cultivating my own dirty imaginings, then led me back to the same room. It was still cold, but with the light of a new day pushing through the window. A jug of water sat on the floor, alongside a chipped cup, and a piece of bread. I took both into my mouth hungrily, and lay on the bed again.

The imagined scene in my head would not be pushed away – of the knock on the door at my parents' house, them pushing past

Mama, Ilse running down the stairs with curiosity, and Papa's ashen face. Too vivid. I couldn't stop its flickering, pecking at my conscience, knowing it was me who had put us all under the Führer's dreaded gaze. Me, whose simple idea of justice had placed us all at the mercy of the worst kind of retribution, from those with little sense of justice.

What had I done?

20

Eva's Strength

My night was long and fitful, although Eva slept soundly, muttering in her sleep. Frau Grunders had set up a cot for me in the room, after I declined it being placed in the adjoining bedroom, with the door left open. The bed – *his* bed – was not offered, and I was thankful for that. Silly as it seemed, I could not bear the idea of sharing the Führer's air, some leftover molecule of his foul insides, something common to us both. He had touched enough of my life already, and I wanted no other part of him.

I checked the baby's heartbeat before I crawled under the covers, and again in the morning – it appeared unperturbed, pumping away happily and squirming irritably under my hand.

'You just stay in there awhile, little chick,' I found myself saying, as Eva slept on, her body limp with exhaustion. Her temperature was back within normal range, and the urine all but clear. The antibiotics were almost at an end, and I was happy to leave her briefly.

I collected some breakfast, and stepped out into the bright and beautiful spring day – that familiar crawl from the cavern of a night shift, the sun's rays catching you unawares. I had slept, but woken almost every hour to place a hand on Eva's forehead, and my eyes were subsequently at half-mast. I took my plate onto my porch, for a slice of solace and privacy. Yet I didn't mind when Captain Stenz walked up the path, his gaze slipping naturally towards the peak view.

'Good morning,' he said brightly.

'Morning, Captain Stenz.'

'Dieter, please. I thought we agreed no formalities when not needed. I'm glad to see you out here – I assume it means you have no concerns?'

'Yes, I think Fräulein Braun is over the worst. The fever appears to have gone and the baby sounds fine.'

'I'm glad – and relieved. For us all.' We sat ingesting the glorious view for a moment or two, until a new curiosity burned a hole in my throat.

'Dieter, do you know anything about injuries to Fräulein Braun?'

'Injuries?'

'Last night, I noticed something on her neck – a wound, something like . . . I'm not sure. It looked like a *gunshot*?'

'Ah.' He wore an expression similar to the one he'd worn during our first meeting months before, as if another cat had leapt smartly out of the bag.

'You say that like you know what I'm talking of?'

'Well, let's just say that Fräulein Braun hasn't always been as content as she is now.'

It took me several seconds to absorb his meaning. 'Are

you saying she shot herself? And *survived*?' My eyes were no longer half open.

'The suspicion is she aimed at her heart, but thankfully missed. It was a long time ago, before the war,' he said. 'It became a statement, a cry for help. It wasn't the only time.'

'A cry to whom?'

He looked at me quizzically. 'Him, of course.'

'But she loves him, as far as I can tell. She idolises him.'

'And love isn't complex? Are you sure he returns the affection?'

I pondered over the question, all the conversations with Eva coming back to me – her moods, her need to have contact. The longing was strong on her part, desperate at times. And yet she was the only woman at the Berghof, the appointed mistress. Surely that meant something?

'She's pregnant,' I said, and knew instantly I was being naive.

'All men have needs,' he said. 'It doesn't always equal love. Or commitment. But now – now Eva may feel she has her ultimate trump card, more powerful than any threat.'

'And will it work?'

Dieter drew himself up and scanned left to right, checking the patrol wasn't passing. 'He doesn't treat her as well as he should. Any woman, in fact.'

'What do you mean?' I countered. 'Is he cruel to her? I've never seen any evidence.'

'Cruelty comes in all forms,' Dieter said bluntly. 'In the Führer there is contempt – deep contempt – for intelligence in women. I've seen it myself. Put it this way, Anke,

173

you and he would not get on. Not at all.' He managed a weak smile, and I took it for the compliment it was meant to be. He picked up his gloves and walked away, eyes on the vista.

21

Recovery and Reflection

I couldn't give any serious thought to this latest revelation, as I was called to meet with Dr Heisler and give my report. He examined Eva briefly and pronounced himself happy to leave – his face said deeply relieved – and told me to telephone him later in the day. He would return if there was any sign of a relapse, but he hoped not. He really hoped not.

Eva woke later that afternoon, groggy and needing a careful explanation of the past twenty-four hours. Her blue eyes showed alarm as I told her, but once I had listened to the baby, with several limbs responding to my touch, she was calmer. The relief in her face was obvious – not for herself, but for the child. For all her silliness and ignorance, her infuriatingly blinkered nature about life outside the Berghof, Eva remained as on the day of our first meeting, selfless where the life of her baby was concerned. She caught my hand as I fussed with the covers.

'Thank you, Anke. Thank you for looking after us. And Lena too. We are grateful.'

The 'we' was ambiguous – I couldn't help wondering: did she mean her and the baby, or the absent father? Did he even care?

Disengaged from her tubes, Eva was well enough to get out of bed and into the bath, and she looked instantly brighter once her hair was washed, and with a little make-up. I took the opportunity of a bath myself, and was on my porch, the afternoon breeze tickling at the roots of my wet hair, when Captain Stenz appeared again. This was getting to be a habit.

'Afternoon, Anke.' He sat down instantly, formalities erased.

'Good afternoon, Dieter. I'm surprised to see you here again so soon. I thought you might have meetings to catch up on.'

'Unimportant compared to the events up here,' he said. 'My priority remains the smooth running of . . . well . . . like I say, events up here.'

'Do you mean the pregnancy? Eva's baby? The Führer's baby? Is that what you mean?' I was prickled he wouldn't speak plainly to me.

'Yes, that's what I mean,' he said, eyebrows arched. 'Why so irritated?'

'Well then, why can't you say it?' My voice was urgent, if not raised. 'Why always the guarded hint, the cloak and dagger, like some Shakespearean tragedy? Is that what they teach you as officers – that if you infer, it's never as bad as the raw truth? This poor child, it's like it's hidden before it's even born.'

I pulled fingers through the wet strands of my hair, letting frustration fly. His face fell, crestfallen. For a second, he was a little boy hurt, that I had made him just one of them, the dark weave of his jacket instead of the man.

He stood up, his face turning white. 'I think . . .'

'What do you think, Dieter? What do you *really* think? Tell me.'

The veins in his neck stood proud, as if the words were fighting to spring forth. The conditioned diplomacy beat them back.

'I don't think you understand how complex this is, Fräulein Hoff. The tightrope this baby will walk upon.' He looked like he had said too much, wished he could suck back the last sentence.

'What do you mean?' I flashed. But he was already turning.

'Good day, Fräulein Hoff.' His back was towards me, and I saw the shoulders square and tense.

'Dieter, come back! I'm sorry, I didn't mean to . . .' But my words were lost on the breeze.

I slept fitfully again that night, even with the comfort of my own bed. Dieter's last words rolled continually around my head – did he believe the baby was already under threat? Poor scrap of a thing, innocently somersaulting around its mother's insides, destined to be pushed from pillar to post once born – already a pawn, a devil, an angel, and yet only flesh and blood. Like its father. Much like the camp babes, better off inside, safety in gestation.

I thought also of the wound on Eva's neck, of the moment when she'd felt so desperate for the love of her man that she pointed a gun at her own heart. Badly aimed, but snug to her skin nonetheless, sure to create some damage and possibly death. How deep was her longing for the attention of another? I was certain she wanted to be a mother – I had seen enough of indifference at the Lebensborn to know she felt deeply – but she couldn't fail to be aware that this baby might also be her ticket, perhaps to his hard-won heart, marriage, and possibly her place as the mother of Germany.

Dieter was right – unfair as it seemed, this baby *was* more than mere flesh and blood, and I had been naive to think we could treat this as just another birth among thousands. We might need more than midwifery skills to secure everyone's future.

22

New Demons

Eva had a visitor the next morning. Magda Goebbels swept up to the Berghof, laden with flowers and chocolates 'for the patient' I heard her say. I was duly summoned to the terrace and quizzed as to the progress of the pregnancy. On these visits, Eva was like a frightened child in the presence of an overbearing aunt, while Magda gushed at how relieved she was that everything had settled down and the baby was healthy. I mused on her words of false delight sticking in her thin, white throat, to see Eva looking well, the baby unharmed. Her own longing crushed.

But the visit wasn't without joy. Soon after, Christa's slim form rounded the house and walked the path towards my porch.

'Anke!' We hugged like long-lost colleagues.

'How did you find an excuse to make the journey up here?'

'Cranberries,' she said with a broad beam. 'I convinced the mistress they were good for warding off future infections, and I don't think she could be seen to refuse.'

'Well, they are, and I'm delighted. I've been aching for some company, someone to talk to.'

Christa brought me up to date on the politics at the Goebbels'; with the Allies in a strong position, Joseph was stamping his mood on an already tense household, where the floorboards were a carpet of eggshells. The audible exchanges between husband and wife were bitter and strained as Joseph became desperate for production of his new propaganda tool to be complete.

'The way he talks about it, I'm sure he thinks of this baby as some kind of new tank or aircraft,' Christa scoffed.

Suddenly, she cast around at our surroundings, spotting a single patrol making his rounds on the perimeter. The guard was young, bored and easily swayed by her pretty face, her maid's uniform assuring him neither of us was about to make a break.

'We're just off down the path to pick some flowers for the mistress.' She threw her sweetest smile in his direction, and he nodded, staring longingly at her pert figure as she pulled me off down the path towards the Teehaus. I felt strangely out of my comfort zone, without Eva or permission.

'Why are we out here?' I asked as we slowed to an amble.

'Well, you never know,' said Christa. 'I'm beginning to believe walls really do have ears.' Her eyes tacked towards the overhanging trees with suspicion.

'Why? What's going on?'

'I've been contacted.' She looked directly at me, a mixture of fear and excitement in her eyes.

'What do you mean, *contacted*? By who?'

'I'm not entirely sure. She was German, told me *they* knew. About the baby.'

I stopped walking and tried to digest what she had said. 'In what way do they know? And who are *they*?'

'They know it's the Führer's baby, roughly when the baby is due – but as to the "who", they weren't clear. I'm certain they're not friends of the Reich.'

'The Resistance, perhaps? Allied spies?' I was guessing, since my knowledge of the opposition within Germany was limited to what I'd picked up in the camp. A good portion of the inmates were Germans, imprisoned because of their refusal to follow the Führer. It was entirely possible this had come from inside our own country. 'What did they want, from you, I mean?'

'Information,' said Christa, tugging at my arm again to get me to continue walking. She talked in a light voice, rather than a whisper, as if we were having an everyday conversation about the weather. 'Somehow they knew I had contact with the midwife, but they didn't say your name.'

'Did you tell them anything? Did they threaten you?'

'I didn't say anything, but I didn't feel in danger. I was walking in the town when a woman caught up with me and just started talking. I could have stopped and shouted, called for help, but I didn't. It's strange, Anke, and I have no experience or reason to think it, but I had a feeling they were friends of Germany. Not enemies.'

The idea that Christa and I had been thrust into a scene of deep political intrigue made me feel light-headed. Life at the Berghof was becoming increasingly surreal.

'Friend or foe of our beloved leader, it's a question as to whether they are friends of the baby,' I said at last. 'You know, Christa, I haven't changed my mind – I'm here to ensure safe passage of the mother and baby. I may not empathise with Eva, approve her choice of mate, but that's not my concern.'

This time she stopped. 'I know, Anke, and I respect it. I'm just as confused as you are. I'm a maid, not a messenger or a spy. I just want this war to go away so I can get back to my father.'

I sighed heavily. 'You and me both.' We plucked absently at some wild flowers, to have something to show for our excursion. 'So, how did it end, this encounter?'

'The woman just said they would be in touch. Then she walked away. What do you think we should do?'

I had no doubts on that score. Information matured like good brandy. It gained value the longer you held on to it – that much I had learnt in the camp. Letting this out in the open could have dire consequences for all.

'We say nothing, keep quiet. You haven't told anyone else, have you?'

'No, of course not.'

'Then that's how it stays. We carry on as if nothing has happened. Trust no one. Except each other.'

She looked at me, a face of innocence – she was probably the same age as my sister, Ilse, maybe even younger – yet it masked a mind much wiser than her years.

'Just each other,' she said.

Now seemed a good time to ask. 'I've been thinking it for a while, after Sonia's baby, and now I'm more convinced that I need you to help,' I said. 'At Eva's birth, I mean. Someone I can rely on, someone who knows me. Is that too much to ask?'

Christa's lips spread and she put a hand on my arm. 'I

would be honoured and I'm touched that you want me. I'm scared stiff, mind, but there's nothing like a birth to lighten up life. I know that now.' Her face darkened slightly. 'Do you think they'll let me?'

'Well, I haven't blotted my copybook so far. Eva is easily persuadable, and what the Fräulein wants, she seems able to get. And Captain Stenz, well, he's been reasonable up to now.'

She narrowed her eyes at me, surprised I was extolling the virtues of an SS officer. Me of all people.

Communication up and down the mountain was our biggest barrier, we decided. If Christa was contacted again I needed to know, but her trips up to the Berghof were rare. Involving someone else, even innocently, was perilous and Daniel, the driver, was an unknown quantity. Food parcels went via the kitchen, and I couldn't be sure of intercepting them in time. Christa had the brilliant idea of adjusting some baby clothes, with good reason to send packages directly to me. We could only hope they reached me without being searched.

We walked back into the complex as Magda Goebbels was saying her goodbyes on the steps. Christa handed me the flowers, and hastened towards the car.

'Ah, there you are,' Magda said in disapproving tones as she waited for the car door to be opened. She spotted me as she turned.

'Fräulein Hoff, I trust we won't see each other until after the big day now. At least I hope not.' She gave her half smile, carefully cultivated. 'Please do let me know if we can help in any way.' And she stooped elegantly into the seat and was gone. Perfect – she had offered her assistance, and I would take her up on it, in requesting Christa. Two could play at the propaganda game.

Back on my porch, I thought about this latest twist. I wouldn't have been surprised if Goebbels and his calculating mind were behind the approach to Christa, testing my loyalties and using her as a go-between, watching for our reactions. But being in league with Goebbels posed its own dangers, and I squirmed at the thought of his attentions.

I couldn't confide in Dieter − I didn't know enough of him to guess at his deepest beliefs. Of course I had sympathy with any group who plotted against Hitler and his heinous ideas, but if this was a true resistance group, could I trust their motivations in involving a newborn? The stakes were high and it might be that they were no better than Goebbels in intending to use Eva's baby as a pawn − or, worse, see its loss as collateral damage. No, I reasoned the best plan was to keep silent and hope the Minister for Propaganda had more on his mind than my dishonesty, or that there was a resistance we could more easily ignore.

23

Nurturing

Eva regained her strength in the next week, a testament to her body before the pregnancy, hardy and resilient. Perhaps shaken out of a dangerous complacency, we began talking about the birth. Sitting on the wide veranda, or walking with Stasi and Negus towards the Teehaus, I tried to relate the length and intensity of an average first labour, without weighing too heavily on the exhaustion or the apparent agony of some women.

How to describe a contraction, the feeling as a web of muscles squeezes together to create a sensation that to an outsider looks like the worst pathology, but is perfectly natural? Midwives struggled, with or without their own experience, to paint any picture. I was careful to pepper my conversation with positives, aware that Eva could opt for a caesarean at any point, at the intense peak of the journey, and the doctors would be ready to comply, eager to ensure the safety of the Führer's baby at any cost.

Eva's natural tendency to see the world through rose-tinted

glasses was a distinct advantage; she didn't appear over-confident, but she was also cocooned from the real world, enough not to have been thoroughly infected by Germany's inbred fear of birth, or exposed to stories of dread from well-meaning gossips.

When I explained about Christa's vital calm at Sonia's birth, Eva was easily won over. I knew she didn't possess any loyalty to the Berghof maids, most of whom she had abused in her rages against loneliness and the Führer's neglect. She sent a letter to Frau Goebbels immediately and Daniel was dispatched to collect Christa a few days later. The two got on immediately. Taking tea on the balcony, Christa was suddenly much more than a housemaid, and Eva's expression reflected what she'd been craving these last months in her virtual exile – companionship and friends. Strange that she had found those among a prisoner and a maid.

Sitting back, I was aware of something intrinsic about the two of them that, despite Christa's true feelings about the war, created a gel I didn't have with Eva. Perhaps it was their traditional upbringing, not sprinkled or confused with the liberalism of my parents, which made them both somehow more *German*. I was pleased they had a connection; it would allow me to relinquish the role of supporter on the day itself, and concentrate on smoothing the clinical journey. That and keeping the predators at bay.

Eva's mood was generally upbeat, buoyed by several letters bearing the Führer's mark and a visit, finally, from her sister, Gretl. As the intended wife of an SS officer in Hitler's favour, Eva's younger sibling played the part perfectly, sweeping up the driveway in her black sedan and stepping elegantly from the car, lips a siren red, her hand firmly on the arm of the pristine driver; the kitchen gossip hinted Gretl's reputation for flirting with officers of varying ranks.

Gretl came laden with boxes and gifts for her new niece or nephew, and the two of them tattled endlessly over tea in the parlour, or lying out on the terrace under umbrellas chattering about plans for 'after the war', and 'when Mama and Papa come to stay'. They also planned celebrations for Gretl's upcoming nuptials at the Berghof, set for early June and unchanged – even with Eva's due date around the same time. Whether Eva truly believed any word of Gretl's happy families I couldn't tell, but when I was called to be introduced to Gretl as 'my indispensable midwife', Eva looked the most cheerful I had seen her in weeks, as if she was truly preparing for blissful domesticity on top of the world.

It was the absence of Captain Stenz that concerned me most. With preparations to be made, I worried I had broken the thin strand of friendship we had weaved. I sat on my porch each morning willing his car to draw up, to see his tall form striding towards me, that blond head at half turn.

Eva was thirty-four weeks pregnant and lumbering characteristically when he reappeared. She and Gretl had driven down to the lake a few miles from the Berghof and I was watching for their return. Ironically, I was absorbed in writing the Captain a letter, reminding him about the equipment we had agreed on, as a shadow sliced across the paper.

'Fräulein Hoff, good day,' he said.

'Oh! Oh, Captain Stenz, I . . . I thought you wouldn't be returning again.' My voice was high and sounded ridiculously frivolous.

'Why not? This is my primary concern at present.'

'Well, after the . . . you know, how we . . .'

'You mean our cross words?' He was half smiling.

'Well, yes, I suppose so.'

'Fräulein – may I still presume to call you Anke? I have a score of encounters each and every day far more bitter than our conversation. Although none of those have given me cause to worry in the same way.'

'Worry about what?'

'That I had lost your trust – if I can presume to own a little of that – or your friendship.'

'I trust you to . . . to be human,' I said. 'And I consider us friends, despite the circumstances.'

'Well, that's all I can ask.' He smiled. 'In the circumstances.'

He sat down and we resumed plans for the birth. Although it was still uncertain, the Führer was unlikely to be present in the house, he said, but the medical team would arrive at thirty-six weeks, and set up a room with their anaesthetic equipment, sterilising apparatus, and everything needed for an impromptu operating theatre. It would be led by an experienced doctor, and a junior. I would act as anaesthetic nurse, if need be, as I had been through my training. I had expected as much but I couldn't stop my face projecting concern.

'But I have insisted – to keep the Fräulein as worry free as possible – that they stay in a house at the bottom of the mountain, until she goes into labour,' Dieter said quickly. 'I imagine you wouldn't want them hovering for days or weeks on end.'

'You imagine correctly,' I said, relaxing a little. 'And when she's in labour?'

'Well, that's your decision as to when you alert me. Then they will make their way up to the Berghof, and position themselves – discreetly – in one of the rooms on the complex, unless or until you call them. That's as much as I can manage, Anke. I don't have total control, as you know.'

'I understand. And the Goebbels, when will they be told?'

'Herr Goebbels has asked to be informed when Fräulein Braun goes into labour. I imagine he will make his way here as soon as possible, for the happy event.' Dieter's disdain was apparent.

'No doubt Magda has her congratulations speech already worked out,' I said, my own sarcasm unchecked.

'Undoubtedly,' he agreed.

A short silence drew a line under our business, and Dieter took off his cap, the signal that he ceased to become strictly SS. He disappeared for a few moments towards the house, and came back looking very pleased with himself.

'I've asked Frau Grunders if we can have our supper out here. I'm not sure she was too impressed, but I said we have a lot of business to discuss.' He grinned like a cheeky schoolboy.

I might have reflected shock instead of the innate pleasure I was feeling, because he looked suddenly alarmed. 'Have I presumed too much? Should I eat inside?'

'No . . . no! I'm just surprised – pleasantly surprised – at the thought of having real conversation with my meal. It's been quite a while.'

Aside from the brief days with Christa at the Schmidts' house, I hadn't eaten with someone in over two years. Food at the camp had been so like inhaling crumbs of survival that I didn't consider it sharing a meal, and eating in the

189

servants' hall was strictly a dormitory affair – necessary and sombre.

Lena brought out the meal and set it down with a wry smile.

'The light is going – would you perhaps like a candle, Fräulein Hoff?' she said, and I shot a look in response to her spirit.

'No thank you, Lena,' I said. 'We can see very well. I'll bring the dishes in when we're finished.'

We shuffled the plates on the small table, and Dieter poured two glasses from the small jug of beer.

'Frau Grunders may be a tough nut to crack,' he said, 'but I have to say she runs a good kitchen. This is far better than anything back at the barracks.'

He tucked into the chicken stew, but seemed distinctly uncomfortable at the small table, his long arms awkward and the folds of his jacket skimming the dishes. The distinctive runes on his collar caught the little amount of remaining light, and his braided cuffs pushed at his plate.

I sat back, looking at him. 'Dieter, do you want to take off your jacket?' I was wearing only a loose blouse, and the evening was still warm. His neck was flushed and red where it met the stiff collar.

He stopped, mid-forkful. 'Do you mind?' he said, and then laughed. 'Well, clearly not, since you've suggested it!'

'No, I don't mind in the least.'

He began unbuttoning the parade of silver down the front. Wary of staring, still I couldn't take my eyes off him. As each button came free, there was a palpable release of tension, pushed up into the air. Underneath, his shirt was white and creased only by the jacket, no doubt crisp before he pulled it on. Who pressed it for him each morning? He wore no wedding ring, and had never spoken of a wife. Or even *seemed* married, if you can give off that air to strangers.

His shoulders were broad, but in shedding the jacket he lost some of his bulk; the wide, black braces pulled the shirt material in to his chest. I tried to imagine him wearing only the trousers, braces loose by his side – I wanted to see him in my mind's eye working in the garden with his father on a hot summer's day, hauling an engine aloft.

'Anke?'

'What? Oh sorry – just lost myself for a minute.'

We could have been sitting outside a nice restaurant on a spring evening, surrounded by the zeitgeist of a city, the heady chatter of Berliners, instead of the twitter of birds beginning to nest for the night. It felt like a real dinner, and the conversation flowed, about life and families, my work and his study. Incredibly, we managed to sidestep the monolith of the war and the Nazis, and it gave me hope that below the ground-in horror, the layers of distrust, we could be people together, stripped of allegiances to one side or the other.

The plates clean, he sat back in his chair, and this time his sigh was obvious, pushing back his head towards the sky and releasing the day's stress as a vapour. I fixed on his prominent Adam's apple, so often shrouded by his jacket collar. It moved as he swallowed and something inside me – a taut string deep in my pelvis – tweaked, and I felt like a schoolgirl from years ago, tainted with guilty thoughts.

He pulled a pack of cigarettes from his pocket and offered it up. I took one and held it awkwardly between my fingers, rolling the unfamiliar paper, staring at the tobacco beneath the translucent covering. I hadn't had a cigarette since Berlin;

food was a far more valuable currency in the camp. And at the Berghof, it was well known that the Führer hated smoking. I had seen Eva surreptitiously indulging as she walked down towards the Teehaus, but I knew she would never do it in full view. I had smoked occasionally back home, never in the house, but sometimes on a night out. Everyone indulged then; it was part of the social wallpaper, to be lifting it to your mouth, seesawing it with a glass of wine or beer, words and laughter filling in the gaps.

Our heads were suddenly close as he offered a light, a strand or two of hair almost touching. I could smell his skin, a stronger scent of the general aura around him. I noted, too, that his hand trembled slightly in holding the match. The first drag made me cough violently, and Dieter laughed good-naturedly.

'It's been a while?'

'Something like that.' The taste was of good German cigarettes, rich with pleasure instead of sour from sheer need. Much like the coffee, I decided to enjoy and savour it, knowing it would be my last for a while.

The dark descended and a silence with it. We both stared at the nightfall and the stars for at least ten minutes, watching our smoke clouds consumed by the navy sky.

'I can never believe it's possible for the air to be so clear,' he said at last. 'So unencumbered.'

'Why? Because you live in the real world most of the time, down there?' I chided him playfully.

He considered for several seconds. 'Because of all the mud being slung.' He was suddenly serious. 'There's so much of it, I can't fathom how every particle in the world isn't heavy with filth.'

I didn't answer. Much like that first day at the Berghof, I had nothing to add.

A sudden chill broke up the evening and I began to shift and shiver. I saw in his face that he would have offered me his jacket but his features weighed up the gravity of such an offer, and he simply said: 'Time to turn in, I think.'

We carried the dishes in together, stopping awkwardly by the kitchen door.

'Well goodnight then, Fräulein Hoff,' he said.

'Goodnight, Captain Stenz. I take it we'll continue our business on another day.'

'Absolutely.' And he was gone, down the corridor to whichever room he occupied at the Berghof.

I lay on my bed, unable to switch off. Like every pleasurable experience in the last few months, I measured it carefully, heavy weights fighting with each other on a pair of imaginary scales, like the solid set in my mother's kitchen. As a teenager, I would have considered such an evening my right to experience, and as a middle-class German woman, to be part of transition towards marriage and children.

Now, everything that made me forget the camp or the war, even for a second, injected a remorse so strong I wanted to physically purge myself, drag it from my being, like a wire embedded deep in my brain, tweezered from my soul. Worse still was the enjoyment I gained from the company of a Nazi – by name, if perhaps not by nature. Was I a collaborator? One of those we women had despised so much in the camp? I hated myself for liking him, for wanting his company. What if I was wrong about him? What if he was complicit in the cruelty, first-hand? I considered the possibility he was playing with me for his own enjoyment – a cat who catches but can't quite kill the mouse. Suddenly, even life in this sky village seemed far too complicated.

24

A Growing Interest

I chanced upon Dieter again the next morning, on my way to breakfast. He had his back to me, towards the vast air between us and the next mountain, and so it was difficult to tell if he had been waiting for me to pass. A thought inched its way into my head: is that what I wanted? For him to seek me out?

'Good morning,' I said as he spun around sharply. 'Oh sorry, I didn't mean to startle you.'

'No ... I ... Good morning, Anke. I hope you slept well.'

'Very well, thank you.' I slipped him a small smile as his eyes went back to the landscape. Seconds prickled, though not in an awkward way, more of an accepted space. I almost walked on without another word, but I realised I simply didn't want to.

'Are you looking for something in particular?' I asked finally.

'No! No, simply watching the changes,' he came back,

eyes still focused. 'I'm always amazed at how nature is continually shifting, even when it doesn't necessarily need to.'

'Isn't that a comfort?' I pitched. 'That the world moves on?'

'Mmm, sometimes.' He turned his head to look at me, his features serious. 'And yet sometimes I crave to look at an edifice in this wild landscape – something solid. Immovable.'

I laughed good-naturedly. 'So, do you think buildings have more integrity than people or nature? Surely not.'

His eyes widened, pupils black and tiny in the brightness of the morning, amid a sea of blue. Then he smiled, joining the joke. 'And would you challenge me if I said that yes, I think sometimes they do.'

'Well, you'd have to prove it before I came on side,' I said, gently needling.

'Have you ever been to New York?' he said.

'No, not yet, but I'd like to.'

'Then if you do, you must see the Chrysler Building in Manhattan.' His eyes were suddenly alight at the memory of his pre-war travels. 'It's a thing of great beauty – tall, shining, imbued with the love of its designer, and yet functional. Most of all, it does not waver. Each side sustains its beauty, through all weathers.' He smirked. 'It remains solid, day in, day out. I find that comforting.'

He looked towards the vista again, lips pursed. 'There are no nasty surprises tucked in corners.'

Another pause, a lawyer resting his case.

'Then I have to say I can see your point,' I conceded. 'Though I am still resting my own hopes on human nature – it may be labile, but it has a good record of triumph.'

'Each has its good and bad sides,' he added wistfully. 'I can see now that change isn't always bad.' He looked directly at me as he spoke, intent. Then his face brightened instantly. 'So there! You seem to have won me round again.'

I smiled broadly as I turned. 'And equally, New York and the Chrysler Building are now top of my list,' I said over my shoulder. 'Good day, Captain Stenz.'

Odd how I could best think, talk and imagine a future beyond this world in his presence.

Dieter drove away soon after breakfast and Gretl departed later in the day. The bride-to-be left in characteristic style, even daring to flirt with the reliable Daniel as he helped her into the car. Eva waved her away with tears, affecting the telltale waddle of late pregnancy as she contemplated another stretch of boredom and loneliness.

Daniel returned with a parcel, clearly from Christa, with no evidence of tampering. Inside were a dozen or so napkins expertly sewn, a knitted hat and several linen cloths we might use at the birth itself. In the folds was a small sewing kit and thread, and a note that said: *Just in case you need to make adjustments.*

Christa wouldn't have missed an opportunity to communicate, and I fingered each garment carefully, eyes closed, like the blind grandmother I once watched at a birth. She had been sewing baby clothes during the labour, palpating each section for stray dressmaking pins, letting her finger pads walk over the fabric and making it safe and soft for her grandchild. Above her dead pupils, her eyebrows danced with the labour rhythm, up and down, knitting together as the noises wavered. The old woman's

197

cues for action fitted exactly with mine, with the strength of the contractions, the despair and the need, and it wasn't long before I swung my own eyes from the labouring woman to her, forcing my ears to sense the changes as she did.

I closed my eyes and pulled each napkin close, feeling in the padded gusset, manipulating the same material Dieter and I had bought in town. On the tenth or eleventh napkin, I sensed the faintest of crackles. Picking at the delicate stitching with the needle, I carefully manoeuvred a sliver of paper towards the opening. It was gossamer thin, yet the weight of it translated as concrete contraband. This was me – us – breaking the rules. With consequences.

I had never been a determined rebel, either at school or in the hospital, but in the camp I had learnt to shift the boundaries and taken great satisfaction in fooling the guards, securing that extra carrot or potato for someone who really needed it. I hadn't lost a second of sleep abusing their so-called trust. Up here, I reserved the same hatred for the Reich. Loyalty to Eva as a mother? I still wasn't sure. But with Christa's safety, with her life, I knew I couldn't play games. She had too much of a future. So, was it my poor judgement that had led her into this? Passing notes between desks was innocent enough at school, drawing a reprimand from the class mistress at worst, but in this war it would get us killed. Stone dead.

I unfolded the note with deep regret, reading her young hand.

They found me again. Made an offer. Need to talk.

I sighed heavily. Ignoring this other interested party looked to be harder than I had imagined. Why had I ever thought this might be simple, a straightforward trade? The war was like a sea creature, an octopus with countless tentacles, sucking in everyone who tried to hide on the calm of the sea bed. Birthing Eva's baby safely was rapidly becoming the least of our problems.

I didn't risk a return note. Instead, I introduced the idea to Eva that another meeting with Christa would be beneficial, to go over the birth plan. In a stroke of good timing, a package of equipment arrived for me, via Sergeant Meier. He crowed in his authority, making a good deal of the fact he had necessarily reviewed the contents, 'for the Fräulein's safety, you understand. You realise you are being entrusted with items not normally afforded to . . .' He hesitated.

'Prisoners?' I offered.

'Yes, well. Please do us the courtesy of honouring that trust.'

There was no restraining my sarcasm. 'Sergeant Meier, I hope that – if I were to be thinking of an escape – I might be creative enough to do it without a pair of umbilical or suturing scissors and some surgical wadding. Besides, if this equipment is of the same quality I am used to in the hospital, these blades won't be sharp enough to cut through paper, let alone the barbed wire that surrounds me.'

Winded by my sheer temerity, he shuffled some paper to mask his fury. No doubt he was craving to unholster the gun at his side, snap off the virgin safety clip, and shoot me, there and then, for my sheer dissidence. And his pleasure. Instead, he merely sweated.

'So, am I to take them, Sergeant Meier? Or will you be sterilising them for me, in readiness?'

'No, no, you may take them,' he said, willing me out of his sight.

Christa came three days later, and after doing our duty with Eva, we gained permission to go on a walk towards the Teehaus, where Christa said she had spied some camomile, and wanted to pick and dry it to make tea for the birth. Her thoughtfulness caused Eva's eyes to well up and I was struck by the guilt of our deception.

'So tell me how they found you this time?' I said as soon as we judged ourselves to be out of human earshot.

'There was a note in the laundry pile at the Goebbels'. Someone who knows my daily routine put it there, I'm sure of it. But I don't remember anyone unusual coming to the house that day.'

'What did it say?'

'That the safety of Hitler's prize was their priority too. They were anxious for it not to become an icon and a jewel in Hitler's crown.'

'That's all very literal,' I said. 'Anything else?'

Christa stopped and looked suddenly grave. 'They say they can get us to safety, Anke. Our families too. They mentioned my father, and your family in the camps. They say they have the power to get us out of Germany.'

'In return for what?'

'Alerting them to when the labour is starting, and when the baby is born.'

'Is that all? Nothing else?'

'No, just that.'

'And how are we to communicate with them, if we need to?'

'To leave a light in the pantry window if we agree.'

I walked on, feet leaden, wishing the Teehaus wasn't so far away. I wanted to stand on its pretty balcony, look out over the expanse towards Austria and wait for the landscape to give me answers. I was suddenly so tired; the branches were dappled overhead, and the day seemed peaceful, but I was weary of living on the razor-thin precipice of those distant mountains, of the feeling that every decision might be the one towards a wrong turn and inevitable death.

'Anke? What shall we do?' Christa had caught up to my side. 'Do you think they can make us safe?'

I stopped, and looked directly in her eyes, crinkled at the edges with concern.

'No, Christa, I don't.'

She looked heartbroken, crushed. 'But why? If they have influence enough to find us here, to apply to us directly, surely they have influence elsewhere? Surely, we should . . .'

I took her hands firmly, only just holding back from shaking them, like a mother with a hysterical child. 'Christa! Think! Your father is hundreds of miles away, my family dotted around two or three secure camps. Even if they have some high-ranking Germans as friends, it would take more than that to spirit us all away. It's a pipe-dream and they know that war makes us desperate enough to believe in those dreams – they are *relying* on it.'

Her eyelids drooped, shoulders sagged.

'I'm sorry,' I added. 'But we are dispensable to them, and we deserve not to be.'

She sighed. 'No, it's me who should be sorry. I know my war has been easy compared to some, nothing like your suffering, but I just want it to be over. To be away from here.'

'I know,' I said. 'Me too. What I don't quite understand is if they think they can get to the baby, why don't they just target Hitler himself? Wouldn't that have more effect?'

'I think it would be almost impossible,' said Christa. 'On the few times he's been to the Goebbels', it's like he wears an armour of people so close to him. No one would get near enough. Besides, the Führer would become an instant martyr, and someone else would step into his place – Himmler maybe. He's just as determined, perhaps more so. Joseph talks all the time about the Nazi "machine" – he needs the baby to feed the machine.'

I looked at Christa and the understanding in her gentle features. It was fortunate the Reich didn't know what an effective spy they had deep in their own nest.

I tried to lighten the gloom. 'I may be wrong, but I think our best chance of getting away, of surviving this, is to stick together, just our little team. What we're doing isn't collaboration—' I had to say it out loud to make myself believe it '—it's what we would do for any woman in need, with a baby to birth. To keep alive, all of us.'

If I said it enough times, would the idea get any easier, the strangulation of my guts any less frequent?

We agreed to do nothing – no spy-like lanterns in the pantry, no courting the resistance. Christa and I would care for Eva and her baby, and hope that good fortune smiled upon us in some way. It wasn't much of a plan, but it was the only one we had.

25

New Arrivals

Unlike the majority of babies, reinforcements arrived earlier than planned at the Berghof. Captain Stenz found me early one morning, while I was sweating over a large pan of water in the kitchen, sterilising the birth instruments we would need.

'Fräulein Hoff.' He strode in, cap in hand. 'That looks like hot work.'

I swivelled at the sound of his voice. 'Captain Stenz!' I couldn't help smiling. 'Yes, it's never been my favourite job, but a necessary one.'

I wiped at the perspiration on my brow and wondered if I looked as red and broiled as the laundry maids. He shuffled his feet for a second, and then looked to the floor. Apologetic.

'I've come to tell you that the medical staff are following on behind me.'

'So soon?'

'I had hoped for two more days, and to send word in

advance, but the doctor is keen to settle in. I just managed to drive on ahead to give you some warning.'

'Well, thank you for that at least,' I said. 'I'd better go and tidy myself up. I can try to give a good first impression.'

He caught my arm as I walked past. 'You look fine. Very well, if I may say.' His eyes were that fabulous blue, even through the steam. But I made a face that questioned both his eyesight and his judgement.

'Well, all right, perhaps a little grooming for the top brass,' he joked. 'But nothing too much needed.'

'I thank you for your confidence, Captain Stenz, and perhaps some stretching of the truth. But I will go and change.'

A single staff car arrived within the hour, followed by a small truck – more equipment than even I had imagined. Captain Stenz fronted the welcoming party, with Sergeant Meier to his left, rigid and sweating in the early afternoon sunshine. I stood a good pace behind, aware of the hierarchy and the need to maintain Dieter's position as the man keeping his staff in order. My aim was to attract as little attention as possible, so they would leave us well alone.

Hopes of minimal interference were dashed the moment Dr Koenig stepped from the car, the grey-green of his Wehrmacht uniform showing few creases, and his Nazi cross proudly pinned to his ample breast. He looked army first and a medic second, a man born into his bumptious face and the three-lined crease above his full eyebrows.

'Welcome, Dr Koenig,' Dieter said, with a salute that made me wince internally.

'Thank you, Captain Stenz,' he replied. 'Heil Hitler.'

They raised the salute, and Sergeant Meier was introduced,

along with the doctor's assistant, Dr Langer, a slight younger man in army officer's green. His tiny pupils swept back and forth as he stepped from the car, like a beady-eyed bird about to catch a worm.

I recognised him instantly – he was hard to forget, not so much because of his appearance, which could have been modelled on Joseph Goebbels', but because of the way he had embraced the 'learning' during his short time in the camp. As I remembered it, his speciality in gynaecology was in eliminating babies rather than producing them; new ways to sterilise women, which he approached with gusto. I had heard tales from the hospital block of his practices and witnessed the bloody trauma more than once. His departure from the camp after a month signalled profound relief among the women.

My heart sank. I wasn't sure what I'd been expecting, but the relative ease of the last few months – dare I call it virtual freedom – had lulled me into a false sense of security. I had no doubt the Reich would ensure competent doctors on hand for the Führer's mistress – the best in their field – but I thought they might be civilians pressed into the task. I was shocked by my own naivety; this was a political baby, and therefore the birth a political manoeuvre, devoid of humanity.

'Fräulein Hoff?' Dieter was calling me forward, and I stepped into the circle.

'Dr Koenig, this is midwife Anke Hoff, late of the Central Hospital in Berlin, and the midwife requested by Fräulein Braun.'

'Fräulein Hoff.' He nodded dutifully. 'I hope we can work together. I was at the Central myself recently – when was it you were there? On the labour ward?' His facial muscles were a thinly disguised smirk, diplomatic and dangerous. He knew my history, and was needling nicely.

'Some years,' I said, without embarrassment. 'I've been engaged in war work since then. But my practices have been kept up to date.'

The lines on his forehead, like a child's crude depiction of waves, straightened as his mood flattened the pink skin. 'I see,' he said, as a full stop to our conversation.

'Shall we?' Dieter was playing the perfect host. 'Fräulein Braun is waiting inside with some tea, I believe.'

The men walked up the steps to the house, and I hovered, unsure whether to follow, suddenly adrift in such familiar surroundings. In sweeping up the party, Dieter looked behind and beckoned for me to follow, but the doctor saw his intention.

'We'll be fine, Fräulein. I'm sure we can gather all the necessary details from Fräulein Braun.'

I had been dismissed, and I turned and walked away smartly, not wanting to catch Dieter's expression, in case it was indifferent, or worse, in agreement.

26

The Good Doctor

Restlessly, I read the same page of a book at least ten times over. In the hospital, I was used to being dismissed by doctors, by men who had a high opinion of their knowledge and themselves. Equally there were some who gave credence to our skills – that we as midwives could coax babies into the world with patience, pulling on a mother's strength instead of merely shouting at them to push. And I had been spoiled at the Berghof, being left to my own devices for this long, flattered by Eva's choosing me. It was a luxury I had foolishly grown used to, like the fresh sheets and good food.

At dinner, I heard their deep tones in the dining room upstairs – the men, though not Eva. She had probably retired early to read her letters again. I heard Dieter's voice, Sergeant Meier's obsequious mutterings, and Dr Koenig's booming laughter. Dr Langer's shrewish voice managed a dark, sinister edge without ever being raised, and so he appeared absent.

I took solace in my room and my letters – just one more each from Mama and Papa had filtered through the previous week. Already, the page edges were fibrous from my constant stroking, as if each letter were Mama's soft skin or Papa's silken beard. I drank in the words again.

Ilse and I, we have joined a singing group and I'm so enjoying it, she wrote in her upbeat, diary style. *Ilse teases me that I'm tone deaf, but I think I may carry on once the war is over. It's been so uplifting!*

I had to smile at her forced optimism, even if it was just for my benefit. Papa, by nature, was more philosophical. *My heart is constantly swelled by the nature of men and their tenacity when we have little to see but the horizon,* he wrote in an increasingly spidery hand. *Their little acts of kindness to me bring tears to my eyes, although you know, my lovely Anke, that it takes little to make me weep over the beauty and the beast of mankind!*

So many messages in a few, simple sentences: couched in front of the wireless in those last days before we were all taken, Papa and I had talked over endless possibilities for us and Germany, sometimes both of us wet with tears. Always, always, though he ended with the sentiment: 'Mankind will triumph, Anke. Be sure of that.' In his scribbled words, he was finding a way for his ethos to live on. I knew then that his thinking, and that of thousands like him – imprisoned or free – would drive out bullies like Koenig. We just had to wait. And survive.

I was still awake when the staff car left at about midnight, to their base down the mountain. But they would be back, hovering; there was no doubt. I felt impatient to gauge Eva's take on the situation – she had always given the impression it was to be just us at the birth, and now Christa. But her flighty mind was easily swayed; any suggestion of the Führer's in favour of the doctors and she might yield. The thought of trying to practise midwifery with Dr Koenig's overbearing presence in the room brought me out into a cold sweat. And Dieter? I knew he understood, but even as SS he had limitations. Depressed, I drifted uneasily into sleep.

The doctor was certainly keen. He was back before breakfast, supervising the transformation of a large guest room on the same level as Eva's bedroom. They had brought an operating bed, portable lights, and an anaesthetic machine – appropriated from a needy field hospital, no doubt – plus an array of instruments. The maids had been up since the early hours scrubbing the floor and walls, and the curtains had been replaced with blinds. My nose wrinkled with the overpowering smell of carbolic.

I ghosted through the corridor towards Eva's quarters almost tiptoeing past the new theatre room.

'Fräulein Hoff, may I have a word?'

I tensed at the sound of Dr Koenig's voice. 'Certainly, Doctor.'

He beckoned me towards Sergeant Meier's empty office. 'Please, sit down.'

Taking his place behind the desk, he sat back as if the chair was moulded to his own, broad shape.

'Well, Fräulein, you do appear to have made something of an impression on Fräulein Braun,' he said, fingers weaved together and resting on his girth.

'She tells me you have made a plan, which stipulates that as medical doctors—' the stress heavy on *doctors* '—we are to remain on site but outside of the delivery room, until or unless you request our help.'

'I believe that is what the Fräulein wishes,' I said, eye contact dutiful but minimal. 'I am, of course, led by her wishes.'

'In which case, I feel it's prudent that we are both clear on our realms of practice.' In other words, my limitations as a midwife, and his scope to do anything in the name of medicine.

'Certainly,' I said.

The list he reeled off was predictable, but constricting: any delays in the labour beyond a certain number of hours, any change in the baby's heart rate, bleeding, discoloured fluid once the waters broke, changes to blood pressure, pulse or temperature. Eva would need to be a textbook case to avoid his large, overbearing hands on her. I was to report the progress of the labour personally to him at every hour.

I nodded at each request, knowing that without his or Dr Langer's actual presence in the room, it was only me who could assess the clinical facts. I was experienced enough to detect real signs of danger, and ignore those grey areas straddling normality.

'Fräulein?' He seemed impatient I was showing no signs of reverence. 'Are we clear on your role, and when to hand over?'

'Yes, Doctor, we are,' I said. 'Although I have every confidence Fräulein Braun will cope with the labour and birth her baby without needing our help to any great degree.'

He grunted, disbelieving of any woman to birth without his expert aid.

'Is that all? Fräulein Braun is expecting me.' I moved to stand up.

'I shall expect to see your notes daily,' he said on parting.

'Of course. Good day, Dr Koenig.'

I held on to my breath until halfway down the corridor, letting it out in one huge sigh as Dr Langer emerged from the theatre room. He stopped, remembered to click his heels, and nodded – his beady, black pupils set on my face. I worried for a second that he might recognise me, but my appearance was so far from that of the waif at the camp I didn't think it possible. Now, I had a recognisable head of hair, pink skin covering my cheekbones, instead of a deathly grey, and a light in my eyes. I was no longer a shadow.

'Fräulein,' he said quietly, and moved on.

Eva was quite perky, as though the mere arrival of the doctors signalled the baby was on its way. Her complexion was that of the healthiest sportswoman, hair thick and glossy as it swung above her shoulders.

'Morning, Anke,' she said. 'The baby is very awake today. I've been up since the early hours. We saw the sunrise together.' She beamed with pleasure, and cupped her bump with both hands.

'That's wonderful – a moving baby is a happy baby, as we say.'

She was glowing the readiness of a woman about to enter another realm, another life. Truly blooming.

I busied myself with the check, though I was anxious to get her talking.

'So, you've met with Dr Koenig and Dr Langer?' I said.

She lay on the bed automatically, and I bent to listen to the baby.

'I did.' She almost held her breath, as she did every time I reported on her baby's wellbeing.

'The baby sounds wonderful. It's a train today, instead of a galloping horse – lovely and steady.' And she laughed, like she always did. 'Anke, what do you think of the doctors?'

I paused deliberately. 'I think they are doing the jobs they were sent to do, in ensuring your safety, and the baby's.'

'But they don't have to be too close, do they? If it's all going well?'

'Not if you don't want them to be.' I sat down on the bed and faced her, puffing out my cheeks theatrically to relay true concern. 'I can keep them at a distance, but only if you make it clear it's your choice. I'm a midwife, Eva – we don't hold rank over doctors. But you do.'

Her plumped features were suddenly relaxed. 'That's good. You know I'll do anything to ensure the baby is safe, but I feel I can do it – with you and Christa. I really do. We just need this little one to behave.' She talked towards her stomach, and – right on cue – the baby made a wave of her abdomen.

'I'm not afraid, you know,' she said as I turned to leave. 'I'm not afraid of giving birth, of everything that goes with it.' She smiled, as if convincing herself. 'It's just after . . .'

'I know,' I said. 'I know.' There was no more to be said. We were all afraid of the after.

I sought out Dieter in Sergeant Meier's office, his under-secretary being conspicuously absent the whole morning.

'Am I interrupting?' I said, when he seemed preoccupied.

'Ah, no, come in – you're a welcome relief from the frustrations of correspondence. I sometimes think this war will be won or lost on typewriters instead of the battlefield.' He offered the chair opposite.

I told him what Eva had said, and waited for the inevitable, long sigh.

'I expected as much,' he replied. 'She was very quiet over dinner last night, and I don't think either of our illustrious army medics made a terribly good impression. Dr Koenig came across very bullish and condescending, and Dr Langer was a mouse in comparison.' He clasped his hands in a prayer-like stance and propped up his chin. 'But I don't think Dr Koenig will take kindly to being sidestepped, by you as a midwife or any other woman. I'll need to let him down, let's say, *creatively.*'

He was deep in thought and seemed to forget I was there, until I forced a cough.

'Dieter, can I ask you something else? Who is in charge here? Herr Goebbels, Magda, or the doctors? I don't understand why we haven't a directive from the Führer himself, about his own child.'

A turquoise light narrowed under his blond lashes. 'I'm not entirely sure either, other than that I know the Führer has never made a secret of the fact that he doesn't want children. From what I can gather he treats Eva badly, but he is fond of her in his own way. He tolerates her, as much as any woman. But not enough to be present.' The next words crept out of his mouth, teeth set together, almost by accident: 'He's too busy being the father of Germany. No, this is the Goebbels' baby, Joseph's little starlet.'

Later that night, tracing the flecks of light on my dark ceiling, I had plenty to mull over. Childbirth was, by nature, a series of unknowns, but had its own assurances. There was a pattern, a labour script, but it was also like the plays I used to watch

213

in a little theatre just off the Alexanderplatz, where the drama could veer wildly in every performance, labile and fluid. I loved that it was experimental and erratic; it had been fun to fall off the cliff of expectation, sitting there on the edge of our seats.

As a midwife, it was the natural adrenalin that drove you on to seek out each new chapter with fresh eyes. Before the war, the next scene had been set firmly, when loving mothers took home their newborns, babes who went on to be loved in a thousand different lives. In the camp, that script was virtually torn up, and yet, in a hateful way, I had got used to even that. Now there was just a wide unknown. The baby would be born – that was a certainty – but as to the narrative after, I could only hope Eva figured largely somewhere in the Goebbels' tightly written drama.

And the fate of my family? Perhaps they were only bit parts. Easy enough to put a line through.

27

The Sewing Room

Dieter was gone for the rest of the day, and I busied myself going over notes for Dr Koenig. In the afternoon, Eva asked me to accompany her on a walk to the Teehaus, a thinly veiled excuse to pump me for more birth stories, which I didn't mind. She liked tales of homebirths especially, and I dipped into my memory – the good side – naturally skating over whether they were Germans, Czechs, Hungarians or Jews.

To Eva's clouded perception, all the babies were plump and pink, blond and blue-eyed, and her face lit up when the labours came to fruition. She loved to know what women giving birth were like – what they said, who they called out for, and the sometimes funny requests they made. 'Do you think I'll be like that, Anke? Oh, I hope not too much moaning!' She clutched at her bump as if to say: 'That'll be us soon.' I couldn't fault her willingness to move forward, fearless in her own little universe.

As for me, I waged a daily battle with impatience, up

there in the static sky. Lena came to my rescue early the next day, asking if I wanted any sheets made into cloths for the birth. She could easily run them up on the former housekeeper's old sewing machine.

A machine! The prospect of some employment made me smile. Daniel got out his oilcan and gave the dusty machine a service, and one of the kitchen boys heaved it onto the little table just inside my chalet door. It was verging on ancient, but totally familiar to me – my grandmother had one almost identical, passed on to Mama and now sitting in the small room in my parents' house. I had a brief vision of her bending over the table, muttering and cursing quietly as the thread stuck frequently in the bobbin, and I swallowed back the image.

Sorrow for another day.

The breeze trickled in as I laid out the cloth. Lena brought me the kitchen sewing box with all manner of threads and needles, and several pairs of large shearing scissors – if only Sergeant Meier could have seen, his well-oiled hair would have fallen to the floor in shock! I was no seamstress, despite my experiences, and certainly nothing like Christa, but I could do a decent seam and hem, and those were all the skills needed. And I had plenty of time.

I was soon humming in time with the treadle, and feeling quite . . . was *happy* too strong an emotion? Perhaps it was contented or fulfilled? I was alive, not under immediate threat of death, and perhaps my family had some chance too. There were reasons to be hopeful.

28

Release

I cut and stitched through lunch – Lena came out to see how I was doing, and brought me a sandwich, sweet girl. By dusk I had a pile of neatly hemmed cloths, which I would boil, ready for the birth. My eyes were tired and sore as I tidied away the threads, and I didn't see the figure move onto my porch. His face in the doorway startled me.

'Dieter!'

'Sorry, I didn't mean to—'

'No, no, I just wasn't expecting you.' I said it like a wife welcoming a spouse home from work, and realised how frivolous I was in his company.

'I see you've been busy?' he said, eyeing the fabric debris.

'I've found a task at last to keep me busy. Any jobs gratefully accepted, no repair too small. Though I can't guarantee the results.' I smiled like a shop girl peddling wares, sounding ridiculous, though equally it seemed beyond my control.

'Well, it's nice to see you . . . content. If I can say that.'

He hovered in the doorway, looking jaded. 'Anke, would

you like to join me in a drink? I could certainly do with one.'

I adopted that stunned look again, but made light of it, for his sake. 'I can't promise the effect it will have – I may just fall asleep – but yes, I would.'

He disappeared into the gloom of the evening, and came back minutes later with a bottle of brandy. Good brandy.

'Will this do?' he held it up, with two glasses.

We sat on the porch and sipped. The liquid on my tongue burned, and like that first drag of the cigarette, I almost coughed it back. Gradually, though, it became a glow, and I recalled the joy of good alcohol on a pleasant night out.

The evening was still, the breeze having dropped, and there was no one in sight, the guards presumably at dinner and the rest of the household having retreated indoors. It felt somehow . . . empty. A distant radiance from the snowy mountain peaks glowed through the arena of blue and there was only a slight rustle of the surrounding trees.

'So, how is the good Dr Koenig?' I said into the air.

He laughed. 'Is it that obvious?'

'Well, you look like you've worked hard at being the diplomat.'

He sighed, and took a large swig. 'That's not the half of it. I've had to spend a whole evening and a full day with him and that . . . with Dr Langer, listening to tales of medical school and how the ungrateful citizens of the Reich owe their lives to their skilled hands. All of them, it seems. It took that much to pacify him about Eva.'

It could have been the alcohol, I don't know, but I was suddenly irked. A minute blister of irritation somewhere deep inside grew into a swell of hate, at how fat, pompous, little-talented individuals like Dr Koenig needed their egos stroking, in order that others should be left alone.

'Did you really need to do that?' I tried disguising the edge to my voice.

His eyes were closed, face to the dimming sky. 'You know I did, Anke. It's what I do – my purpose.' He said it lazily, as if the alcohol was having a numbing effect.

'Have you thought about *not* doing it?' This time, a definite slice. I didn't want an argument, but like my flirting, it was out of my control.

He sat up, eyes open. 'What do you mean?'

'Do you know, Dieter, do you really *know* what is going on in your country – *our* country? In Poland, Hungary, in this glorious Third Reich?'

His features flashed red as he stood up, casting around to check we were truly alone. 'Of course I know! Do you think I'm ignorant, or worse – a monster?'

'No, but—'

'Like I told you before, it was expected. There was no choice but to join, it was *not* an invitation.' His voice was a bitter whisper. 'We all have sacrifices, Anke.'

I couldn't help myself. 'And are your parents in a labour camp, surrounded by death and destruction, seeing one human's cruelty pitted against another, day in, day out? Or is it their comfortable lifestyle they stand to lose – a servant or two, the nice meal on the table?' My own voice was hot with fury and brandy.

'No!' His voice spewed out and his eyes panned, watching to see if his bile had travelled.

He brought it under control again, a low boil. 'Now it's

219

you who's being naive, Anke. Do you honestly believe that you can toss aside a uniform like mine at will? Quite apart from the shame to my parents, they would be at real risk — all of them — if there was the slightest doubt about my loyalty. SS officers don't just turn tail and retire. They are prone to car accidents, and suicides. Their families die in house fires.' He swallowed hard. 'More often than you imagine.'

An ugly chasm sat between us as I absorbed the reality of his words.

Dieter sat, slumped and looking utterly exhausted, a hand pushed through his hair. 'I'm a prisoner of sorts too,' he said quietly. 'I may not have seen what you have, have suffered as others, but I know what goes on. I have ears and eyes, and sometimes wish I hadn't.'

Right then, I believed him. Why, I don't know — sitting there in the jacket as leaden as a storm sky, murkier than hell, those hideous skull bones on his collar reflecting what little light we had. But I did.

'So, how do you live?' I asked.

He sucked in a large breath. 'I do everything I can to limit my effectiveness without raising suspicion. If I appear incompetent they will simply replace me with another who is efficient — viciously efficient. So I push paper, sometimes in the wrong directions, slowly. A typing error here, a lost paper there, so that a name falls off a list, lost in the mire.'

He looked at me, squinting in the half light. 'I don't pretend to be hacking at the foundations, Anke. I'm not that brave, but I can weaken the scaffold just that little bit. Just enough to divert time and resources away from doing real harm. It's not that much, but it's all I can do.'

Dieter sat back, gazing at the sky and empty of words, and I saw the moon's silver catch the lines around his eye and the crease of anxiety at his mouth's edge. The air was so, so still – life totally suspended. In seconds, a small breeze blew up and it gave me the courage, a push. I moved towards him, touching his cheek lightly as I bent my head down and pressed my lips against his soft mouth, gently at first, and then hard. He was taken by surprise, but in a split second had yielded, drawing my own lips into his, and we stayed almost motionless, only the tiniest of muscles rippling. Seconds? Ten or more? Who knows? Eternity has no clock.

It was me who drew away first, anxiously looking to gauge his expression. It wasn't one of shock or disgust, but of relief, and – dare I think it – pleasure. Our pupils locked, both of us scanning and judging. Eyes still fixed, he stood up and took my hand, leading me into the chalet, like a girl being invited onto the dance floor for the last waltz. Everything in me gave way, and I let myself be guided.

There were no words. In the near darkness, we undressed and he draped his jacket around the chair. I watched him do it, and he caught me staring, taking his shirt and covering the slate weave with the white cotton so it was almost unseen, his cap out of sight. Then I saw him as he might have looked in another life: braces by his sides, a lean, taut chest just visible in the shimmer from the window, his lungs pushing breath in and out, hard and fast, ribs like pistons.

I pulled the curtain across the window before I took off my vest and stepped out of my knickers, ashamed of the body I had lost and only semi-recovered since this other life began. We slipped under the sheets – still no words – and measured each other, inch by inch, hungrily matching each

221

piece of skin so that nothing wanted for contact. I sucked breath from his neck, smelt the nape where his blond hair ran into the bones of his spine and he moved to the place where my breasts had once met, greedily taking solace from the flesh that was there. He smelt of brandy and cigarettes, and that mysterious light cologne, but not of sour filth or hate.

There was no going back. This was war, no half measures, no barriers, no 'let's wait and see'. Love or lust? When there was little time to analyse either; you made up something in between and lived the moment.

He was tender with the spindle of my body, taking care to hold where I had gained new flesh, and skimming over the flaccid excuse for a figure. By comparison, he was firm and chiselled – naturally so, muscles earned in the football fields of childhood or in his father's garage, firmly rooted. I took pleasure in palpating every curve, each proud sinew as he held me, and he cloaked himself around me and in me, and I felt as I hadn't done in so, so long.

Safe.

On the Move, February 1942

A gap between the tarpaulin joins in the back of the truck meant I could see real life whizzing by as we drove away from Gestapo headquarters; army uniforms, cyclists, mothers pushing prams at a pedestrian pace. Life carried on for those at liberty, unaware of the horrors so close to them, as I had before the past few days. There's nothing like craving freedom when you haven't got it, and I could just taste it in the chill air billowing through the gaps.

The tarpaulin was as solid as any prison boundary with the armed guard presence, but afforded little protection against the bitter temperatures. The two guards were stiff and impassive in their heavy coats and boots, while the four prisoners shivered uncontrollably. I was the only woman, alongside an older man, and two younger men opposite. Their faces were noticeably bruised, but the older man seemed unmarked. Unconsciously, we didn't speak, flashing looks across the truck gangway, and reassuring smiles when the guards closed their eyes with fatigue while we rattled along.

My lips trembled with the cold, and one of the men opposite began to take off his suit jacket. It sparked a hasty reaction from one guard, who barked at us not to move, and the man gestured at his offering. Finally, the guard nodded it was acceptable. I protested at first but the man's face showed such willing.

'I have a shirt and sweater,' he said quietly, pointing to the thin, sleeveless wool under the tweed material.

'Thank you,' I said, and realised it was the first time I had uttered a single word in the last day or so. I felt the immediate warmth of fabric and humanity combined, the material heavy on my shoulders. I tried showing real appreciation in a smile, and he looked buoyed by the act of giving. He would never have known how that simple gift saved me from suffering in the next hours, or how often I thanked him from afar, hoping he wasn't too cold in his own thin coverings.

We seemed to be going north, judging by some of the streets and buildings we passed. But as we left the confines of the city I lost sight of the geography and fatigue caught hold. I rested my head back, bobbing in a half sleep, lulled by the growl of the engine. I roused to a sharp stop, shouts of men outside, and our guards snapping to attention, rapping their gun butts on the floor of the truck. 'Listen! All of you! No talking.'

We — the cargo — were unloaded in some type of goods yard, with multiple train tracks side by side. I was held back as the men peeled off behind a goods train and out of sight. A weak sun sat behind a grey mask of cloud, and I guessed it was around midday, the faint glow tracking sideways while we — six women in total — stood shivering for almost an hour. Only one bored guard stood watch, shuffling his feet and looking anywhere but at our faces, although he didn't stop us talking amongst ourselves.

The women whispered similar stories of cultivated fear; I imagined that somewhere, in an office in Berlin, there was a team of beady-eyed psychologists busily devising new ways to break down their own countrymen, devoting themselves to fracturing humanity without a thought for reassembling the soul. The mere notion depressed me more than anything.

I stood beside a woman called Graunia, a journalist on the wrong side of Goebbels' thinking. She struck me as bright and stoical amid the grey of the day and I was attracted to her tenacious spirit even then. I often thank fate we were pitched together in that moment, a prop for each other's future survival that we could never have predicted.

Eventually, out of the milky distance, a goods train rolled slowly towards us. The brakes squealed painfully to a halt and several guards appeared, forming a semi-circle around one carriage, rifles at the ready. They barked orders loudly, apparently to whatever was inside: 'Keep back! No noise! Attention!' The women looked at each other, alarm drowning our features.

The door to the cattle truck swung open, and an invisible but foul cloud puffed out, desperately seeking clean particles of air. It caught in my throat — the stench of human degradation. The guards looked on in disgust, openly covering their noses, and I struggled not to do the same. The faces that peered out of the darkness looked ashamed of their own filth, then crowded towards the entrance, eager to suck in the air of the yard, heavy with engine oil.

'Back! Back!' the guards barked, prodding at the air with their rifles, then ushering us towards the opening. A retch rose in my throat and I pushed it down with every ounce of my being. I knew this, too, would soon be my own stench, wallowing for Lord knows how long in my own swill. Another point to those wily psychologists.

We pushed inside the carriage, and although it wasn't shoulder to shoulder, there wasn't enough room for all to sit, so some of the women stood in clumps, as if making small talk at a party. The door clanged shut and my eyes adjusted to the gloom; I saw it was mainly older women who were sitting, and one younger woman who was already skin and bone, as if the spindly limbs folded underneath wouldn't hold her. Graunia and I were pushed close, no words said. What could we say? There was nothing to justify the sheer bewilderment.

Instead, one woman next to me spoke. 'Have you any water? Anything at all?' Her lips and voice were cracked and her tongue leathery. She kept her mouth to the side, already aware of her own breathy revulsion.

'No, sorry,' I said. 'We have nothing.'

Her eyes died and she turned away, stumbling over some seated bodies and collapsing like a puppet, weeping quietly.

'She's not doing well,' one of the women murmured. 'She was one of the first on, and I don't how long it has been since she's had a drink.'

We stood close, Graunia and me, talking to those who had been in the carriage since the last stop. They hadn't been travelling for long spells, maybe thirty minutes at a time, but the standing time in between had been hours, stretching to most of the night. Just once, the guards had pushed on a canteen of water, but the train lurched violently almost the second it appeared, and half of the fluid had been lost on the floor, the rest shared among those who needed it most.

Outside, there were occasional shouts, a flurry of voices, silence, then more activity, several gunshots in the distance and then a continual hiss of the steam climbing, the engine breathing its release

226

and building again. My calves ached and my feet burned inside my shoes. It was fortunate I'd never been precious about my appearance, now that I resembled some of the patchwork ladies who stood in a line daily outside the hospital, begging for a pfennig or two, cheeks brown and leathered. The difference was that they smiled. And they were free. Poor and homeless, perhaps, but in charge of their own destinies.

I was in a half doze, propped up by the clutch of bodies, when we set off. Light was still coming through the slits in the wood, our only marker of time. There was a small gasp of relief that maybe, maybe the journey was nearer to its conclusion, but no one spoke. Just the mixture of heavy hearts and resignation, twirling with more worldly odours. One unspoken thought united us: where would we end up? And how much more like hell could it be?

29

Friends

I lay in the crook of his arm, watching a tiny sliver of moon-light make an arrow on the wall. He was silent, breathing hard, his other arm stroking my back, tracing over one of my few curves, his chin nestled into my hair.

At last his breath slowed, and he cut into the moment.

'Well, Fräulein Hoff, you are something of a surprise.'

'Not so predictable yourself,' I countered. 'For a captain.'

We squeezed and giggled under the covers, and took time in kissing, now there was no urgency.

We didn't talk of what it meant – what lines we had crossed or the consequences if discovered. There was a time and a place for that, but not now. For those precious minutes, stretched into hours, we drank in the intimacy, fastened together against the cold, hard world outside, amid the warm spring evening.

He explored my rack of ribs and the horns of my pelvis, and I the scars from his first battle, deep ridges in both shoulder blades, and we neither asked nor explained. It just was. It was war.

Both of us must have slept for a good while, and woke – Dieter with a start – when the patrol came by at first light. I usually slept through it, but the two young lads were sniggering at some joke as they passed. We tensed against each other and then relaxed, my smaller body curled under his curve, like tiny kittens in the universe of their mother's limbs.

'I need to go,' he whispered into my ear. 'It wouldn't do for me to be seen tiptoeing out of here – for your sake.'

'I know,' I said.

'Let's hope Frau Grunders doesn't prowl the corridors on her own patrol.' He laughed as he pulled back the covers, and I rolled into the empty impression, eager to occupy his shape for a few minutes longer.

He dressed in the half light, just his trousers and shirt, kissing me on the lips before bundling the jacket and cap under his arm and turning towards the door.

'Dieter?'

'Yes?'

'Tomorrow – today – no regrets, eh? Don't let it make us different. We can be friends.'

He turned to face me again. 'We are friends, Anke, and we can be more. No regrets.'

He smiled and was gone.

I dozed a little more after Dieter left and roused myself for breakfast, taking care to appear no different. I wanted the old Anke to mask the fireworks erupting inside my toes and springing from the top of my head. Dieter wasn't at breakfast, of course, as he always took his in the dining room upstairs, and I felt relieved to avoid contact. My face would have been a sure giveaway. Lena and Heidi were laughing in the kitchen; I could hear them giggling over the new, young patrolmen, weighing up who they would choose.

'That Kurt, he's just a boy,' said Lena. 'If it's a man you want, then it would have to be Captain Stenz. I wouldn't say no to dating an officer like him.' Her voice peaked in admiration.

'Oh no!' countered Heidi in mock disgust. 'You don't want to get mixed up with the SS—' she lowered her voice '—a dangerous game, that is. Stick with the regulars. More muscle and less brains but at least you stay alive.'

Their girlish laughter drowned out the rest of the conversation, until Frau Grunders' gruff rebuke sent them scurrying off to clean the rooms.

My heart plummeted like a stone in a millpond. Had I been foolish, my desire running rings around any sensible reason? Had I seen too far beyond the uniform, into a man I had moulded inside my head? I guessed it wouldn't be unusual, or even frowned upon, for SS officers to bed women at will. Perhaps even applauded in some quarters. How much of a hold would he now have over me, if he wanted to extend and exert the power he was used to? Had I, in my moment's need, been very, very stupid?

And yet, in the next second, I swung towards the memory of his warmth, his tenderness, the quest in him for affection instead of brutal lust. The way he'd finally said my name as we'd climbed towards the peak reassured me: it was me he wanted, and not a convenient vessel for his own frustration. I didn't feel used, or bedded out of greed or need. I felt we had come together craving a soft shoulder, some gentleness in the granite shards of ugliness surrounding this bad world. That we'd found more in each other than we had come looking for. Could I have been so wrong?

Through the window, I glimpsed the cigarette smoke of a guard as he leaned against a fence, perhaps daydreaming about his sweetheart back home, and I wondered how we'd ever got here – both of us, atop the beanstalk, in the middle of a bloody, annihilating war. So much of me craved to be back in Berlin, even if it was reduced to mere dust under a cloud – to be in a stark reality, instead of floating in this bubble of the Berghof. I wanted things to be *real*.

30

Clouds in Springtime

You know what they say: be careful what you wish for.

I returned to the chalet, fingering the bed sheets and plumping the pillow, though not before drawing in his scent, still there, and finding a small blond strand attached to the cover. Then guiltily looking about, as if I might be caught. Nothing but my own insecurity for surveillance. Making room on my table, I tried heaving the sewing machine onto the floor. As I shuffled the heavy metal to one side, something other than off-cuts of material flopped down, a light scuff of paper parachuting its way to the floor. It sat at my feet, a small, folded square, pulsing white as a beacon. A pencilled scrawl said only: *Anke*.

For a brief moment, my heart leapt teenage beats and I thought it was a note from Dieter. But even in affection, I knew he wouldn't be so naive as to leave any trail. I watched my fingers tremble as I opened up the folds and read the message:

You have the power to change everything for our beloved country. The Reich needs an icon — you can deliver it into Hitler's hands, or to safety in ours. Think of your family and your fate. And of good Germans. You can change lives.

Real or not? I couldn't decide. Except it was there in my shaking hands, an increasingly tangible fantasy. I still wasn't sure what they were asking of me — to betray the baby and steal it from Eva? Or to act as go-between and feign ignorance if they — this unknown group — staged a coup just after the birth? Either way, it was the baby who would suffer. And Eva along with it.

I pocketed the paper, and went quickly to the door, casting about for any bodies slipping away down the path. But I'd been out of the chalet for a good while and anyone could have crept in, with no lock to my door. Still, I felt invaded, as if I'd clawed back some of my personal dignity and space since the camp, and now someone was picking at its thin crust again.

I felt angry at their invasion, and then immediately powerless, sapped of any capacity to find out who or why. I could trust no one aside from Christa, but equally I had no power within myself to decide on a definite course. A combination of will and fate had taken me through this war, and though I had never believed in any higher being, I wanted desperately to surrender to something outside of myself. For me not to pluck at any one route, but just to be taken along. Let life choose me for a change.

The hours until lunchtime dragged, the wisp of paper in my pocket causing agitation, carrying that lead weight of betrayal. I fingered it nervously as I saw Dieter walk towards the porch, his gait stiff and his cap firmly fixed. I smiled at the first welcome thing in my life that day. He didn't. His eyes flicked up briefly and the expression was stern and devoid of colour; my heart muscle twisted with the knowledge of my own misjudgement. I had read him entirely wrong. He was SS, nothing less.

'Dieter?' I searched his starched face.

He came onto the porch, dropped his eyes and took off his cap, placing it dutifully under his arm. He fingered at his gloves, a sign of his own agitation.

'Anke, I'm sorry,' he began.

'Oh, um, for last night? Listen, we can forget—'

'No, it's not that.' He was grave and serious, not angry or embarrassed.

'Then what? Dieter, tell me – please.'

'It's your father,' he whispered. 'I'm so sorry.'

There was no ambiguity in his voice; a gravelly delivery of the dead. A rolling crest of fear and sorrow welled up into my throat and became something between a cough and a tearful retch. I staggered before him and he caught me by the elbow, lowering me onto the chair. I dissolved into a sea of sobs, my hand trying to hide the contortion of my face. I had learnt over years in the hospital to mask some emotion – it was expected of us – but when it broke free, my floodgates were unbounded.

I wanted to know how, when and why, but I couldn't form the words beyond gulps of sorrow pushing out of my throat. Dieter spoke low and even over the tears, holding my free hand. His back was towards the house, and looking from a distance no one would have guessed at an exchange so heavy with emotion.

235

'I have been in touch personally with the camp doctor,' he said. 'I'm reassured he died from pneumonia, as a result of his asthma.' Pinprick pupils tacked back and forth, searching my own. I only stared as the sobs subsided into the pretend hiccups of a child. 'Anke, did you hear me?'

'I hear you, but I don't believe you,' I said angrily, tears streaming into my neck. 'I know how many death certificates have pneumonia, or heart failure, pasted onto them as truths. It's all a lie, it's just what they say.'

'No, I—'

'How can you know? It's all one big lie. He was probably herded into a truck and taken to the place no one comes back from . . .' and I dissolved into tears again. *Please, please, oh Papa, please don't tell me you died under the gas.*

Dieter took both my hands, drawing them down sharply to grab my attention. 'Anke!' He looked almost angry. 'Please believe me when I tell you he did not die in one of those places. I have done the most thorough of checks, and I have evidence your father died in the camp. Of natural causes.'

I flashed fury again. 'There's nothing *natural* about being starved and worked to death, because you hold beliefs close to your heart.'

'I didn't mean it like that,' he said quickly, 'you know I didn't. But your family – you know what the agreement is – your family is not in danger of the transport.'

'As long as I behave – isn't that the deal?' My anger and petulance were rising above sorrow, and as much as I was aiming at the Reich, Dieter was in the firing line. 'And how can you possibly know the details? Are you intimate with the Commandant?'

He pulled back, and I knew I had gone too far again, in aligning him with the side of the Reich he found more than unsavoury. Unlike me, he didn't kick back, but let his hands fall away.

'Because I have made it my business to know,' he said quietly, 'and because I have taken an interest, for some time now.' He pulled out an envelope from his pocket. 'This might explain a little.'

I took it from him, and our fingers touched lightly again, this time with no crackle of acrimony. He reached out to push away a tear on my cheek but stopped short as a patrolman rounded the corner and came into view.

'I'll leave you in peace,' he said. 'I'll come back later.' He stood up and surveyed my curled, deflated body. 'I'm so sorry, Anke, I really am.'

I watched him, as I had so many times, step down from the porch and walk down the path. This time, though, he didn't turn his head automatically towards the golden sun and the vista of blue. He put on his cap and looked straight ahead.

The letter was in Papa's hand, dated just a week previously. I might have had trouble knowing it was his, if it hadn't been for the ornate way he wrote his Ts and Ps – the 'academic's artistry' I had always called it. The script was spidery and disjointed, that of a man struggling to hold pen to paper.

Darling Anke
I would like to say I am well, but the winter has taken its toll and my old body hasn't emerged from the cold with as much gusto as before. However, I am in the

infirmary and the conditions are good, with nice sheets and kindness.

Please tell Mama I am thinking of her — of you all — and remember so much the happy times we had at home, together around the table, when we laughed and told tales. Franz especially told the tallest ones! I remember too, all the times we two sat around the radio on a Sunday, and read our papers — those special times with my lovely daughter.

I hope to hear from you soon, my precious girl, and know that you are strong. Keep the sun rising in your world.

All my love, your Papa x.

It was, undoubtedly, a farewell letter of the dying. It might have taken him hours, or days to write. He could have dictated it to someone, but I knew he would have fought, between the fire in his lungs, and the effort of sitting upright, to write this last goodbye, because he'd known I would sense it as genuine. There was his message, too — keep the sun rising. Ever hopeful, my Papa. Humanity will bear out, he was saying. Keep the faith.

I stared at his telltale writing for an age, and although the tears rolled, I was not consumed by a crippling, burning sadness. The anger, I knew, would come later, but I pushed back my own images of the camp, the wide-eyed resignation of women sitting in the trucks, ready to roll towards their fate, the hospital block, the conditions. I could not allow myself to think of that now.

In a strange, distorted way, there was some relief; a curious reprieve that I would no longer worry about my father and his fate, that he would not – in his frailty – face the split second of realisation when the shower heads did not produce a freezing spray of fluid, but the insidious hiss of death. We knew from the gossip in the camp that that was when the screams reached their peak of panic. No, I could not – would not – think of that now.

I couldn't do anything other than believe Dieter when he said that wasn't Papa's end. The letter was proof, wasn't it? He wouldn't have told me about the sheets, and the kindness, otherwise. As a dying man, Papa would have been a prime candidate for the transports, labelled a 'useless mouth', but there could have been strings pulled, favours asked. As Dieter said, he had some power – just not enough to save them. I rolled the possibilities around in my head, seesawing beliefs and wishing above all my faith was right. I had to believe my father had died in a bed, and not in the bowels of inhumanity.

I woke to a short rap on the door. The low light told me it was late afternoon, one foot warmed by golden rays pushing into the room as I lay curled on the bed. I watched the door handle turn and Dieter's head peek through. He slipped in and pulled the curtain across the window.

'How are you?' he said in the new gloom.

I rubbed my eyes, and thought for a second: how was I?

'Uh, I'm all right. I must have fallen asleep.'

He moved towards me, sitting alongside like a mother attending a sick child. My face was streaked with salt tracks, gritty as I brushed them away. He cupped one hand around my cheek, and stroked a thumb over the swollen skin around my eyes.

'It's too much,' he said. 'I know you are stronger than an ox to have survived this far, but it's too much. I'm so sorry.'

I sat up, rubbing both hands over my face, trying to inject some life into the parchment skin. 'The funny thing is I've imagined getting such news for the past two years – about all of them – but I feel slightly numb. The numbness feels worse than being broken inside.'

He took my hands again and brought them to his lips, kissing the tips of my fingers. 'I hate this war, I bloody hate this disgusting excuse for a fight between children pretending to be grown men,' he said quietly, into the flesh.

I looked at him and swallowed hard to ingest some courage. There was just one thing I needed to know, one thing I could not ask last night, but that I had to question now.

'Dieter, do you have anything to do with the transport? The picking and choosing, the lists?'

His eyes flashed alarm, but were directly on me, no hiding. 'No. I promise, Anke, I promise. I wouldn't – I *couldn't* – do that.'

'But you said . . . you mentioned names falling off lists, going missing?'

'I sometimes deal with visas, granting transport out of Germany. Academics, doctors, families with foreign roots. I stamp a few more than I should, lose the rejection letters. Like I said, not much.'

'It's something,' I said, with a weak smile. 'Something is better than nothing.'

He cocked his ear towards the door, at the rumble of an engine, and said he needed to go. Could he come back later, after dinner? Did I want to be alone? No, I said, I didn't. I wanted his company, his warmth, not to be left to eat away at my own sorrow.

'Won't they suspect where you are?' I hadn't seen much of Frau Grunders in recent weeks, but I didn't doubt her eyes were everywhere.

'I'll give Rainer the night off and he'll take the car into town,' he said. 'It's the advantage of being a roaming officer – I have no set agenda, or home.'

He kissed me lightly on the lips, stroked my hair as a farewell, and was gone again.

I washed and tidied myself, and sat on the porch until dinner, perhaps my happiest place until last night. My stomach was growling with hunger, typical after a daytime sleep, and I realised I'd missed lunch, but equally I wasn't keen on facing the servants' hall, so I ignored its gripey protests at first.

The breeze was cleansing, pricking at my sore skin, and I stared at the falling shadows, indulging myself with thoughts of Papa. I pictured him at home, before the angst and the conflict, as the wise one with a sharp sense of humour behind his paternal seriousness. He had often laughed so hard at the dinner table that Mama shot him a look to halt his childishness, yet in the next breath, she was giggling too, unable to hold back. The image was so fresh, and I made a decision there and then not to let the injustice stir up a bitter stew, one that would infect my insides and make me brew a hatred so filthy that it coloured me, forever. Papa's body had succumbed to circumstance, but this madness could not beat us. It would not.

31

Relief

My growling stomach forced me eventually into the servants' hall for dinner, although I took care to bathe my reddened eyes before I went. I didn't want to answer awkward questions, and was unsure if Dieter would have told Frau Grunders about Papa. I hoped not – the grief was mine, and I didn't relish forced sympathy from any quarter, least of all supporters of the Führer's war.

To my relief, no one paid any special attention, and dinner was as muted as always. Only Lena and I talked, about sewing, and she was animated about the dress fabric she'd just bought in town. Perhaps I could help her with making a dress for a local dance in a few weeks' time? I said it was Christa she needed for a skilled seamstress, but I'd do the best I could.

There was no sign of Dieter, Rainer or the car after dinner, and my heart deflated a little. I tried reassuring myself it was the duties of office keeping him away. Later, I sat under the navy sky – the chalet seemed too claustrophobic – as wheels scrunched onto the drive, a door slammed, and the car moved off again. He strode up eagerly, casting about for the patrol, and not speaking until he was on the porch.

'Evening,' he said, face darkening. 'Are you all right?' His eyes scouted mine for clues.

'I'm fine,' I said, and smiled to drive it home. He cocked his head to one side and raised eyebrows in half belief.

'Honestly, Dieter, I'm all right. It was a shock, but not unexpected in some way. I hate where he was, I hate that it should ever have happened, but it's also a kind of release for him. I'm determined it won't destroy me.'

He took off his cap and reached for my hand. His flesh was warm, finger pads soft, and his fingers kneaded at the bones above my fingers, creating an instant tingle inside.

'You are amazing,' he said, looking at me. 'I like to think I would react in the same way, but I don't know. I'm not sure I could be that forgiving.'

I flinched at the word. 'It's nothing like forgiveness, Dieter. It doesn't come close. But I refuse to be further damaged by this . . . this soup of hatred. That's their triumph, in making me hate the way they do, just because of what they are. They won't make me like that.'

He nodded understanding. 'You are one very determined lady,' he said. 'And I'll say it again: you are amazing.' His mouth was beautiful when he smiled, teeth even and straight, with just the slightest chink in a top tooth. I hadn't realised it until then, but that was what gave him such a boyish look – despite his height and stature – as if he had stepped off the football field after a tricky tackle, grinning triumphantly.

'Well, I won't argue with any man who tells me I'm amazing,' I said. 'You can come onto my porch any time.' We were good, and flirting again.

This time it was me who cast around for any stray witnesses, squinting into the darkness. When there were none, I took his hand and led him off the porch and into the chalet. Curtains closed, it was the same scenario, the same anticipation, but without the unknown ahead. It was slower, and we ambled over each other instead of racing to drink in the moment, more certain that we held the space. He was patient and giving, and we took turns in leading until I could no longer delay that moment when we climbed and fell into a nest of feather-lined bliss.

My head was on his chest for an age after, his arm securely around me, my finger tracing over his chest. My eyeline settled on his navel, and a strange bump in the skin. I pooled my finger in the dip and then around a small nest of hair above. Yes, there was a second hole above, not as deep as his umbilicus, but unmistakably there.

'Dieter, what's this?'

He roused from a semi-dose and bent his head upwards, as if he could only half feel where I was touching.

'Oh, that. It's, um, an injury.'

'From the war?'

'I was careless,' he said. 'A stray bullet.'

'It's not hard to take a bullet in war,' I said. 'Was it in battle?'

'Yes.'

The clipped reply sent a firm message, and I decided not to let it hang awkwardly.

'So, were you in hospital long? Were the nurses nice to you?'

'Nice enough,' he said, 'but not as nice as you would have been, I'm sure.'

'Don't be so certain – I'm a better midwife than I was ever a nurse. I might have been an ogre of a matron to you – a young whippersnapper of a soldier.'

He pulled me close to him and kissed the top of my hair. 'Well then, I'd better behave myself, hadn't I?' He pinched me playfully.

'Did it hurt, the bullet?'

'Like hell.'

'In that case, I'd better administer care and compassion to the best of my ability.' With a wry smile, I pressed my lips against the wound, a waxen crater amid his softened belly, and it was the only signal he needed. The gravelly tiredness in his voice disappeared and we sank under the covers and into the warm balm of safety again.

32

Waiting

He left again at first light, skulking across the no-man's land of the complex towards his own room, and I wondered how much of such bliss would be allowed before this war took it away again, the way it sucked everything tender and kind into its black vortex. For now, though, the morning sky was painting itself a crisp mountain blue, the curtains puffed gently inwards, and I allowed myself a few moments of self-pity. Then, my mind turned towards Papa, Mama, Ilse and Franz, and I roused myself to begin another day of survival.

Eva's mood matched mine, although she wasn't aware of anything other than her own discomfort, complaining of backache and 'odd pains', most of which sounded like twinges of late pregnancy.

'When will this baby come, Anke? Surely there's something I can do to move it along, something you can give me?'

'No,' I said matter-of-factly, 'nothing but a healthy dose of patience, and a smattering of faith.'

'You and your faith,' she grumbled. She glanced sideways

like a cunning child. 'I'm sure Dr Koenig would oblige, if I asked him in the right way.'

'I'm sure he would,' I countered briskly. 'Always assuming you wanted to end up in a hospital, when your body decided it didn't like being pushed and pulled into labour. And the baby along with it.' I was in no mood to deal with her silliness, or be centre stage in a minute power struggle.

'Oh,' she said. 'Really? Is that what happens?'

'There's a fair chance,' I said truthfully. 'Babies don't take kindly to being forced out. Besides, what you're feeling is a good sign the baby is descending, and is getting ready.'

'Are you sure?' Her face lit up, like I'd given back the lollipop I'd just taken away.

'Nothing is sure at this point, but the baby's head feels nice and low, and it's pointing in the right direction. So, it's all good. But if you're asking me when, I simply don't know. Only the baby does.'

'Come on, baby!' she said urgently into her bump. 'Come on, your mama wants to meet you.' With superb timing, the baby kicked again and she giggled like a schoolgirl. 'Oh, it heard me!'

Arrival, Somewhere in Germany, February 1942

I'd never given much thought to what hell might look like – youth gives you that luxury, plus my father's general distrust of religion meant the rhetoric of hellfire and damnation didn't feature in our household. On that juddering journey, neck aching as my heavy head tick-tocked in synch with the train's motion, I repelled any images of furnaces and black holes pushing up through the cracks of my half sleep.

I needn't have worried about any fiery predictions. Because hell is grey – grimy, vapid and devoid of any pigment designed to lift the spirit. As the doors were finally pulled back on a dusky, barren world, the image couldn't have been any bleaker.

There had been a twitch of noses as we ground to a halt, to orientate, gain some idea of the geography. I detected a faint saltiness, and there were mutterings: 'Are we near the sea?' 'Will they ship us out?' We settled ourselves in for a wait, some women giving up their floor spaces for others to rest their legs. There was shouting outside, but senses piqued when we heard female voices among the low bark of men and dogs. Then, the heavy scraping of the latch, and the door sweeping back, followed by the recoil of those outside to let the foul odour fly.

'Out! Out! Quick!' the men growled, while we stared wide-eyed at the women who were holding back the dogs, canine teeth large and looming in the gloom, spittle foaming against the pull of their leashes. On the other end of the leads, the women faded into the background almost, the crisp lines of their grey uniforms and hats only just visible. Their faces were granite but the shoulders jerked with the dogs' strength. They made a play at restraining and then seeming to let the dogs leap forward in turns, the snarls jibbing at our space.

Graunia and I stayed close to one another, shuffled onto a rough concrete ramp. They poked us into lines of ten, and it became apparent that more than a hundred women had been in that one carriage.

'What a shoddy lot they are,' one guard laughed. 'I wouldn't give any of them the time of day back home.'

'Yeah, but at least they're not Jews, or prostitutes,' another said, and their cackles were as filthy as I felt. Marching off the slope, there was gravel underfoot, the tincture of the salt mixing with a strange, singed taste in the air. I couldn't hear the sea and something in me sensed we weren't at Germany's coastal edge. But I might have been deaf, dumb and blind for all the sensory clues misfiring inside me.

Our feet crunched for what felt like an age, made longer by having to help along the weaker among us. The woman with the dead eyes and the other with twig-like legs needed two shoulders apiece for support, which the guards tolerated with cruel cajoling, the women without dogs prodding with long, heavy coshes strapped around their wrists.

250

'Come on, no stragglers,' they crowed. 'You've got to be fit to be here; you've got to hold your own. Be something to the Reich.'

Large, iron gates swung open and we were halted in an open space, made square by the boundaries of the huts, while underfoot it was a finer, slate grit. Faint lights came from one or two windows in each hut, and I glimpsed faces bobbing behind the small panes. The guards surrounded us, barking orders to 'Stand straight,' 'Heads up,' the women circling with the dogs, wolves tenderising their prey.

After an age standing, the cold seeped into the core of my bones and I felt them physically splinter inside me. Then, a numbness that was almost a relief. I couldn't remember a time, even in the last two weeks, when I had been so cold. Had it not been for that stranger's jacket, I felt sure I would have succumbed there and then.

The woman with twigs for legs was the first to fall. Her body made a gentle thud as it dropped and the guards were immediately on her. The woman next to her bent to help as a reflex, and was pushed back by rifle butts. 'Leave her!' they barked.

'Fucking weakling,' one shouted at her unconscious body, stabbing at her midriff with his bayonet. When she didn't even whimper, they hauled her up roughly, her head lolling as if she were dead. I glanced briefly at one of the female guards, and I saw a wry smile creep across her lips, ruby with fake colouring. Was she wearing lipstick? Adornment and vanity in this utter madness? Or was it my mind playing cruel tricks?

The tiny woman was dragged away to a small, brick building, her legs making tracks in the gravel, the soles of her feet pinker where the arches hadn't been infected yet by the grime. Maybe they stayed that shellfish pink. I never saw her again. Plenty of twig-like limbs in the months ahead, but none belonging to her.

★　★　★

It was dark by the time we were formally addressed, snowflakes dancing and settling, making us a job lot of brides-in-waiting. A woman emerged from a solid three-storey building, its windows brightly lit, revealing bodies moving with purpose. Her uniform was the same grey, and as she came closer to the square I noticed her skirt didn't part as she walked — like the others, she was wearing thick, woollen culottes. On her upper arms, her jacket sported several lines of embroidered red and silver diamonds. Heaven knows why I paid attention to such detail, as if my mind was searching for anything in this sea of drear, like a blind person seeking a sliver of light to create sense.

She stood before us, grey hair swept under her small cap, stockings smooth against toned calves. When she spoke, her voice was that of a kindergarten teacher, matriarchal yet capable of being kind, hugging a needy child who'd bumped their head. As she raised her hand, thrust it towards us and barked: 'Heil Hitler,' the image popped like a fragile bubble.

'You have been brought here for a number of reasons,' she began. 'Whatever they are, you are no friend of the Reich or our glorious leader, and do not deserve your liberty. You will therefore contribute to society, with our guidance. Ravensbrück is a work facility, with an emphasis on work. Those who cannot labour will be directed elsewhere.' It was clear that 'elsewhere' was not preferable.

Her eyes panned right to left, pausing for effect. 'If you abide by our rules, if you work hard, you will be treated fairly. But discipline is vital. We will not tolerate any dissidence — punishments will be severe, that is my promise.'

Her voice moved up the register, something of an 'all girls together' tone, but what she said next was pure ice. 'Ladies, this is no holiday camp. Make no mistake, you will give back to the Reich. Or face the consequences.'

I felt eyes swivel in the rows, women terrified to move heads but desperate to gauge reactions. Suddenly, I was eighteen again, when Matron Reinhardt had addressed us on our first day as trainee nurses; bewildered, expectant, scared. Only then, there had been light, the brightness of our snowy cotton uniforms, the barely suppressed giggles, the hopes we held inside of improvement, of moving on. Here, there was just abject gloom. The gates clanged shut behind us and I couldn't see any way out or through this mire.

33

Empty Space

The next days were a patchwork of empty hours, punctuated with spurts of activity. Dieter was absent for several days, but the disappointment was in myself, already missing the night-time curl of his limbs around mine. Wary of any physical touch within the walls of the Berghof, he had simply winked goodbye: 'I'll be back – soon.'

Lena and I spent her free hours working on the dress for her dance, which was perhaps the longest time I had stayed in the house, since the servants' quarters had the biggest table for cutting material. Frau Grunders ghosted in and out, wearing a variety of disapproving looks, although I caught a wry smile glancing across her lips as Lena twirled during a fitting. It was gone in a second. Was she ever that girl, young and carefree, with butterflies in her heart, before the mask of loyalty took hold? Before her passion for the Führer?

'Lena, remember the dining room needs clearing,' she said as she clipped out again.

I spent some time alone in deep thought about Papa,

mentally boxing him away into parts of me no one could ever reach – not the Reich, the Gestapo, this war, or Hitler himself. They were mine. With no prospect of a body or a burial, I did the only thing I had in my power and wrote him a letter. It was long and sometimes rambling, my pain bleeding out through the pen, mixed with fat tears that spilled over, making the paper wet and fibrous. The page looked war-torn itself, warped and smudged as I folded it and walked towards the gardens. A fire burned continually in the brazier, low flames crackling and popping at stray ferns and garden waste, carcasses from the kitchen kicking up tiny limbs. I hovered the letter over the glow and released it from my fingers.

'Goodbye, Papa,' I said, and watched the paper crimp, blacken and die, the ashes floating into the breeze, skywards.

The calm was interrupted by a visit from the good doctors, who professed to be 'concerned' at the preparations made so far. Facing me in Sergeant Meier's office, Dr Koenig sat while Dr Langer stood, arms folded as they took turns grilling me over what action I would take over in a variety of scenarios – a long labour, shoulders that were stuck, a compromised baby. They had a long list.

'Have you delivered many babies by the breech?' Dr Langer pitched in, mouth pursed, adding to the weaselled nature of his whole being.

'I have,' I said. 'Both at home and in the hospital. I find they rarely need help if you leave them well alone. But I'm quite confident Fräulein Braun's baby is not breech.'

I smiled inside as they exchanged dark looks. It was a bonus to be irritating these two heinous individuals, without the need for obvious dissent. The interrogation lasted half an hour, with my answers short, clinical and to the point. Dr Koenig sweated frustration.

'I will, of course, share my concerns with Fräulein Braun this afternoon,' he puffed. 'I make no secret that this arrangement is not, in my professional opinion, the safest and the most appropriate for such a lady of the Reich.'

He paused and waited for an answer.

'I'm sure she will receive you and listen to your concerns,' I said flatly. 'If there is any change in requirements, I will, of course, respect the mistress's choices.'

Tiny blood vessels seemed to pop in Dr Koenig's fat cheeks, and I could virtually hear his blood pressure hissing like a pressure cooker. Dr Langer, by contrast, did nothing but look intently at my face, unblinking. It was my turn to squirm inside, at the depth of his jet-black stare, and the darkest thoughts behind it. The blustering, pompous Koenig was a parody of himself, but Dr Langer was simply dangerous – a willing butcher – and I made a mental note to remember it well.

Later, I learned from Eva that she had feigned tiredness and postponed Dr Koenig's visit until his next trip to the Berghof, and I had to stifle a smile at the thought of the great man being sent away with a flea in the ear of his overinflated head.

Sewing Room, The Camp, North of Berlin,
November 1942

The noise of the sewing room was ear-splitting when production was at its peak, a combined dancing of a hundred or so machine wheels creating a blanket roar across the hut. Oddly, the intense sound afforded a little cloak of privacy as the noise wrapped around each woman sat hunched over her table, an automaton as regards the task but jealously guarding thoughts as her own.

The eight months in the camp had variously dragged and raced by; cruelly, the warmer months had flashed forward, to be replaced by freezing nights when we huddled together in the huts, the one blanket we were each afforded too thin to repel the cutting chill, cocooning our bodies, three at a time, in the bunks. My precious tweed jacket, donated by a fellow inmate back in Berlin, had been confiscated on arrival, along with our clothes and all bodily hair, razed in an instant and scalps scorched with boiling hot water as part of our cleansing. I hadn't seen a mirror since. Nor did I want

259

to. The crust on my head felt ugly to the touch, and my body itched with patches of raw, broken skin. And that was before the lice came to stay.

Graunia and I managed to stay together in the same hut, although were separated by work divisions. After that first bewildering night on the floor of a block building, then being shorn and clad in regulation dresses of coarse wool, we were interviewed for our various skills.

'Tell them, tell them what you do,' Graunia urged in a whisper. I couldn't imagine there was any need for a midwife and – with Papa's advice still holding strong – I didn't want to attract attention. I stretched the truth and told them I could sew, hoping my limited experience at my grandmother's old hand-cranked machine and in stitching perinea would allow me to bluff it out. Graunia's writing skills secured her a position in the office, drafting letters and transcribing, with her knowledge of Polish and Russian.

My gamble worked, as the sewing was by rote and involved no real skill beyond a steady hand and ability to follow instructions. And work fast. The overseer in this workshop was a civilian, from a factory somewhere in a former life, where he'd no doubt scolded poor housewives to keep up their quotas, using money – or the promise of it – as his cosh. Here, Herr Roehm was happy to use the real thing, prodding us in the back with his long, polished rod when we attempted to stretch our sore shoulders, hitting bone when the work was shoddy, or the machines clogged with thread, as they frequently did.

'What do you call this?' he screamed, when he called a halt to the whole hut, flashing the lights on and off as our signal to quit. He held up the grey-green uniforms of the Wehrmacht we sewed, day in, day out. 'If I put this on I would be the laughing stock of any invading army. Look at this seam. It's shit. You are all shit. Do better.' His face, a round, pink pudding, pulsed with anger.

One woman's punishment was always shared and Herr Roehm regularly allotted the whole room another hour of work, knowing we would miss the arrival of the soup pot in the hut. Graunia would campaign to save my meagre portion of soup – greasy water with thin slivers of cabbage – but there were those so hungry that she would have to work to keep my cup safe, let alone warm. The one square of bread would be stale anyway, dense and with the texture of sawdust, but a tasteless lifeline.

Had I adapted? I suppose I had, as much as you can sink to a life so low. In that first week I functioned in a daze; every one thing, comfort or person I'd known gobbled up overnight and spat out in an oily ball of phlegm that was this life. The newcomers were either shoved, pushed, or piloted by kind camp veterans. You got through or you fell, simple as that. As a midwife I had learnt that women were resilient beyond imagination, and in those next weeks I saw for myself how humans can and will cling on to dignity and life in equal measure.

Hunger was a constant companion; my own mother wouldn't have recognised the scant flesh on my willowy frame, with only my lower arms maintaining any kind of wiry definition, from the constant pressure of pushing fabric through the machine. Even without a mirror, I didn't recognise the contours in my own face, my cheeks so sallow I must have looked as if my neck might snap from the effort of holding up my bulbous head.

The camp itself was run efficiently. It was filthy, disease-ridden and a haven for death, but it functioned like clockwork and dished out punishment with vicious regularity. Officially, it was commanded by male SS, but in reality the female guards kept order and thrived as overseers. They presented the appearance of a tailored, coiffured and

261

painted posse, having bizarrely set up a small hairdressing salon on site, where prisoners teased their locks into the latest styles. When they weren't goading the dogs to snarl at us, they lavished untold affection on their 'babies', grooming their fur and slipping them treats of meat that we could only dream of. Each of them could have given the male SS officers lessons in cruelty, as if concrete had been stitched into that grey uniform.

Beatings were common, vicious and visible, the punishment block often overcrowded, and death a part of daily life. Days when the body cart didn't leave for the lakeshore were rare, bloody feet poking through a thin shroud, although Graunia told us that — officially — the death certificates only ever gave a cause of heart failure or pneumonia. I only hoped they were buried in peace, instead of a thousand souls bobbing for all eternity around the mud-laden waters.

I kept my head down, sewing at a rate of knots, and took solace from the company of Graunia and several others in the hut. There were eighty or so in our barrack, a human mosaic of cultures and creeds: German, Hungarian, German Poles and Czechs, but no Jews. Our unity came in that we were anti-Nazi, some Communist, some Social Democrat, and so by definition all failed patriots. We called ourselves The Pests and took pride in it.

The rest of the camp was a lesson in how to divide and rule. Jews, prostitutes, native Gypsies, Jehovah's Witnesses — all deemed 'undesirables' — each had their own hut or huts, depending on the numbers, and the guards took pleasure in pitching the groups against each other. It would be heartening to think that women forced together in adversity would band as one, all looking out for each other, the strong supporting the weak. But human nature isn't like that. Survival, I learned swiftly, is the most basic of human instincts, and the Nazis' strongest weapon was that they knew it. They used it.

Reissen, the chief overseer, was shrewd. She took time in recruiting prisoners as enforcers – or Kapos – to act as hut leaders, giving them titbits of privilege to make life more bearable, and a smidgen of power to exert over women in the hut, in return for information on dissidence. They were also called on to do the guards' dirty work for them. Some women, those who doubtless thought they had no morality left to lose, worked in the punishment block and dished out the beatings personally. The lust for life – your own life – is a powerful motivator.

Because I kept myself under the radar, I was never singled out. Instead, I formed a tight trio with Graunia and Kirsten, a Czech-born German whose crime had been slipping Jews onto trade ships out of Germany. Together, we pooled food, stories, wishes and dreams. We kept each other alive. Each night, before lights out, we linked hands and whispered: 'Another day gone, another day alive, another day towards freedom.' It reminded me of the words I said almost daily at the hospital, to mothers who felt they would never reach journey's end: 'One contraction less, one closer to seeing your baby.' Each day, that life seemed further and further behind me, like sand through my fingers.

Until Leah. The industry in the sewing room that day was frenetic, with Herr Roehm even more ferocious than normal, due to an urgent order from the Reich's upper office. There was a reward of a new Mercedes-Benz as a thank you for his 'loyalty' – Graunia told us as much when she typed the letter from Roehm, assuring the Reich office it would be ready on time, 'whatever it takes'.

That day, two women had already fainted from dehydration, and a snowstorm of fabric motes clogged the air as the cutters worked at full capacity. I had time only to concentrate on not catching my fingers under the machine needle, which was jumping at breakneck speed. The noise was endless and cacophonous.

Leah was working two machines over from me. I had glimpsed her that morning walking into the room at six a.m., stooping slightly, with a hand clutching at her belly. Monthly bleeds were rare among prisoners but urine infections were common, causing intense bladder pain. I had flashed a look at her as we'd entered, bringing up my brow, as if to say 'All right?' She had smiled weakly, but didn't nod. She was small and slight, and I hoped she would make it through the day. Graunia had told us the entire shipment was to be on the train by ten that night.

All of us felt the end of Herr Roehm's stick that day. Fast wasn't good enough – he wanted the uniforms to fly off the machines at an obscene rate. By midday, when he saw the hope of his shiny new car rolling from view, his voice had reached fever pitch.

'You bitches! No coffee at lunch until we have over half the order. Faster! Work faster, you bitches. Work for the Reich!'

There were sweat patches on his jacket, and he looked as if he might need a doctor before some of us. Leah had already been prodded once, plus given a crack on her shoulder when she visibly slackened. When it was long past our missed break time, the woman between us shot out a hand to grab my attention.

'She's in trouble,' she mouthed, and we both glanced towards Roehm, occupied on the other side of the room. Leah was slumped forward, head nestling on the material. She wasn't dead; I could see the bony ladder of her spine through her shift dress, rising and jumping as if she were receiving a gentle jolt of electricity.

We both froze. Rule number one, drummed into us day after day at the five a.m. roll call, barely awake in the grey square, was that we should not help any woman who fell. Weakness was not tolerated, even if it was created by the Reich itself. The instinct to help a fellow human in need earned you a swift beating and time in the solitary confinement block. More effective psychology.

I knew if Roehm spied Leah looking as if she was napping, his cosh would come down hard on her tiny body, maybe even her head, with fatal consequences. One-handed, I continued sewing and waved the other arm in the air, hoping to attract the attention of the duty guard walking the lines of machinists. She was new to the camp and I hoped we might take advantage of what humanity was left inside her. The Kapo talking to Roehm was particularly brutal and, ironically, we had more chance with the guard.

She approached. 'What is it?'

I pointed at Leah and the guard clomped over, pulling on her shoulders. 'Come on, girl. Don't get into trouble.'

One eye was on my rattling machine, the other to my side. Leah's head lolled heavily, and the guard pulled again. Leah came to sharply, and clutched at her belly. I heard that familiar wail even above the din of the room. Braying, bearing down. Labour. A baby. Unmistakable.

I didn't think of the consequences, the nights I might spend alone in a dark cell, nursing multiple bruises. I was up and out of my chair, peering under the rim of Leah's dress, where the shape of a baby's head was already moulding her skin, ready to show itself any minute.

'She's about to have a baby,' I told the guard.

'What? Can you see it?' She looked worriedly for Roehm, but he was still distracted.

'Not yet, but it won't be long.'

She looked at me suspiciously, and our eyes met. I pleaded with all my might in that look not to alert Roehm, but to ghost us out of the door before he could wield the cosh. Leah moaned again, and the guard's eyes flicked towards the nearby door. She may have reasoned the mess of a birth would halt production and earn her a rebuke.

We half pulled and half shuffled Leah from the room, into the small vestibule of the hut.

'We need to get her to the Revier,' the guard snapped, looking behind her for Roehm following.

'She won't make it,' I said. 'The head will be here any minute. Trust me.'

'What makes you an expert all of a sudden?'

'A big family, lots of nieces.' I brushed it away. 'We need something to wrap the baby in, some material.'

Leah was on the floor now, seemingly unconscious, but brought round by the pain of the contraction. She was straining and pushing down visibly, the stretch of her skin paper-thin as I glimpsed a penny-size circle of black hair. The back of her dress was slightly damp, where the tiny pool of waters surrounding the baby had broken. Malnutrition meant it had been no tidal wave.

The guard appeared again, with a length of off-cut material, her eyes darting uncomfortably. 'This better happen soon, or Roehm will be out here,' she barked. Even so, I saw her hands go automatically to Leah's shoulder and give fleeting support.

'It will.' I was talking low to Leah, although she seemed in her own world. 'It's all right, Leah, you're doing fine, nearly there.' The patter was as much for me as her.

Leah gave one almighty push and the baby's head was born rapidly, black hair against chalky white skin. The features were still, lips a mottled maroon, and I couldn't tell if there was life or not. With only a half push, the body slithered out like tiny puppy, flaccid and unmoving, a scrawny cord around his neck spindle. Instinctively, I rubbed at him with the material. 'Hey, little man; hey, baby, come on,' and then bent to blow life on him and in him. I didn't think, I just did it.

With no fat on his rack of ribs, it was easy to see when he *breathed, a balloon of life hitting his sternum, and he coughed and whined. Leah came round in that split second, and her eyes registered alarm, and fear, soon joined by a smile. A real one. Several workers from the Revier, the hospital block, arrived and we moved her across the yard, still attached to her baby, drops of blood giving light, life and colour to the grit underfoot.*

Inside the medical block, I worked in my own world, encouraging the placenta away with a rub on Leah's abdomen. Turning to dispose of it, I was met by the hard stare of the Revier Officer.

'Do you have something to tell me, Prisoner Hoff?' she said, eyebrows arched. 'It seems you may have been hiding something from us.'

34

Beginnings

Midnight on the fourth day since Dieter left, and I woke to the squeak of the door handle. His lofty silhouette moved towards the bed, feet tiptoeing in his socks.

'It's fine, I'm awake,' I whispered.

'Is this too late, do you need to sleep?'

I propped up on my elbows. 'No, I want to sleep with you – eventually.'

The past week had seen my sex drive – depressed to almost zero since the real conflict began – reawakened, whetted by his presence. Sleepiness subsided at the mere sight of Dieter. His jacket relegated to the furthest corner of the room, he padded towards me and slipped under the covers.

Bright sunlight was pushing through the thin curtains when I woke. It took me several seconds to realise I was still curled in the conch of his long body, that he hadn't ghosted away as the light rose. He stirred as I stretched.

'Dieter, it's quite late. Shouldn't you go?'

He squinted at his watch, and fought the fog of sleep, squeezing my midriff as he burrowed down again.

'Dieter?'

'Huh? Oh, I gave Rainer the car for the night – he visits a woman down in the town. He won't be back until midday.'

He dozed as I stared at the curtains, dancing a jig in the breeze. My stomach groaned noisily and I would have given anything right then to have been in a Parisian hotel room in peacetime, the smell of coffee and pastries nearby, tempting me to run out from under the warm covers and steal them back to bed to share with Dieter.

Gradually, I felt his breathing rise and he stretched awake. His lashes caught and tickled the back of my shoulders. He lay back and I shifted to fit like the last piece of a jigsaw under his arm.

'Do you think we'll ever wake up in a nice hotel room and have breakfast together?' I mused.

'Does it matter?' he murmured. 'I could go halfway and ask Frau Grunders to bring in a tray, if you're really that keen.'

I dug him playfully in the ribs. 'Never hurts to have dreams, Captain.'

He pressed his chin into the top of my head and I felt the warm air of his nostrils.

My curiosity grew with the length of our silence.

'Dieter, what do you think will happen to us, to Germany?'

He pondered for a few seconds. 'Us? I have no idea about that. But Germany, I don't even like to think. It's ironic that Hitler is probably in some bunker underground trying to manoeuvre a victory and yet we're digging ourselves deep and deeper into a very dark hole.'

'Is it that bad?'

'I think so, judging by what comes across my desk. The high command has always been good at putting on a show, but underneath they are scrabbling like mice. I think Hitler has underestimated the Allies hugely. They are tenacious and Churchill is a wily fox.'

Aside from the outburst that had first led us into bed, this was the nearest we had come to discussing the war in detail. Still, he seemed unguarded, as if purging was a comfort.

'Goebbels still has control of the newspapers, so your average German thinks we're marching over Europe unabated, heads high. In truth, the Allies are taking key points in Italy, and we've suffered major air attacks. German cities are destroyed and we're limping like a wounded animal. There have been several attempts on Hitler's life too, from inside his own troops. No wonder he's not up here playing happy families.'

A breath caught in my throat at the mention of an assassination attempt, and I worked to let the air release slowly. The words almost tipped out – the messages to Christa, the note under the sewing machine, the potential threat to the baby. Something in me, however, held back. I trusted him, I really did. I didn't think Dieter would hurt or betray me. But, even now, I wasn't sure how big the threat was, or if it would be very real on the day. I didn't want to burden him any more, make him choose one side or the other. Too many choices might break us, and right now, he was the only bright thing allowing me to limp through. After Papa, my own propulsion wasn't enough. I needed a reason to push through into tomorrow.

'Dieter, are you afraid?'

He took a long breath in and held it there – I felt the taut bellows of his chest against my ear. Finally, he let go.

'I'm not sure I know what fear is any more. I lost it a good while ago, along with anxiety and worry. It all merges into one – you live every moment expecting to meet death like a long-lost friend around each corner. Even in my world. A drunk Nazi commander with a grudge and a gun is as dangerous as a battlefield sometimes.'

'Do you have hope?' was all I could say.

'I do now,' he said, squeezing me. A tiny, wet sensation snaked its way through the hairs on the top of my head and hit my scalp, but I didn't look or feel to see if it was his tear, or the spark of my entire being pushing up to meet him.

He dressed properly while I was in the bathroom, kissing me goodbye before I shut the door. I wandered into the servants' hall as the table was being cleared, putting the kettle on to boil and busily setting my own breakfast. Cap under his arm, Dieter stepped uneasily into the room.

'Morning, Fräulein Hoff. I appear to be too late for breakfast upstairs,' he said, a smile curling at the corners of his mouth.

'So it seems, Captain. I'm rather late myself.' I could barely suppress my laughter, in serious danger of giving us away. But I dipped my head and held on, our secret being the best of motivations. 'I'm just about to make coffee. Can I interest you in some?'

'I would be very grateful, thank you.'

And so we had our breakfast together, not in an ornate hotel room, naked and smelling of sex, but fully clothed in the midst of the morning bustle, and with a steely, sideways glance from Frau Grunders as she sailed in and out.

I moved towards Eva's room with a definite spring to my step. Unusually, she was still in bed – it was gone ten by this point – but she called me in and rolled over with a groan. Her face was pale and puffy – telltale signs of a bad night.

'Eva, how are you? You look tired.'

'Oh, Anke, is it going to be like this for weeks now? I must have been up until about three. It feels so tight, like everything below is being crushed. But the baby is wriggling a lot, so that's good, isn't it?'

'It is. It's probably the baby's head going down and turning, which is also good.'

Just a minute into the check, however, tiny wires pulsed in my brain. As I palmed the bump, it tightened under my fingers and Eva's face crimped visibly, flushing just under her chin and creeping up her neck, subsiding as the flesh softened again. Her blood pressure was up slightly, and her pulse a little raised. If I wasn't much mistaken, Eva was in early labour.

The baby's heart was sound as always, and I played down the tightenings – if she believed it could happen imminently, the whole house would be on high alert. Even if I was right, we could still have days of rumbling and brewing towards the real thing.

'Well, it all seems fine. I'm sure it will settle down again,' I told her. 'Perhaps you ought to go for a walk, and then make sure you catch up on some sleep later.'

Strangely, she seemed satisfied by my advice, and not for

the first time I thought Eva Braun was stoical enough to withstand the physical demands that would soon face her.

I found Dieter in the communications room, and gestured for him to talk outside, privately.

'I can't be sure but I think Eva is going into labour,' I said as we came out of earshot.

He looked slightly alarmed. 'Is it too soon? I understood it would be another three weeks.'

'Well, that's women and babies for you. But no, it's not too soon, she's thirty-seven weeks and no longer premature. It's just that I don't want to say for sure until I really am. I don't want the troops descending.'

'What do you need me to do?'

I wanted to kiss him right there and then, for reacting in the way I hoped he would.

'I want to get Christa up here, but without alerting the Goebbels or Dr Koenig. Is there a way we can send for her with a good excuse?'

'I can, if you think of one that's credible. I do know Frau Goebbels is away at the moment, so her suspicions won't be aroused.'

The news was a profound relief, and we settled on calling up Christa on the pretence of keeping an eye on Eva at night, as she was up and down to the toilet a lot, and to put the finishing touches to the baby's layette. Questions were bound to be asked, but we could easily counter those. More important was protecting the space around Eva, so she could and would labour with this baby.

The Camp, North of Berlin, November 1942

'So, you are a midwife?' Gerta Mencken squinted at my file. 'And yet you are in the sewing room?'

'I thought I would be of more use there,' I said in a deadpan tone. I had become adept at lying, stripping all emotion from my voice, features flat and my eyes seemingly sightless.

Mencken had a reputation for being a loyal Nazi, but one who maintained her ethos as a nurse in pre-war Germany. Looking at the top of her bleach-blonde hair, cropped into a masculine style, I wondered how the two even began to mesh.

'Yes . . . well.' She wasn't convinced. 'You're here now, and we could benefit from your skills. We have more women than first anticipated.' She looked at me and softened her mouth purposefully, though that wasn't convincing either. 'The women will benefit from your experience.'

Like every true Nazi, Frau Mencken knew how to elicit the best from her prison-workers, using a subtle form of moral blackmail.

275

I could help to make the experience more tolerable for them, she was saying, and serve the Reich at the same time.

'Report here tomorrow morning, six a.m. We'll take you through the procedures.'

I'd had an itch since arriving at the camp. Unlike the numerous bugs and lice resident on my body, causing me to scratch wildly until I was raw, this barb was on the inside, pricking away at my brain. It was the knowledge that babies were being born in the camp. Naively, I'd imagined all pregnant women were screened out before boarding the transports, since this was no place to grow or birth a baby. It was a labour camp, only children aged twelve and above – those who could do a day's work – were permitted. But most of my new clientele hadn't been obviously pregnant when they became separated from their husbands and some had been brutally raped by German soldiers on capture. Even so, as the camp opened, the numbers of births were small.

Elke, an inmate since 1939, told me the first babies were treated with real reverence in the Revier – clean sheets, baths for the mothers, even a glass of milk after the birth. For all the fussing, though, the newborns didn't survive camp life, succumbing to malnutrition at days and weeks old when the mothers had no milk in their breasts, or transported at a day old and 'Germanised' if they were lucky enough to be born with blue eyes. Most babies were sons and daughters of the political prisoners, German or non-Jew at least, and therefore just tolerated. The few Jewish babies didn't make it past a day, even then.

As the war raged on, the camp population increased and, with it, the amount of Jewish women arriving already pregnant. Scores had been raped with the invasion of Warsaw, and their numbers swelled along with their bellies. Yet the Nazis were shrewd. The camp provided essential supplies for the troops and labour for

276

the engineering factories around us, and Poles were good workers, Jews especially. I overheard Mencken one day telling her chief Kapo that pregnant women 'were like mules – if they're strong enough to carry the child, they have more stamina. One week after the birth they're back on their feet and we need that strength. They're worth more to us then.'

Her thinking didn't stop the enforced abortions. Any woman thought to be under twenty weeks was taken to a separate block and a certain end to either one or two lives. Their screams could be heard at intervals as junior Nazi doctors arrived to hone their skills without anaesthetic. If the women bled out, it was. put down to experience and collateral damage – although I often saw Mencken stomping through the corridors, cursing the medics for reducing the numbers of 'her girls'. But she was thinking only of the figures, and not the sorry corpses lying on the slabs.

Women can be equally determined, though, and their zeal to preserve life in the womb easily outstripped the Nazi will. Some women knew of a baby only once they felt a telling tickle inside, since monthly periods – through stress or malnutrition – stopped almost on arrival. A baby's movements and a slightly rounded abdomen were often the first signs of a pregnancy. Even then, the loose woollen dresses hid the tiny bumps well, and some women concealed it to all but their barrack mates until the birth itself.

On my first morning in the Revier, a woman was brought in from the 4.30 a.m. roll call, having stood no doubt for hours on the grey square, collapsing with labour pains. By the time she reached the building and I was pushed towards her, she was in advanced labour, dripping sweat and flushed from shoulders to brow. She was Czech, rambling in a dialect I couldn't catch, and I had no choice but to apply the universal language of childbirth: a soft touch to her hand, massaging its rough skin down towards her scarecrow fingers, a cooing-shushing of my voice as I talked evenly to her in German. 'Let me just have a look there, can I have a look under your dress?' I didn't even know her name.

After one contraction, she stopped muttering and opened her eyes. Our pupils met, I smiled at her and nodded. 'It's all right,' I said. 'You're having your baby.'

'Bebe,' she said, and bore down to show me her child.

The Revier had seen better days. It was a solid building at least, without holes in the planking, though its weathered walls peeled with neglect. The clean sheets of Elke's memories were also long gone – now grey and ripped, torn to make napkins for those babies who survived. The chief guard, I learned later, did not share Mencken's ethos about healthy pregnant women and tolerated her efforts rather than encouraging them. There were no instruments, or drugs, and it was only a clutch of prisoner-midwives from across Europe that made it anything other than a building to house birth. Their experience and humanity transformed it into a maternity unit that bore life.

Whatever our skills, the ending of a life was never close behind the giving of a new one. All the non-Jewish babies – those without blue eyes – were moved to a Kinderzimmer after just two days with their mothers, who were allowed to visit only briefly in daytime. At night, the door was locked, and the window left open, even in winter. Mothers frequently found their babies stiff and lifeless come the morning. Other newborns starved slowly over the weeks ahead and only a handful lived beyond a month.

For the Jews, however, there was a more certain fate. I will never forget the first time I heard the splash of a newborn hitting the water barrel; my stomach wrenched and my throat burned with the realisation that a life was being brutally snuffed out. The pain each mother endured at that sound could not be fathomed. As a midwife, having been driven by the light of life at each shift – a mother united with her baby – my entire ethos was shattered. What would I be doing? Simply aiding the brief transport between life and death? Would I be servicing the Nazi machine to hone a new workforce, helping Hitler in his despicable aim for a clean Germany, bathed in moral filth?

After that first day in the Revier, I twisted in my bunk, not from the itch of bedbugs, but a conscience wrestling with my brain. The truth was, I had little choice. It was either comply or be taken out into the forest and shot for dissidence – many had never returned after making less of a stand. Or face the ominous threat of transport to the East. At that time, no one knew quite what 'the East' held but we all sensed it wasn't good.

Over the following weeks, the moral wrestling waned and I found a new purpose, a light that can only ever be described as dimmed – a chink in the greyness, yet something to take from the horror of this alternative world. The women who came into the Revier were amazing; to reach beyond twenty weeks without miscarriage was miracle enough, but to do it with a baby whose limbs pushed proud against the scabietic parchment of their abdomens, saying: 'I'm in here, I'm alive,' seemed unbelievable. They had preserved their babies with every depleted cell, eyes sunken with lack of nutrition and worry, tiny bumps top-heavy on legs sometimes as thin as reeds. They never once thought of giving up. Ever. To give life was everything. Most knew it would be a short existence, but all harboured a slim hope that the war would suddenly end, with a swift liberation by the Allies and a last-minute reprieve for their newborns.

I soon realised my role – and that of the ten or so other qualified midwives in the camp – was to bring dignity where we

279

couldn't prolong life. We could create memories, perhaps of only hours or days, where kindness and humanity won out. We sat, we coached and cooed, we scavenged what little extras we could to make every woman feel they were party to the best care money might buy.

Each of us had our way of creating a small world impenetrable to the harsh reality of noise and stench around us. It was a tiny cosmos where we cried and laughed with them, where we held a space – perhaps only for a few minutes – so pure that only their child, their baby, existed for that time. Their history. The burning ache of a baby's parting was no less painful, but alongside the sadness sat memories of what they did for their babies – memories of being mothers.

And in that sickly arena of skulking death, I came alive again.

35

Brewing

Unusually for me, I was agitated after Eva's check, hovering around the complex and virtually spying on her from a short distance. She emerged onto the terrace around noon, and I went to tell her Christa would be arriving to help with the last of the preparations. She seemed pleased, but also preoccupied – shifting uncomfortably on the sun lounger, unconsciously clutching at her bump as she did. Her face was less pale now, and flushed a lot of the time. She asked me to stay to keep her company, and so for a while I sat leafing through a magazine, with my ears tuned in to her breathing and eyeing the contortions of her body. Looking at her, I felt certain she was – in midwife-speak – *on the cusp*.

We parted for lunch, and Christa arrived an hour or so later, collected by Daniel. I felt true relief at her presence. Untrained and with little medical background, she was nonetheless what I needed most, a trustworthy ally – like Rosa before her. She came armed with bundles of material and her sewing box, convinced she would be settled in for at least three weeks before the birth, and her face fell when I told her of my suspicions.

'Really? So soon?' Her large green eyes widened.

'It's still possible it could all fizzle out again, but the signs are good.'

'Are you relieved?'

'Yes and no,' I said truthfully. 'I've been slightly caught out, but to be honest if Eva went past her due date, we would be under scrutiny much more. Better that this baby comes when it wants. We have to face it some time. If there's one certainty about birth, it's that no one is pregnant forever.'

We both laughed, to break the tension that lingered above our heads, a brooding raincloud that would track us now until either the sun broke through, or it cracked with a tyrannical thunder.

'What was the reaction at the Goebbels'?' I asked.

'The mistress and master are both away – separately. I don't doubt they have their spies in the house, but I think I was casual enough about the reason.'

She said there were no more messages from the resistance group. 'And you?'

'No, nothing.' I should have told her, because of our trust, but I reasoned it wouldn't change our plan, only add to the tension. We were set on giving Eva a healthy baby, and getting out with our lives.

We decided Christa would sleep in Eva's room that night, to keep up the pretence, but I did want Christa to call me if needed, rather than one of the maids. There was still no telling who was in the pocket of the Goebbels, or the resistance.

Just after three that afternoon, Eva called me to her room, her face bathed in alarm.

'Look!' she said, guiding me to the bathroom. Her silk knickers were on the floor, soiled with a mucousy coating, streaked pink and red. 'What is it?'

'It's just a sign you're getting ready, a good sign,' I re-assured her. The 'show' – a jelly-like plug guarding the womb entrance – could come away two weeks, two days or two hours before labour began, but with everything else I'd seen, it was another indication we were close. 'Come, let's listen to the baby.'

She was still tightening, the skin a solid shell as she lay down, but she didn't squirm or react. I'd known women in tears at this point with exhaustion and despondency, but Eva was showing her stamina yet again.

Christa helped her into the bath, and we agreed the plan for the night. Still, I didn't mention the 'labour' word, playing on Eva's innocence. I also knew I needed to sleep – in case of being called in the early hours – and I headed back to the chalet after dinner. Christa joined me briefly on the porch, but even she was tired and soon left. In the dusky backdrop, I glimpsed a shadow hovering around the house. For an anxious moment, I imagined it was the resistance trying to make direct contact, but the patrol was circling, and the body didn't flinch as two sets of boots neared. The patrol gone, the bobbing silhouette of a cap took on a familiar shape.

He approached with a grin, cap in hand. Wordlessly, we both cast a look around and disappeared into the chalet, closing the curtains. He took off his jacket, and we kissed before speaking, my fingers snaking under his braces and clutching at the solid ribs through his shirt.

'I've been itching to do that all day,' Dieter whispered, as we parted our moist lips. 'If I'm honest I'm willing Eva to hang on, so I can have more of you.'

'Me too,' I said.

'Is there any news?'

I told him of the signs. 'She'll either labour tonight or it will go off and we'll be in for a longer wait,' I said. 'To be honest, I can't tell. She's quite hard to read.'

'Well, well,' he mocked, 'a woman who beats the intuition of the great Sister Hoff! Eva Braun has my respect.' I dug him playfully in the ribs, and that was our cue to slide into bed and delay my precious sleep.

36

A Night Shift

'Anke! Anke!'

A hoarse urgency saw me battling towards the surface of sleep, swimming against a tide. As I broke free, a rap on the glass.

'Anke! Anke!'

'Coming,' I managed, only just feeling Dieter was beside me. As he roused I turned and put my finger to my lips, signalling his silence. Christa's face was close to the door; she was in her nightdress, hair loosely pulled into a ponytail.

'I think you need to come,' she said.

Strange that I'd been dreaming about Eva giving birth – this time at the Teehaus, with Negus and Stasi as my trusty assistants – and yet it took seconds for the present to fall into place.

'Anke.' Christa's tone pulled me further towards waking. 'I think her waters have broken.'

At that, I was fully alert. 'All right, you go back to her, I'll be a few minutes behind. What time is it?'

'Two–thirty a.m.'

She might have wondered why I kept the door ajar, why I didn't say, 'Come in, and tell me all about it,' as I dressed swiftly. But in the circumstances I didn't care.

As I retreated inside, Dieter was propped on one elbow, rubbing the sleep from his eyes. 'Is something wrong?'

'Nothing wrong, but it's happening,' I said, pulling on my stockings awkwardly. 'Christa thinks Eva's waters have broken, which means it's likely to move on.'

He swung his legs to the side of the bed, palming away more fatigue from his face. 'What about Dr Koenig? When shall I call him? You know we have to, Anke.'

'I know.' I stopped buttoning my blouse, cogs spinning. 'But you are actually in your own bed, aren't you? And you know nothing about this until I call you, or the house wakes up.'

'Don't leave it too late, Anke,' he warned. 'Koenig is already riled. He could make things worse for you. I'll do my best to keep him at bay but . . .'

'I know.'

'You know what?'

'I know to be careful, Dieter. Honestly, I'm doing this just to keep alive, for my family. I won't risk it at the last minute. But I am Eva's midwife. To me, that counts.'

'And I love you for it.'

I froze at his words, one shoe on, as he beckoned me towards the bed. He put out both hands, long, strong fingers curling into mine, and squeezed them tightly.

'It's crazy, it's the strangest time,' he said into the floor. 'And it's war. But this . . . it's love.' He pulled up his chin and pushed those turquoise eyes into mine, the hue obvious even in the darkness. 'I love you, Anke. I love you and what you are.'

I moved my lips towards him. My heart was tumbling beats – adrenalin from Christa's news and lust for the man in front of me, a heady cocktail. 'I love you too. Every ounce of you. What we've had, even if it's—'

'Shhh – we don't need to talk like that. Just get through today, and we'll work it out after. We will, I promise. We'll leave this life behind.'

Our kiss was long and we pressed in hard. Despite what he'd said, it was born of desperation and longing. I kissed the top of his head, sucked in the smell of his boyishness. I never wanted to leave that space.

'Anke,' he called as I headed for the door, 'here, take this. You'll need it.'

He held out his wristwatch into the air, and I took it. It wasn't Reich standard issue, but more of a personal style, a wide plain face and the strap well worn, a ridge in the leather to fit his slender wrist.

'Thanks.' I smiled, slipping it into my pocket and walking through the door to an uncertain day.

I crept through the front door and tiptoed the corridor without shoes, stopping briefly and tuning my ears in to the night sounds. No obvious activity. In Eva's room, Christa's relief was clear, though not Eva's – her head was buried in the pillows as she lay on her side, knees brought up and her nightdress just covering her buttocks. One hand cupped her bump and the other covered her eyes, even though the light was low, just a single lamp on the bedside table. She was breathing steadily, but not moaning or crying.

Christa had already gathered some of the equipment, and I'd brought the rest.

'How long has she been up?' I whispered.

'She began stirring around midnight, tossing and turning. She got up at about two and was on the toilet for a while. She called me in just before I came to you.'

'What did she say?'

'That she felt a pop, and then water coming away. The pains were stronger almost immediately.'

'Did you look in the toilet, see what was there?'

'A small amount of blood – I know that's all right – but the water looked a bit dirty. I left it for you, I didn't flush it.'

'Perfect, Christa, you're a marvel.'

A low moan rose from the bed as a contraction started, Eva breathing more deeply, and then a rolling wail, though not panicked. Her upper hand went to the pillow, the material and her face crimping together. Christa went to her, rubbing her back and murmuring encouragement.

In the bathroom, Christa's report was exact. The blood was a good sign of the cervix beginning to open, the brown stain of the water not so encouraging. Certainly Dr Koenig would view it as a reason to intervene, but if the baby was fine, I wasn't concerned. Eva was lying on a white towel, and it was easy to see the meconium wasn't thick, only a light colouring of the amniotic fluid – the much preferred variety.

'Eva, it's Anke,' I whispered. 'Can I listen to the baby?'

As with so many times before, she rolled automatically, although this time in obvious discomfort, and it took her time to fidget onto her back.

Under my hands the baby's head was low in the pelvis, but unlike the days before, I couldn't locate a back, just limbs on either side. I closed my eyes and checked again, not wanting to believe it. But with a blind man's instinct, the translation was the same. It was a guess, but a good one – this baby was back to back, its spine spooning into Eva's own backbone. It didn't cause the alarm of breech babies in midwives, but it often meant a long, slow and exhausting journey, as the baby either tried to spin a full hundred and eighty degrees inside, or negotiate the mother's pelvis back to back – said to be much more painful as the line of the birth canal was less giving. With a head this low, I felt Eva's baby would be unable to turn properly. We could be in for a long night and day.

With contractions clearly regular, Eva gave consent for me to examine her, and it confirmed what I suspected: a telltale space behind the baby's head and a head trying – but not quite managing yet – to snuggle in to the bony confines of her pelvis, best described to women as an egg 'not quite in the eggcup'. On a good note, her cervix was a thin four centimetres dilated, working and labouring, and I thought I felt a thick coating of hair on the baby's head. There was no going back now.

The baby, thankfully, sounded fine, a steady hundred and forty beats per minute, and another contraction took Eva onto her side. Extreme backache was another factor with the baby's position, and Christa was already employed in rubbing hard into Eva's spine during the contraction. Eva whimpered more with the low soreness than the contraction itself, one hand dancing over her sacrum as she breathed.

Quietly, I told Christa my suspicions, not to alarm, but

as a way of preparing her. This would not be a labour where the baby beat the arrival of the overbearing Dr Koenig.

'So what do we do now?' Christa said.

'We wait, that's all we can do. We listen to the baby, we see to Eva and we keep her going. The rest is up to her and the baby.'

'And hope?'

I managed a light laugh. 'Yes, Christa, you're learning fast. We hope a lot.'

With Eva, I focused only on the positives. 'You're doing fine,' I told her, my face close to hers.

She grimaced as if unbelieving.

'You're in good labour, your baby is well on its way.' With certainty, I promised: 'Today is your baby's birthday,' and then remembering her fussing about the timing: 'It'll be here well before Gretl's wedding. You'll be showing off your baby to all the guests.'

This raised a smile at least. 'She'll be so envious,' she murmured into the pillow as another contraction welled up.

Christa padded along the corridors to fetch more fresh water, and reported the house was still quiet. The kitchen maid would be up by five to light the stove, and after that, we might have to reveal ourselves. I figured Dieter would be smart enough to send Daniel to collect the doctors rather than employ a car already in town – adding another hour to their journey, if not more. Then I would begin the defence of one wall while trying to break down the other.

The Camp, North of Berlin, April 1943

'Well, if she won't come in, we'll have to drag her, or she'll die in her bed. It will serve her right.'

Mencken shut her desk drawer with such force several bodies recoiled, as if a gunshot had sounded right inside the Revier. She was in a foul mood – her workforce had been cut yet again, which dented her pride and put her reputation under threat.

Only a month before, Mencken had received the highest of all Party accolades, a letter signed by Heinrich Himmler himself, praising her for an 'exemplary record of workforce provision' in the camp. With the letter neatly framed and locked in her desk drawer at the Revier, Mencken was driven to maintain Himmler's confidence in her work. She didn't spare a human thought for the labouring woman in Hut 16 who was refusing to come into the Revier – but if she bled out and wasn't at her work post within a week, it would reflect badly on the Chief Nursing Officer.

'Send the guards into the hut,' Mencken barked at one of the Kapos. 'And make sure they take the dogs.'

A sudden, crass vision of a contracting woman faced with snarling dogs and the fear welling up inside her made me speak out. 'I'll go,' I said. 'I'll attend her in the hut.'

Mencken's face crinkled with distaste. Hut 16 was an all-Jewish barrack, and as much as she hated Jews tainting her dominion, she wanted eyes over all births — and us midwives, no doubt. Only those babies born rapidly during Appell — roll call — or in the toilet block were outside the Revier.

'Why would you do that?' she said, soot-dark pupils directly on mine.

'The dogs will only halt the contractions. If it stops the baby could suddenly turn and we'll have a transverse or obstructed labour, and she's more likely to bleed.' I was exaggerating wildly but Mencken was a nurse, not a midwife, and it was easy to blind her with jargon. Two midwives on either side of me nodded, joining the conspiracy. Mencken's mind churned, thinking no doubt of the moral infection of her relatively clean unit and the tiny room set aside for Jews, already full to capacity.

'All right,' she said. 'But I want to know the minute she delivers. It's on you, Hoff — if she's not back at her place within the week, you may just lose yours. Or be going East.' It might have been a bluff on her part, but it was enough to make my nerves flutter — we had gradually learnt that transport out was to a place not designed for labour, or life. No one spirited away in a lorry bound for the East ever came back.

Hut 16 was almost deserted, with all prisoners on work duty. The only noise was a low moan from the front of the hut, backed by the clatter of the camp. It was as much silence as I'd heard in months. A young woman stood as I entered, shoulders stiff, her expression on alert. She relaxed a little on seeing I wasn't a guard or a Kapo. At just seventeen, she was an aged head on young shoulders.

'I'm Rosa,' she said, obvious worry lines on her young brow. 'I've tried reasoning with Mama, but she won't go. She says the baby should live and die in our home.'

'It's fine,' I told her, a hand on her thin flesh. 'We can stay.' At those words, Hanna came out of her labour bubble, rolled to one side, and we began the journey towards birth.

We waited and tended, Rosa by her mother's side constantly. I sat vigilant as the roles were reversed, daughter dissipating her mother's distress, reassuring when she uttered the inevitable, end-stage words: 'I can't do it.'

'Yes, you can, for us, for all of us,' Rosa reassured, and she watched — wide-eyed but with silent maturity — as her mother birthed a surprisingly bumptious boy. His sandy hair and light eyes confirmed what Rosa later told me: Hanna had been raped by a civilian factory foreman, taking advantage of his well-earned 'perks' as he called them, as he stole from her. He plundered her body, and the Reich thieved the resulting life just hours later. Hanna, though, was alive, Rosa still had a mother, and the warped scales of justice in this new world told us we should be grateful for that.

I stayed until the work detail returned. Almost a hundred tiptoed in, the news having somehow been spread among the camp. Quietly, they moved to the bunks, and then by degrees towards Hanna and Rosa, each offering a hand or a hug. Almost all gave up a meagre portion of their dishwater soup that day to Hanna, so that when they sat singing in a circle around her, she fell asleep in Rosa's arms, with the fullest belly she'd had in months, but a heart left scraping at its own empty insides.

★   ★   ★

Hanna was up and at her work post in six days, and Mencken noted the extra days' toil, reluctantly affording me a nod as I passed her in the Revier. Over the next months, more births occurred in the huts. They were Jews mostly, but it wasn't treated so much as dissent, as long as I or another midwife was willing to go out. Mencken revelled in keeping her tight ship morally clean, despite the ever crumbling walls and filthy floors; they had fewer rats there than the huts, only by virtue of the building being up on wooden stilts.

However, since most babies died well before infection could set in, dirt wasn't my main concern. Besides, when a baby was due to be born in a hut, a general rallying and hoarding of rags or paper by all the women made the area cleaner than the hospital block, making it oddly safer against infection. And in their own 'home', they were surrounded by friends and love, a vital balm to their inevitable grief. I felt, in a small way — as I had on my community stint in Berlin — among strong women who understood each other, spiders spinning elegant webs of love and protection, who would weave repeatedly, never mind how many times that web was brought down.

Even so, I set out to each birth with a heavy heart. No matter how close the community in the hut, the end result was always the same — a mother without a baby, either in hours, days or sometimes weeks, if she was unlucky to watch her child mew with hunger for that long. The separation was agony every time, and we could not battle against the cosh or the gun. I composed myself before each birth, an icicle wedged somewhere deep in my own heart muscle, and then sobbed on Graunia and Kirsten when the level of injustice became too much. It was they who reminded me what we were doing — affording dignity inside the Nazi machine. But I needed reminding often that it was good, and not simply aiding the bad.

Over time, I was trusted enough to move from hut to hut, tending the ante-natal or post-birth women, and using my nursing to help with the rounds of the sick, the endless sores and wounds that needed dressing. Soon, I was rarely at a birth in the Revier and I became known as the 'homebirth midwife', though it was sad to imagine any woman would think of those hovels as home. After that first birth, Rosa became my official helper, and we worked as a team at countless arrivals.

It's true that we never lost a baby at birth. In pregnancy, yes – and after was the norm. Our only success was in the recovery – that women survived. Tended by their friends, they were cradled in love and shared sorrow, and as long as Mencken's workforce provision was healthy enough to stand, she tolerated my efforts.

The mobility meant I was a good messenger, practised at hiding minute, folded pieces of paper around my body or in my shoes, with larger items nestled well among the sodden rags post-birth. None of the female guards ever wanted to delve into these with their manicured nails, and the male troopers were even less likely to. The best gains were on visits to the vegetable kitchen – each of the workers was searched religiously in and out, but I was often too filthy for even the guards to touch, given my proximity to birth blood and pus. Sometimes, I managed to smuggle a small potato, on a good day a badly grown turnip.

One fortuitous day a new guard was so clearly sickened by a newborn's end that she forgot to ask for the return of a penknife she hastily gave me for cutting the cord. She was either too ashamed or afraid of the consequences from her superiors to ever challenge me about it. With a sharp edge, I could distribute tiny pieces of contraband among the huts, a potato shaving here, a sliver there, to the sickest or weakest women.

The knife gave both calories and comfort. At each birth I severed a wisp of the baby's hair, while Graunia had spirited away a printing pad and some paper (she got two days in solitary for her incompetence at the 'stationery count'), and we were able to create hand- and footprints as memories. It was a poor substitute, but as they cradled the precious paper, the women held on to a brief life that became history – tangible and real. For some, in their post-birth grief and madness, it was the only thing that tethered them to reality.

And so we lived, and survived. Much like Berliners who came to barely register the flutter of Nazi insignia through the city, our expectations of life slowly lowered by degrees.

37

Watching and Waiting

Dieter's watch signalled we had managed to get to almost six a.m. before there was a gentle knock on the door. He was dressed, newly shaved and his cologne came through the gap in the door, pushing down the anxious pulse of my heart.

'How are you doing? Anything to report?'

I slipped outside the door and laid myself flat against the wall, hoping to sink my voice into its fabric. Our fingertips met briefly, ears scanning for nearby bodies.

'Well, no baby yet, but Eva is in good labour,' I said. 'She was four centimetres at about three, but it's always best to be conservative – two for the doctor's benefit.'

Dieter's face reflected confusion at my midwife's tongue.

'It means she's almost halfway to pushing the baby, but still a good few hours to go.' I sighed heavily. 'I suppose you'll have to get a message to Koenig now. We can't hide it any longer, and we'll need help from the kitchen soon.'

'All right, if you're sure,' and he turned to go. I caught his arm.

'Dieter, when they arrive, please come and collect me. Don't let them come knocking on the door. And no maids lingering in the corridors.'

His face took on a look of concern.

'I know it's a big request,' I added. 'But I don't want Koenig bulldozing in here. It might send Eva off balance.'

His eyebrows went up. Was it Eva, or me, whose calm would be upset?

'Seriously,' I said. 'It could delay the whole labour. Trust me on this.'

He looked at me intently, no facial theatrics now. 'I do trust you, Anke. Implicitly.'

'Thank you,' I said. 'I promise I'll keep you well informed. I won't leave you in the dark.'

Christa and I took turns tending to Eva, who was generally uncomplaining for a woman experiencing so much back pain. She simply needed reassurance that the agony was normal as the contractions became more intense. Every half hour, I listened to the baby, and we spooned camomile tea into Eva's mouth and warmed the lavender leaves for relaxation, the odour strong in the room. We drank insipid coffee to counter the lavender's soporific effect and keep us sharp, given the early start. In between, I wrote copious notes on the progress of the labour, choosing my words carefully, knowing they would be crawled over by medics and the Reich alike, perhaps even the Führer himself. More so if anything went wrong.

At 8.30 a.m., there was another light knock of the door. Dieter again.

'They're here,' he said. 'I've put them in the parlour and Lena is keeping them busy with breakfast. But they're insisting on seeing you – soon. Koenig appears to be nursing a large hangover, but Langer is razor-sharp. Be careful.'

'I will. I'll be there in five minutes – promise.'

I listened to the baby and left Christa in charge. As I walked towards the parlour, it was obvious some of Eva's moans were snaking through the corridors and prompting a house on high alert. She was getting more vocal, and I could only guess it meant the labour was progressing.

'Fräulein Hoff.' Dr Langer got to his feet as I entered, but Koenig's girth stopped him rising quickly. That and the mouthful of bread and meat he was working through. He nodded in reluctant acknowledgement.

'How is the labour progressing?' Langer's eyes were jet black, more weasel-like than before.

'Fräulein Braun is doing very well,' I replied. 'She was two centimetres at three a.m., the contractions are good, her waters broke at two-fifteen.'

'Clear fluid?' Dr Koenig managed, mouth still full.

'Yes,' I lied unashamedly.

'Heart rate?'

'Within normal limits, Doctor.'

He grunted. 'I'd like to see her.'

Here it was. The distrust not only of doctor to midwife, but also of Reich to prisoner. I took a breath. 'Fräulein Braun has asked that unless there is any reason, she would

299

only like myself and Christa, one of the maids, with her. As planned.'

She hadn't said this explicitly, but it had been every way implied.

His eyes blazed into mine and his delivery was pure pomp: 'I think, Fräulein, if you tell your mistress why we are here, she will admit us to her bedroom briefly. We are present for the safety and survival of her baby. Perhaps she needs reminding of that.'

'With all due respect, Dr Koenig, I think you will find I am also here for the same purpose, and Fräulein Braun is already aware – and grateful – for your concern.' The words were crisp, born out of irritation and a profound contempt of his arrogance. I ignored a shuddering somewhere in my stomach. 'I am concerned, however, that any interference will not help. She needs quiet and calm for the labour to progress.'

'Hmph.' He dismissed centuries of midwifery intuition with one derisive sound. His face coloured to match the boiled ham piled onto his plate. Langer was a ghost in comparison, and they glanced at each other. The temptation to shoot me down must have been overwhelming but they were still mindful this was the Führer's mistress – treading eggshells was wise.

'Very well, but I want to know of the slightest change or delay.' His voice attempted to command.

'You have my word.'

At Eva's door, I stood for a moment eavesdropping on the sounds from within – not out of distrust of Christa, simply a need to switch on my birth radar. With the pressures outside, there had been no time to gauge the change in pitch, the rolling weave of the contractions.

'Christa!' Eva's voice was needy.

'I'm here,' I heard Christa say through the door. 'Come on, one closer to seeing your baby, one at a time, Eva.' She had a perfect midwife's patter.

'But it *huurrtts*,' Eva moaned, as a statement more than a complaint.

'And you are strong, and the reward is your baby,' Christa kept up as Eva mooed noisily into her own body. How many times had she said that already, and how many more would she say it again before we saw this baby?

Contraction over, I opened the door and saw it immediately – the familiar white fold on the floor, just inside the doorway. I scooped it up and pocketed it before Christa could see me. She had enough to deal with already. I listened to the baby, whispered to Eva that the doctors were here, as confirmation the baby was truly on its way. She smiled meekly, and asked me if it would be all right. Eva's wet face showed such need, this lonely princess in the tower. I told her she was the strongest woman in the room, everything was going fine – she nodded, content with such loose assurances.

I retreated behind my notes, slid the folded paper from my pocket:

We're ready and waiting. We have safe transport for you and your companion. Your families will be safe. You have the future of the Reich in your power, and of Germany. We will seize the opportunity, as can you. Leave us a sign, back door by the pantry.

Was it a promise or a threat? Or both? If we didn't deliver the baby into their arms, would they – army generals, German dissidents or even a small group of Allies – take it by force and leave Christa and me to face the consequences? I had lived this war as long as any German, but my experience was overt and brutal, violence not shrouded. I had no experience of these games, nor of an ugly exchange of bullets. And if there were a showdown, up here on the mountain, people would be caught in the crossfire. Dieter would be forced to defend, and he'd already dodged one bullet.

My brain was a quicksand of doubt, fear and bloody-mindedness. How dare they? And yet they could and would. This war had no boundaries, no rules. How could I appease them, delay for more time, and shore up Eva's safety with the baby?

I decided quickly I could no longer do this alone and be a midwife to Eva. On the pretence of checking the gas and air, I found Dieter in the office. He looked up quizzically.

'No, no news,' I said. 'But I do need your help.'

I came clean, as he looked on, surprised but not aghast – about the notes, the unknown mole at the Berghof, the plan to scupper the Reich, the threat here and now to the baby. His eyes hardened as he read the latest threat, a sea glass blue as they narrowed. Was he angry with me? He had every right to be. A furrowed brow meant he was thinking hard – torn no doubt between his defence of the regime he hated, the woman he had proposed love to, and the Germany he aspired to, all twisting uncomfortably around his core of concrete morals.

'Dieter, what shall we do? I'm really at a loss.'

His answer seemed to take an age. 'Well, if the labour goes as you predict, the baby will give us real time, but we can delay the resistance by promising what they want.'

'You don't think they can give us what they say? Safety for us and the baby?' I needed to test his thoughts.

His reply was steadfast: 'Listen, Anke, I don't want the Goebbels to have a tool in their hands any more than you do, but this so-called resistance, it's false hope. They don't care about you, Christa or Eva. They will leave you hanging.'

The analogy was painfully visual and reinforced my own belief.

'So what happens we don't deliver?' I added.

'I don't know, but it gives me time to think.'

'Will you tell anyone else? Meier? Radio for troops?'

He looked at me, his own cogs in furious motion. 'No. We keep this to ourselves. It may be an elaborate bluff and not come to anything.' Still, he opened his desk drawer and fingered a pistol sitting on the top. He caught me looking at him, a wordless exchange like that very first day at the Berghof, and his mouth set in a thin line.

'Dieter, now it's my turn to tell you to be careful. Please.'

'I will. I promise.' He smiled an assurance, but it wasn't convincing.

'I need to get back to Eva.'

'All right, but please give a report to the doctors soon. They're getting restless. I'll write a note and leave it by the pantry door; it will appease for a while.'

Our little fingers linked briefly across the desk, and I

wanted desperately to lean forward, kiss his knuckles and draw him in to me. Even with the jacket, I wanted to meet with his lips and feel their softness, but it wasn't safe. Safety was survival now.

38

Imminence

As I arrived back, it became obvious Eva was approaching transition – the tunnel between dilating and pushing stages. Her pitch had changed, and she was thrashing inside her own head, moving it from side to side, a self-directed 'No, no' coming from her. Christa was permanently by her side, offering honey water and solace with her own aching hands.

I took over massage for several contractions, reading the progress at the peak, looking at the crease in her buttocks as I rubbed around her sacrum, noting a distinctive purple line rising nicely. But an early pushing urge was common with back-to-back babies, and I'd need to be sure she was fully dilated before Eva bore down hard. It was half past ten and a good while since I'd checked on progress internally. Had I been truly in charge I would have waited until she showed signs of pushing, but the good doctors would need placating soon.

My luck was in Eva's stoicism – in her nether world she agreed to almost anything, and I checked her quickly. The baby's head was now deep in the pelvis, and the cervix at eight centimetres, paper-thin and working well. I mapped the position, feeling a tiny kite shape under my fingers at six o'clock – a small gap in the baby's skull bones, which meant he or she was still spine to spine but tucked nicely down. Not perfect but good enough, since the baby appeared to be finding its way through so far. The next two hours would be crucial in making sure Eva didn't push too early; the noise of her bearing down would almost certainly travel through the house – to the doctors, and anyone with resistance ears. They would be hovering for different reasons, but neither in Eva's best interests.

I found Koenig and Langer in the temporary theatre, checking the anaesthetic equipment, like vultures circling. I coughed at the acrid smell of disinfectant.

'Fräulein, is anything awry?' Koenig was quick to look for problems in his tone.

'No. On the contrary, Dr Koenig, Fräulein Braun is a very strong woman, along with her baby. All is well, and the labour is progressing as expected for a first baby. She's now seven centimetres dilated.' I wilfully put her back a centimetre.

'I would have thought she'd have been further along,' Koenig complained.

'But she's only been in active labour for seven hours, Doctor. An average first baby is twelve hours—'

'Yes, I know that!' he snapped. 'I am all too aware of an average labour, thank you. I want a report in two hours. She needs to be fully dilated by then. If not I will speak to Captain Stenz and we will see then who is in charge here.' He was red and breathless from the exertion of command.

Langer stood motionless, a rictus grin chipped into his chalky skin.

'Very well,' I said, and turned to go, sensing Langer's creeping form on my heels.

'Fräulein Hoff?'

'Yes, Doctor?' I was all innocent curiosity.

He dropped his voice as his wide, thin mouth and sour breath invaded my space. 'Don't imagine that we — or at least I — are not wise to your . . . particular practices.'

I cocked my head, a child caught red-handed and yet smiling virtue. 'I am all too aware of my realm of practice, Doctor. We have laid out the rules in detail.'

'Fine, have it your way.' His verminous eyes sprayed cunning on his words. 'But I have a memory for faces, and I remember yours well, despite the good living up here. You are a liar and a traitor, and even if you have the ear of the Führer's mistress, you remain an enemy of the Reich and cannot be trusted.'

I matched his look, desperate to blink, but holding my breath and entire self in limbo.

'And yet, despite that, Doctor, I am a good midwife, capable of bringing this baby into the world. Without recourse to butchery.' On that, my breath failed and I turned before he could see me colour and exhale at the same time, feeling his disgust burn into my back as I walked away.

The Camp, North of Berlin, June 1943

Rosa, my invaluable extra hands, was by my side when Dinah went into labour. It was her sixth baby, five of which she had left behind in Munich on her arrest. This new child was just a nugget in her belly as she was prised away from the others. Both Rosa and I were wary of the birth being quick, and arrived in the hut as Dinah began her pains. We brewed what nettles we had, and drank tea; I'd persuaded Mencken that herbs from the camp vegetable patch were effective in contracting the womb, and she allowed me to keep a supply.

And so Rosa and I waited. Dinah gave up her baby at dusk, in a trickle of fluid and a stream of tears. The baby — only her second girl — was initially quiet, breathing but calm, and we gained an extra half hour or so before her eventual wails meant I was forced to announce the birth. The guard who came in hovered nervously at the door, and had to be reminded to hand over scissors to sever the cord. She edged in reluctantly. We knew she had no stomach for the drowning – that was left to a specialist guard and a prisoner who had been incarcerated for child murder as war broke out, their morals of equal stature.

The guard took back the scissors and retreated, saying: 'I'll call the others.' Dinah wept as she asked Rosa and I to fetch a blanket she'd miraculously reworked and hidden under the flooring, in readiness for the birth.

We were gone only five minutes to the other end of the hut, carefully replacing the boards. As we returned, the tears were flowing on Dinah's face. The baby – Nila – was lost under the thin covering, but her mother had bundled up the cloth around her tiny features, a hand hovering over the fabric.

'I want to spare her that end,' she sobbed, 'but I can't do it.' Her fingers twitched with the need but were equally paralysed. She would have felt the baby's subtle breath through the fibres.

'Please help me – help her.' Her face was molten wax with the pain. It took me an age to understand what she was asking. 'Help her,' she said again.

'I . . . I can't, Dinah,' I stuttered. 'How can I?' Rosa was silent beside me. I looked at her young face, intent. I knew she was remembering the day her own brother was born and taken, all within hours. She had heard the splash, and many since. I swear I saw her head dip in the tiniest of nods.

Dinah's eyes were wide and wet, sporting a sorrow as deep as any well. 'Please,' she repeated. 'For her.'

I couldn't hold the baby as I did it, desperate not to feel the last flinch of life against my skin. But I did bundle the cloth and put my hand over Nila's tiny pout, one eye on the door for the returning guards. She twitched, but with only the slightest of struggles, then yielded as if to make it easy for me. I held firm as Dinah's head went close to her daughter's, kissing her damp head.

310

It was the mother who knew the final flinch. When there was no more breath in those rosy lips, we wrapped her in the blanket. She looked at peace, although my body was in turmoil, everything filthy in this world churning in my gut, detritus bleeding into my insides.

'Thank you,' Dinah said, anger swelling amid her turmoil. 'Her soul is in here.' She dug at her bony chest as she spat the words. 'Not out there, not with them. I wouldn't give them that. They can't have it. She's mine. Always.'

I did my sobbing later in the hut with Graunia and Kirsten, spewed what little food was in my stomach, poured repentance and guilt on their laps as they held me. What I did know, the thought kept close to me every day until then, was that the taking of a life still amounted to murder. Even in this vile excuse for a war. I held on to it, each time I heard the shot, or the splash. It was cold-blooded homicide, carried out by minions but engineered by that man who had promised to be our father, to look after the fatherland. He'd pledged, for those who believed his ranting at Nuremberg, to give us a better life, and here he was, robbing everything that was close and precious to us. Our lives. Our families. Our humanity. How dare he? Adolf Hitler was no father.

And what about me? I had crossed that line, taken a life, for whatever reason. Was it murder, or mercy? Would I – could I – ever come back from that?

39

Strength of the Web

In Eva's room, her telltale growl signalled she was pushing. Low, rasping and primal, it came from deep within her, as if every woman was born with a tiny fire pit nestled in their being, ready to ignite for such occasions. I was thankful the volume was manageable for now, and I watched intently as Christa rubbed hard into her sacrum, my eyes focused on Eva's buttocks and the tiniest of movements. There it was – at the peak of the contraction, the rounds of her skin parted, the line between her buttocks moved upwards and the skin flattened and became shiny, almost translucent. Spine to spine or not, this baby was moving down.

Encouraging Eva to breathe through each contraction, I timed half an hour before I suggested checking her internally again. If she really was fully dilated, then her labour was proving quick despite the baby's position. If she wasn't, we had to somehow stop her pushing.

My heart sank as I felt a definite ridge of cervix in front

of the baby's head: a common but irritating 'anterior lip'. The tissue was thicker than previously – too thick to push away – and if Eva continued bearing down, it would swell even more, leaving us no choice but to wait. And I knew Koenig wouldn't be willing to do that.

'Eva, you're nearly there, just a tiny bit more work to do before you push,' I said, her coppery labour scent obvious as we came face to face. Tears sprang automatically.

'How long, Anke?' she pleaded. 'I don't think I can do much more. I need it to stop.'

'I know you do, and it will, but for now just breathe as much as you can. For your baby.'

She nodded with resignation, slipping back into her role at the Berghof – the dutiful, obliging mistress.

Christa and I spent the next half hour moving Eva around, to the bathroom and back, distracting her from the heavy swell in her buttocks, which broke into a brief push at the peak of some contractions. 'Just breathe through it, Eva, blow your breath out, blow out the candle in front of you,' we urged through each bout of pain.

'I'm trying, Anke,' she moaned, eyelids at half-mast. 'I'm trying so hard.'

Finally, there was no holding back. Pain erupted and a streak of blood came through like lava as she bore uncontrollably – Christa and I felt its power, and no amount of coaching would dampen this brute force. Perhaps it was Eva's former fitness that showed through again, because I could feel no more cervix as I eased inside. The baby's head was low, just half a finger's length away, and moving further forward under my fingers with a contraction.

314

'That's amazing, Eva!' I couldn't help the joy and relief in my voice. 'You can push your baby.'

She looked at me, as if I was an apparition. '*Really?* I thought it was too early. I thought I shouldn't yet.' Her face was flushed and sweat had gathered at the roots of her hair. Now, though, she looked more alive than in recent weeks, ready to receive her child. Just that news had galvanised her, and she visibly gathered energy.

I was prepared for a lengthy pushing stage and I told Eva simply to 'go with urge' for now. It was noon; without the doctor's knowledge we weren't yet on a timeline, and the baby's heartbeat was normal. By one o'clock, though, I would need to send word that Eva was fully dilated, and the clock would be ticking. We had less than an hour to make some progress and get a head start. I sent Christa for some air and to gather more tea and supplies, as we settled ourselves in.

Through the bathroom window, I glimpsed a uniform moving about the grounds, a black shape against the midday glare – Dieter's lean, upright frame, prowling the back of the house. My heart skipped beats at the very sight of him, looking out for us. He turned and I signalled for him to come to the window, his eyes constantly sweeping the landscape.

'Everything all right?' he said, gaze still distracted.

'Yes, Eva's beginning to push, but the doctors don't need to know that yet. Can you knock at one, and I'll send a message to Koenig via you? Hopefully, we'll be well on the way to seeing the baby by then.'

He nodded a yes and went back to his vigilance.

Eva's steadfast grit increased with every contraction, and

I watched in genuine admiration. Instinctively, she seemed to listen to her body – no longer moaning but waiting for the intense urge and using its energy. Instead of howling wolf-like into the air, as so many women did until they harnessed the power, she pushed deep into her own self and her pelvis, with only a low, sustained grunt. Eyes tightly closed, she willed her baby into the world. With Christa encouraging from the top, Eva rocked back and forward on her knees, and I kept watch from below. I wasn't expecting to see the baby for at least an hour, just signs it was coming. We kept her going with a steady stream of banter.

'That's brilliant, Eva, you are moving your baby.'

'Is it coming? Are you sure? Can you see anything?' she panted in desperation.

'Not yet, but it all looks fine. Keep going. You and your baby are so strong.'

Increasingly agitated from the strain on her buttocks, Eva moved to the toilet, with an undulating soundtrack of strong pushes and squeaks of surprise as the baby entered into new areas of its mother's anatomy. I was relieved the noises were pitched low and wouldn't be travelling through the house, alerting friends and foe alike. Unwittingly, Eva was proving a saviour to her own baby and its future.

Back in the bedroom, Eva couldn't replicate the pushing power she had on the toilet, so Christa and I did our best to engineer a human birthing stool, Christa sitting on the bed and Eva spooning into her, astride her chair-like legs. I stayed in front, watching for signs of the head. Had I not witnessed Christa's own strength first-hand during Sonia's labour I might have worried at the strain on her body, but she was more than equal to the task. Pumped on adrenalin, the room was hellbent on having a baby.

At 12.30 p.m. precisely I could tell Eva what she needed to hear.

'I can see your baby!' This time, it was me who needed to temper my voice at the tiny, welcome glimpse of a dark, wet head.

Her own head fell back in relief, but only for a second. As the next contraction took hold, she wanted to see more, propelling her energy downwards, every vessel and sinew in her neck proud with the effort. Each push, each contraction nudged the baby just a millimetre forward.

Dieter's light knock came at one, and I opened the door slightly. 'Just tell them she's fully dilated, the heartbeat is normal, and I'll report again in an hour,' I whispered.

'What's really happening?' he said, already with the measure of a midwife's stealth.

'I can just see the head. Hopefully, we'll have news soon, so keep close. Any activity out here?'

'Nothing that I can see. I'll do another sweep soon and come back. If you need me, leave a coffee mug just outside the door.'

All three of us worked that labour in the next half hour. Having shown itself, the baby was static for a good twenty minutes, despite Eva's huge efforts; a coin-size piece of the head sat tantalisingly at her opening, while I willed it forward: 'That's the one, Eva, that's the spot, just a little bit more, you can do it. Just one more.' My own muscles, lungs and ligaments were at full stretch with every contraction, but Eva

317

was tiring and not even spoons of honey could coax more effort.

Just as Eva began another push, I heard it. A crack in the air – short, sharp and familiar, my brain taking seconds to locate the origin. Then another. A motorcycle backfiring, or a gunshot – as we'd heard daily in the camp. Was that the resistance making their move, come to take what they thought had no right to exist? Would there be scuffles and an exchange of bullets, with Dieter at its centre? One ear tuned beyond the window, and the other on Eva, I couldn't detect raised voices outside or anything disturbing the still air. My battle was concentrated in the room, and I had to trust Dieter would shield us. I heard nothing and focused on little else but the force of energy crackling between the three of us.

We moved into a range of positions – kneeling, a full squat, onto Eva's left side, and back onto Christa's human chair – with little progress. I glanced at Dieter's watch, the hands ticking too fast towards two o'clock. Would this baby need the help of a doctor's forceps, like a lot of those back to back? Would we run out of time and Eva's energy? The baby's heartbeat was holding strong, but it wouldn't forever. Babies tire eventually and Eva was already exhausted. We needed to pull something out of the bag – and soon.

I spied the neatly folded layette of blankets and clothes ready to dress the baby. Eva's mother had sent a beautiful, hand-knitted woollen blanket and I could tell she had been touched when the parcel arrived several weeks before, wrapping it around her bump and prancing like a catwalk model. I took the blanket and laid it firmly under Eva, her head lolling now with fatigue.

318

'Eva? Eva, look at me.'

Her eyes opened with effort.

'Do you see this blanket, this blanket for your baby?' A limp nod. 'Well, I want you to land your baby into the nest that's under you, and it will be safe because I'm here and your nest is lined with this special blanket. Now's the time, Eva, now's the time to have your baby.'

Even through her fog of exhaustion, she heard the tone of my voice, the nuance of real need. The next contraction was a mighty one, matched by her effort, and I grinned as the baby rounded the curve of the birth canal and sprouted forward, the hair now showing itself to be sandy rather than dark. Eva alternately blew and pushed, forced to continue by the contraction but held back by the ring of fire in her skin at full stretch.

'Fantastic, Eva! Fantastic!' It was hard to contain my own excitement. 'Just a little push and nudge, that's wonderful, keep it coming.'

Behind Eva, Christa's face was focused on mine, and I beamed the progress to her.

Once the curve was breached, it moved quickly. The baby's head crowned, and Eva's loudest cry came as her skin slipped over the skull bones, the nose and mouth gliding forward as the whole head emerged, looking up and out into the world, still back to back. Christa's legs were shaking with the weight of supporting, and Eva was on tiptoes with the limbo of a baby part born, shoulders still inside, mother and baby in a half world. We were all hanging on – just. The baby's face was blue, eyes closed, but normally so, and I had to remind myself it was.

'Just one more, Eva. Wait for the sensation – one more

and then we'll have your baby.' My hands were poised to catch, and I glimpsed the time was 1.55 p.m.

The shoulders came a minute later, the body sliding into my hands with gymnastic grace. The cord was loosely around the neck and I unlooped it with one hand and brought the baby up to Eva, who snapped from her dream world at the sight and touch of a wet baby against her skin. Her smile was one of the widest I had ever seen, complete contentment.

'What is it?' she said. 'Boy or girl? Tell me, Anke!'

The body was laid against her and I peeled one leg back to look at the unmistakable genitalia. 'It's a boy!'

Poor child, I thought instantly. A girl may have been ignored – not the macho trophy Joseph Goebbels was craving. But in being less of a treasure to the Reich, she may have had a chance. This boy was pure gold – to both Goebbels and the resistance.

'Is he all right? Why isn't he crying?' Eva sounded alarmed, like all parents who thought babies screamed instantly. His wide eyes surveyed the faces in front of his, and my hand went to his chest, pink with oxygen. I felt his little heart flutter through his ribs.

'He's fine, he's breathing fine,' I told her. He coughed and squeaked slightly in response.

We landed Eva and the baby into the nest as one and Christa's relief was instant. Still bathed in adrenalin, she went instantly into action, moving the equipment and getting sheets under Eva, while I checked the blood flow, which showed nothing of concern. We gave her sips of water while she caught her breath, landing kisses on her baby's head. 'My baby,' she almost sang, 'my gorgeous boy.'

Tightly, I tied cloth strips a few inches apart on the healthy, fat cord and he squeaked again as I severed the complete dependence on his mother. I drew him away to dry and wrap him well, and it was only then that I saw it.

40

A Real World on Top of the Mountain

His right hand was missing. It had been tucked out of sight in the few minutes since the birth, close into Eva's body. Left free, I could see the limb finished smoothly at the wrist – no deformity of fingers or hand, just nothing there at all. I checked both feet and toes – all other fifteen digits, ears and eyes appeared normal, with no evidence of a syndrome or handicap. Thankfully, he had far more of Eva's look than his father's. In his complete innocence, he cooed as I checked him over but he didn't cry. Just minutes old, he seemed to sense a large howl might alert everyone around us to his presence.

Quickly, I wrapped him tightly and handed him back to Eva, who clearly hadn't noticed – yet. She wallowed in her ecstasy while I beckoned Christa into the bathroom. She caught my look instantly.

'The baby has no right hand,' I said.

'What? What do you mean? He looks perfect.'

'He is, in every other way, but there is no hand – nothing.

We need to break it to Eva gently, and keep the others away for now, give her time to adjust. I want to deliver the placenta first before we unwrap him and show her.'

She nodded, and we went back to our tasks.

Again, sheer fortune blessed us more times than I can count that day, with the placenta coming away cleanly. Eva beamed at me, a woman whose fragments of insecurity had knitted together at that intense moment of motherhood. And here was I, about to unravel it.

As Christa and I moved to unwrap the baby, a knock pulled me up sharply. I'd lost track of time and it was after two o'clock. Dieter's face appeared in the crack of the door.

'What can I tell the doctors?' he whispered. 'They're getting very agitated.'

I slipped outside the door and faced him, catching his cologne.

'We've had the baby but . . .'

'But what? Is everything OK?'

'He's alive and well, but he's missing a hand.'

'What do you mean? How is that possible?'

'It's rare – I've only seen it once before. It can be simply genetic—' at the word his frown deepened '—but can also happen where a band forms in the womb and just cuts off blood supply as the baby is forming. It's pure chance. He's perfect in every other way.'

'But not completely perfect.' Dieter spelled out what I had dared not contemplate. His eyes narrowed, signalling deep thought. 'What do you need me to do?'

'I need time to break it to Eva before the others descend. It's likely they'll want to do testing, and after that . . . I don't know.' I thought quickly. 'Tell them we're still pushing, the baby is fine and it's moving but that we might need help with forceps in a little while – don't tell them how long. That way they'll be busy preparing and not pacing. Come back as soon as you can.'

We locked fingers again and squeezed; I swear I felt his pulse flutter on my skin.

Back in the room, Eva was on her bed, babbling with hormones of post-birth, and the baby had attached himself to her breast, suckling with real vigour. She looked down in complete adoration.

'I think I'll call him Edel – I've always liked that name. It's very strong, don't you think? Oh, everyone will be so pleased – a boy. He will, I'm sure he will.'

She stopped short of saying 'Adolf' or 'The Führer' but it went over my head. I was too busy forming the next piece of script.

'Eva, the baby is lovely, and he's perfect in so many ways . . . but—'

'But what?' She snapped a parent's instant defence.

The baby was feeding on her right breast and I peeled back the blanket to reveal the stunted limb. She gasped and put her hand to her mouth, eyes creasing and sprouting instant tears. Aside from no baby at all, this was clearly her worst fear. I tried filling the air with words, explaining how it might have happened, that he looked perfect otherwise . . .

'He's perfect to me, but not to them, is he? Not to . . .' and she really did stop herself saying his name. The name of the baby's father. The man who needed to accept him as heir to his name, and the Reich. As a proud parent. Like

Dieter, Eva had lived in the Nazi inner circle longer than I – they understood the narrow boundaries of tolerance. The saturation of joy in the room dissipated to bleed complete despair. She moved her finger over the baby's smooth stump, dropping tears onto his wispy hair, while he sucked happily on his mother.

Christa and I drew away to let Eva absorb the news, and we hugged each other tightly, partly in relief the birth was over, but also in fear at what might come next. The abnormality was not our doing – it was no one's fault – and couldn't have been predicted, but the Nazi regime was never tolerant of excuses. There would be consequences.

For the minute, though, mother and baby took priority.

'He's beautiful,' I said to Eva, fingering his locks. Battered and bruised, skinny or robust – all babies were bewitching to their mothers and it needed acknowledging.

'He is,' she said, stroking his head. 'But you and I know he can't stay.'

Her words hovered like a dense fog between us.

'What do you mean?' I snapped my eyes to hers.

She sniffed. 'I'm not so naive as to think the doctors won't want to look at him, poke and prod at him. Whatever the reason, they will see it as genetic, as defective.' The word made her shudder. 'And then what will happen to him? At best he'll be an embarrassment, at worst . . . I don't like to think.'

'But he's a baby, an innocent, surely—' Despite what I'd seen with my own eyes, I couldn't believe that *this* baby would be cast aside.

'Anke, you don't know how they are!' She was shaking her head in despair. 'The Führer, he's sickened by handicap.

It's what he fears most. If his son is revealed, it will weaken him, his dream. I could cope with losing him, but for the baby to be ghosted away, to be investigated, prodded . . . by them . . . I couldn't, I just couldn't bear it.'

Silence hung like a stench, until I could stand it no longer: 'Eva, what do you want to do?'

Her shop-girl smile became the steely mask of a mother's newly grown will. 'I want you to take him away, to safety. To live.'

My heart dived – it was Dinah and her plea all over again, separating a mother from her baby.

'Eva, do you know what you're saying? You may never see him again. Are you sure?'

'No, but it has to be done. For him. I know it does.' She gave a weak smile and squeezed my hand. 'Please. Help me one more time, Anke. Help my baby.'

She was right, of course. I had seen officers coming and going at the Berghof, some with injuries sustained in war, limping badly, false limbs and lost eyes, but I didn't doubt they had all been perfect Aryan specimens on entering the battlefield. Handicaps through valour were acceptable, even afforded kudos. But a weak birth line was seen as just that – weakness. Only Joseph Goebbels, with his pronounced limp, seemed to be the exception. The Führer's child had to be strong and complete.

The knowledge ignited my mind to a perpetual motion. How would we get a baby down a mountain, out into the plains below and under a cloak of safety, in a country at war, in broad daylight? And quickly? It seemed impossible.

I moved away from Eva to think – a few steps and the room spun, so wildly I caught the wall for support, sour bile rising in my throat as the colours of the rug became a swirl of confusion. Through the fog, I saw only one image: Papa laid out on his deathbed, pale face and long, wispy beard, looking peaceful, but nothing other than dead. Dead not through war, not under an Allied bomb, but at the hands of his own countrymen, the country he loved with a passion. Those same compatriots I was surrounded by now.

In that second, gripping the doorframe, I thought: why would I do this? Why would I risk everything I had been holding on to by a thread for someone who colluded with – slept with – the architect of my own sorrows? Whose own hands might be tainted black with death? I could say no. I could leave Eva to deal with the consequences of her own making. She wouldn't be under threat, would she? An enforced exile, perhaps, no longer the honoured princess, but not mistreated. Not dead like Papa, imprisoned in the same way as Mama.

My heart muscle wrestled, enough to make me clutch at my chest, and then at my mouth, to stop the nausea bearing fruit. I forced myself to look over at Eva, smiling and sobbing in unison as she drank in precious moments with her baby – the one she had just given life to, and was preparing to pluck from her breast. As his little, bereft limb bobbed, she kissed it so gently that my heart was crushed again. Her innocence may have been in question, her choices morally wrong, but his weren't. He didn't ask for this, had no say in his parentage. He should not have to pay for their judgements or crimes. I was sure of little else, but his virtue right then was a certainty.

Dieter's knock came like a toll bell, crashing into my head and yanking me back to the moment. This time I coaxed him just inside the door, and Eva's eyes went up in alarm at the sight of his uniform.

'It's fine,' I said to her. 'He can help.'

I told him quickly of Eva's request. Strangely, he didn't announce the plan as complete madness or suicide, only nodding that he was thinking.

'Dieter, do you really think this is wise?'

'No, nothing in this war is wise, Anke. But I think Fräulein Braun is right: the baby has no chance up here.'

'Why? Has something happened?'

He dropped his voice to a whisper. 'The resistance made its move, from the inside. There was no need for an attack, they were already here – Daniel, and several of the house patrol. I can only guess they are part of a group whose frustrations have turned them against the Reich.'

'Daniel!' I couldn't believe the mild-mannered chauffeur was anything but that. Except the war had taken its toll on his family – he'd alluded to that. 'Are they here now, threatening?'

'There was a small ambush, which we've contained. They've retreated for now, but my guess is they've gone to regroup, and may well come again. They've dismantled the radio in the meantime – luckily, Meier is preoccupied in trying to fix it.'

'So, how do we get the baby away? Are there any other sympathetic drivers we could call on?'

He shook his head. 'I couldn't ask Rainer. He's loyal to me, but he has a young family. It's too much to ask.'

'We could hide the baby until it's safe to move, after dark?' I knew I was grasping at very short straws even as I said it.

'I don't know much about babies, but I'm guessing they

don't stay quiet for long, especially when they're hungry. And the mountain road will close up soon, once our reinforcements arrive.'

He was right. The baby was feeding now, but we had a maximum of about four hours, if that, before his stomach was empty again. Eva had some milk powder to hand if she couldn't feed, but we had to mix up the bottles without the kitchen suspecting.

Dieter was quiet, deep in thought. 'We need to move soon or we risk not being able to at all,' he said.

'But where?' As I said it, a thread of hope nibbled its way from deep in my memory, and I plucked it into reality: Uncle Dieter's farm. It was here in Bavaria, less than thirty kilometres away, and he had a housekeeper who I knew to be kind, forgiving and – I suspected – no supporter of the Reich. She might harbour the baby until we could arrange somewhere safer. I wasn't certain but we had no choice.

'I know somewhere,' I said, 'but we still need transport. I can drive. If you can find me a truck or a jeep, I can move the baby.'

He looked at me with those intense, penetrating eyes. 'Anke, you know that would be suicide – and the end for your family. Besides, you wouldn't get beyond the first checkpoint.'

He blinked long and hard. 'I'll take him.'

'Dieter, no! It's dangerous for you too.'

'But I'm more likely to get past the checkpoints, if the baby is quiet. At least we'll have a chance.'

He swallowed and refused to meet my stare. He meant the baby had some chance, but beyond that, life – Dieter's life – was a complete uncertainty. He would never be able to return to the Berghof – at best considered a deserter, at worst a traitor and a fugitive. For the Nazis, that ranked worse than the enemy.

'How will you explain away the baby's absence?' he added.

'Leave that to me.' I had absolutely no idea at that point but we would think of something and face the consequences.

'I'll sort out the transport, and hopefully stay out of Koenig's sight. He's on the warpath – so you'll have to be quick in getting ready. I'll be back in five minutes.'

The spark from our fingers was electric as we touched and he slipped through the door.

Eva saw me approaching, and tensed, arm muscles holding tight on to her precious bundle. 'So soon?' she said.

'It has to be now,' I said. 'There's no other way if you're sure he needs to go.'

'Will you take him?' she said. 'How can I ask this of you?'

'Captain Stenz will go. To a place I know – hidden and safe for now. Someone will care for him there. I know they will.'

'Captain Stenz, is he . . .?'

'He's reliable, kind. I promise. Trust me. Trust him.'

'I have to. I have no choice.' She looked down at her son. 'Neither of us do.'

Christa helped Eva dress the baby quickly, and I found a make-up compact on the dressing table – we imprinted his little foot onto the powder and then on a sheet of writing paper. Later, we could think about preserving it. Christa cut a wisp of his hair and pressed it between more paper. Through all of this, he was mercifully quiet, cooing slightly, a little drunk on his mother's first milk – the thick, yellowy nectar crusting around his lips.

Swiftly, Christa collected some boiling water from the kitchen, professing we needed it for the imminent birth, and was soon making up a bottle of milk.

Dieter's knock came all too soon, like the enemy at the gates. He slipped inside and nodded.

'Eva, it's time,' I said gently.

We wrapped the baby in a soft blanket, and then again in a grey, regulation covering – nothing to stand out and attract attention. Asleep now, his body was cocooned and his tiny features peeked out like those of a Russian doll.

Eva could barely speak through the sobs, and I peeled back her fingers, knuckles white as I prised him away.

'Darling Edel,' she breathed, as Christa held her shoulders, grief rocking her entire body.

I handed the baby to Dieter, with a wrapped bottle of milk.

'I've got a motorbike and sidecar,' he said, focusing on the practicalities. 'It's less likely to raise suspicion, but I'll need to tuck the baby right inside.'

'Can you ride a bike, at speed?'

Those blue pools flicked up and the boyish grin surfaced. 'I've grown up around engines, Anke. I'll be fine.'

I babbled to delay the inevitable. 'He should sleep for a bit, with the motion too. Just make sure his face is clear of any covering. If you need to stop just give him the bottle.'

He nodded. It was time for us now. His free hand linked with mine and squeezed.

'I'll find you if I can,' he whispered. 'Be safe, Anke. Survive. You *must* survive.' His eyes were the clearest I had ever seen, and I wanted to kiss his lips so hard and for so long – tumble into bed and forget everything of the past day, eat fresh pastries and drink good coffee while tracing my hands over his pale, beautiful face. And never let go.

Instead, there were only words, insipid and inadequate. 'You too. Stay hidden. Uncle Dieter will help you. He's a good man. But look to yourself.' My hand was so tight on his I might have drawn blood.

I slipped a note into his pocket, a quickly scrawled code to Uncle Dieter: '*Care for this boy, find him parents where he has none. I'm well. Noo Noo.*'

It was the pet name my uncle and I had used since childhood, and proof that the message came from me. The rest was up to trust and fate and his rough, good nature. A noise came from the corridor, and Dieter snapped back into the room.

'I need to go,' he said, turning and mouthing, 'I love you,' that little chip in his tooth just visible.

'Me too,' I mouthed back, but I don't know if he caught it. I saw the jacket disappear through the door, and my future, once again, became as deep and dark as the weave he was wearing.

A minute later I heard the thrust of a motorbike engine, the throaty roar as he revved and receded into the distance. They were away, no sounds of a chase; perhaps he had slipped by without attracting attention – his unblemished reputation paving the way. Then a crack. And a second, third. Gunfire or the engine kicking back? I had no way of knowing, only time and consequence would tell. Eva gripped on to my hand while our futures disappeared down the mountain, each of us keening inside at the loss.

I knew then I could only do what he asked of me and survive. I turned to Christa, whose silent support through the past twelve hours had braced me more times than I could count. All three of us sat in a huddle on Eva's bed, listening to the encroaching heavy steps outside, Koenig's strident boom causing us to link arms and stand firm. A thunderous rapping on the door signalled an end to the momentous birthday at the Berghof, and we three prepared ourselves for the battle ahead.

41

Retribution

From his feet to his collar, he oozed fury, pushed out in the slightest of twitches, pacing hard so that his limp barely registered, blood simmering in his vessels. Above the collar, however, Joseph Goebbels was a set mask of calm, sunken cheeks, black hair not a slick out of place. Only his eyes pulsed with unrest.

He circled me, jabbing at his prey, as if I was a disgusting yet intriguing exhibit in a zoo. I stood perfectly still, resigned, every nerve within me working hard on the blankest of expressions, nothing to rile him, nor show fear.

'So, Fräulein Hoff,' he began. 'This is not quite the outcome we expected, is it?' The tone was not rhetorical.

'No, Herr Goebbels. I'm as sorry as you for Fräulein Braun's loss. It is tragic.'

'I would say it's more than tragic. This was not just any child, as you know. This is a tragedy for all of Germany. So, can you enlighten me as to what happened?'

I sucked in air as discreetly as possible, fighting against

the rising quiver in my voice. 'The labour was progressing as normal – as with any first labour – and there was nothing to concern me until the baby was born.'

'And then?'

'It was obvious from the first seconds that he wasn't . . . coping.'

'And so it breathed?' This heinous man – a father of six himself – could not even attribute a sex, a persona to this baby. I hated him more for that than anything in his despicable history.

'Yes, briefly.'

'Did you attempt to save the baby? To give life?' His tone was still flat, a gargantuan anger kept underground, bubbling like the pot of ham on Mama's stove, puffs of steam fighting their way out from under the lid. Always, always, that pot spilled its dirty scum onto the clean metal stove.

'I did, for a short time.'

'Why only for a short time?' he shot back. Now he was animated, a chink to show my guilt, assigning my own blame. It would save them having to fabricate it later, just for the records.

'Fräulein Braun asked me to stop.'

'Are you sure about that? Are you sure you just didn't want this baby to die, the Führer's baby? For revenge, retribution? We know the Reich has enemies.' His face was inches from me now, spiny teeth just showing. An ugly man, inside and out.

'No.' I said it as calmly as I could, without emotion. The lid on my fear made his nostrils flare.

'And why did Fräulein Braun ask you to stop? Why would a new mother tell you to cease saving her baby from

336

death? I can't imagine it, Fräulein Hoff. I really can't picture it at all.'

'Because it was obvious the baby was not capable of living. The baby had—' here I felt a stab of betrayal to all babies born not quite perfect '—deformities. Significant deformities.'

'So you say. In fact, severe enough that you felt the need to dispose of the body before we were able to view it, to burn it so completely that all proof was lost?' Now his voice was rising, the pot beginning to boil, sour foam bubbling.

'I imagine that was behind Fräulein Braun's thinking,' I said. My own voice was beginning to crack, resolve crumbling. Come on, Anke. Fight for the baby, for the family, for Eva, for yourself. Deep breath.

'Her first concern was that the Führer's reputation may be damaged if he were . . . if the baby was known to be his. She wanted no record, no possibility of an image, to be used against the Reich.'

I looked him squarely in the eye and lied through my own, silently chattering teeth. 'She did it for the love of the Führer. For Germany.'

He was briefly blindsided, drew back, and paced the room again. Then he rallied for a second attack. 'And you, Fräulein Hoff, you didn't think that these actions would arouse suspicion, might create questions?'

'I wasn't thinking of that at the time,' I said, in semi-truth. 'I was dealing with a dead baby, and a very distressed mother, who had just lost her son. My priority is always with the mother, and the baby, if possible.'

'So you have said!' He was shouting now, loud but controlled. 'And yet I am still at a loss, Fräulein Hoff, as to what is the truth. The real truth.'

He banged his fist on the desk at the same time as the door flew open, and Eva launched herself in the room. She had the look of an injured lioness rallying to protect her cubs.

'Joseph!' she cried, and his face swivelled, stricken at probably the loudest and only rebuke she had ever dared aim at him. She stood, trembling, pale and unsteady, loose hair hanging limply, her robe soiled and hanging from her suddenly diminished body. I left my spot, took out a chair and led her to it. Her voice was calmer when she spoke. 'Herr Goebbels, please. This is not Fräulein Hoff's doing. It was my decision entirely.'

He was struck dumb by her intrusion and forthright words. 'You cannot – and will not – hold her responsible,' she went on. 'Her care was unblemished. There was simply no hope and I did what I thought was right at the time.'

He stepped forward, and I saw in his twitch the wily cogs of his brain working overtime.

'Of course, Fräulein Braun, and my thoughts go out to you – mine and Magda's. Our deepest condolences.' His sudden fawning made me nauseous. 'But perhaps it would have been more . . . fitting, if we had been able to prepare an appropriate burial.'

No one in that room believed for a minute he was talking out of respect, rather than control. Not even Eva, as gullible as she could be. She looked at him, her face cracked from crying, and acted like a consummate actress.

'I understand, Joseph, and it is for me to make peace with the Führer, when the time is right. But I did not want anyone – *anyone* – laying eyes on the boy who should have been perfect. I did it out of respect for the Führer, for his bigger creation. Surely you can see that. Or is your faith in the dream waning?'

She didn't weep, or falter. She wasn't supposed to at that point, moulding to the expectation of a Nazi mistress, focused and unyielding, like the scores of Magda models across Germany. But I caught it in Eva's voice, the tiniest glitch, the pain not of a dead baby, but a live child all but dead to her, knowing he was out there somewhere, without her, nuzzled into someone else's breast. And I couldn't help applauding her for it, the sacrifice.

The Reich's ultimate wordsmith, master of the truth twist, was finally silenced. He was Hitler's right-hand man, among the most trusted, but could he – would he – dare question the word of a queen, the only chosen one?

'As I say, my condolences,' he managed. 'Fräulein Hoff, please help your mistress back to her room.'

I felt the tremble in Eva's limbs as we walked out, perhaps from weakness and loss of blood, but more likely from the biggest confrontation of her life. For someone who had spent her life in the shadows, she had come out fighting when it mattered most.

'Just before you go, Fräulein Hoff.' Goebbels' quiet, understated tone jerked on my leash and I froze mid-step.

'Yes, Herr Goebbels?' I didn't turn but held firmly on to Eva.

'Captain Stenz. Do you know anything of his disappearance, the circumstances surrounding it?'

I felt Dieter's watch prickle on my wrist, where I had strapped it, perhaps unwisely, the day before. I slipped it out of sight under Eva's robe. Joseph's beady stare was on me, burning into my shoulders. Had he seen my wrist, the giveaway I couldn't bear to hide away?

'No, Herr Goebbels. I saw him yesterday, briefly during the labour, and not since.'

'As have we all, Fräulein Hoff. I understand from Sergeant Meier that you were . . . friends.'

He didn't see me swallow, but it allowed a second to stop a sob forming. 'Not friends, but we were civil to each other. He was my overseer.'

'Nothing more?' He was probing, would have loved to wheedle, cajole or beat it out of me, given the chance.

'Nothing. It does as well to be on good terms with your captors, Herr Goebbels.'

'Hmm.' I took it as a dismissal, and piloted Eva from the room.

I settled her in bed, checked on her bleeding, while her face turned into the covers, eyes creasing into tears. Her dry, cracked fingers locked into mine.

'Thank you, Eva,' I said. 'For me and for my family.'

She looked at me, eyes red, tears rolling. 'It seems I do get to care for someone after all,' she sniffed, and smiled weakly. 'Just briefly.'

'Yes, you do,' I said, and held her as she sobbed for her lost boy.

Epilogue: Berlin 1990

Anke, aged seventy-seven

From my flat near the Chausseestrasse I can see the Wall coming down, little groups chipping away at years of internment, bodies scurrying away with their piece of concrete history, already marketable. Like ants with their spoils.

I'm strangely sad, not for humanity, because those on the Eastern side might finally know something of democracy in time, but because those bricks assure me I'm not alone in my memories of that time. Each one of us old enough to see the Wall go up would remember the time before, during and after the rage that took hold of Germany, Europe and the world. Today's little piles of rubble are a reminder of that moon rock landscape of post-war Berlin. In an odd way, that's comforting.

Sometimes, I find it hard to remember things – details of daily life – but it's the privilege of age that you can recall events of forty-five years ago with clarity. Some I want to shy away from, but I have long since battled with my demons and we have come to an impasse. They are part of the package.

In those days after the birth of Eva's baby, there was confusion; she with her grief, me with the fear of retribution for my family. I was oddly calm about what I viewed to be the inevitable: the arrival of the Gestapo at the Berghof, being taken from my porch, perhaps into the surrounding forest, and shot for my failures. What I feared was a tortuous and lengthy preamble, to no end other than facing a bullet anyway. Christa had been sent back to the Goebbels' the day after the birth, no doubt where Magda would control her silence. I could only hope she was safe.

At intervals, Magda stalked the rooms of the Berghof under the guise of easing Eva's sorrow, but she was preying on information. She cornered me each time, probing my knowledge about disability and survival, most of which I bluffed with a sheen of medical jargon. Woman to woman, I felt she could see through my mendacity far more effectively than the Gestapo's best agents, but I was vigilant with my words, playing cat and mouse with her questions.

Joseph was elsewhere, constructing lies about the crushing defeats and the impending fall of Germany; I caught whispered talk in the dining room about the war nearing its end. Aside from Lena, no one talked to me directly, dared be infected by my leprosy of failure.

Yet the Gestapo did not sweep up the drive in their black, demonic chariots, and Frau Grunders bristled as if nothing much had happened, eyeing me with a mixture of suspicion and admiration. Her boy was once again safe from the tethers of *that* woman.

He – Germany's great father – did not make an appearance, rushing to the side of his grieving woman. I was sorry for her, but relieved for myself. I had lost hope of hearing about my family, left with only a sliver of faith, wrapped and tucked deep in my heart. With Dieter gone, there was no one to ease the path, and Sergeant Meier's punishment was a wall of silence. There was no talk of whether I would go, stay or be returned to the camp. All thoughts instead were way beyond our sightline, in Europe, scrambling to salvage what they could from the Allied advances. The skies overhead buzzed with aircraft, theirs or ours I couldn't tell, but no one ran or called alarm. We either cast our eyes briefly upwards, or ignored them. The road to inevitability perhaps.

I checked on Eva, as I would do any post-birth woman, but she was engulfed by her own grief, as barbed as the wire surrounding all of us. And she had no one to share it with, aside from me. Yet I knew that just a glimpse of my face brought back her own loss so acutely and so I avoided her whenever possible; I had become a symbol of betrayal to her own child, and the brief intimacy we had was gone, consumed by her guilt. Her eyes were a dull blue-grey surrounded by ripples of red, the amber glint to her hair lost in days without washing. She was no longer that girl in a Berlin department store, all smiles and promise. I recognised the look, having seen it countless times among the bed racks and bunks of the camp – a woman who had lost.

Two weeks after the birth, Sergeant Meier called me to his room. I felt as I had on facing the Commandant on my last day in the camp – resigned, ready. It only irritated me that he would enjoy a smug satisfaction on delivering my fate. Instead, he handed me a month's 'wages' and told me I was to leave immediately.

'To where?' I said, aghast.

'To Berlin, to your freedom,' he said curtly. 'There are some that keep their promises, Fräulein Hoff.' He couldn't look at me, a standing icon of betrayal to his beloved Reich.

'And what of my knowledge, of the things I've seen? Are you going to blind me, like Samson, or cut out my tongue?'

His eyes narrowed to reptilian slits. 'Who would believe you, Fräulein Hoff? Some madwoman from the camps, muttering about the Führer's baby. Besides, your family remains with us, and will do so for the foreseeable future. I have every confidence in your discretion.'

I turned before I might glimpse a perfect smirk settle under the oily bristles of his lip.

I said a brief goodbye to Eva. She managed a wan smile, put out a wrinkled hand – nails bitten to the quick – and squeezed my own weakly, then pulled it away to hug at her other babies, Negus and Stasi. They were her solace now, sprawled among her sheets. On the bedside table I noted letters, handwritten, perhaps from him, perhaps acknowledging her sadness, their loss, but maybe not. The tiny imprint of the baby's foot was beside her pillow.

Rainer drove me to the railway station in Berchtesgaden, and left me with a handshake.

'Enjoy your freedom, Anke,' he said. 'It was hard won.'

There was a look in his eye, one I had never seen before and couldn't fathom, but I was too anxious to shed all traces of the Berghof to give it much thought. In the envelope of money was a train ticket – second class to Berlin. I didn't take the first train out. Instead, I went into the town square, and I sat in the cafe – *our* cafe – under an umbrella. Was it the same spot? I couldn't remember. I drank a cup of very good coffee, the milk froth still rich and active. I raised the cup to my lips, thinking of Dieter, and I let the tears fall over the rim, the brine adding to the bitterness of the beans.

Berlin was in pieces. Under siege of the military, it was unrecognisable as the place of my birth – the city now grey and encumbered, the air singed with the smell of cordite. Hunched figures scuttled through the streets, shoulders cowed, their heads turned upwards only when a noise broke through the fuggy air above – a raid, or falling debris from damaged buildings everywhere. The noise merely made them scurry faster. It was as though Berlin had been a carnival, and the circus had left town. Approaching defeat infected every ashen pore, each stricken face.

I had nowhere to go, so I headed for the only place that was familiar, back home. In the western suburbs, our street looked almost as it did in the early years of the war, with added sandbags as an assault course for the children playing outside, but essentially untouched. The house, though, was anything but abandoned. Several pairs of tiny clogs were stacked at the front door as I made my way nervously up the path, my mother's carefully planted hostas healthy survivors of the raids, pale green and standing to attention.

The door was opened by a woman of about thirty in apron and headscarf, clutching a broom, and with a young, flushed face. When I explained, she welcomed me in, embarrassment evident at the mess her three children had created. But I wasn't perturbed – it felt like the family home it had once been for us, sprinkled with dustings of love. As a

345

specialist engineer, Helen's husband had been excused military service and his family were settled in the 'abandoned' house. In return, he spent long hours keeping power supplies in Berlin flowing.

She was one of the lucky ones, she said, hinting her relief that he was at neither end of a gun. There were no airs and graces to Helen and I liked her immediately. She offered me a room, the attic that had once been Franz's little-boy bolt-hole. I refused, of course, but she insisted, and it didn't feel like charity. Besides, I had nowhere else to go, and limited money to last me. She and her kindness reassured me that, despite this hideous onslaught, honest Germans were the still backbone of our country, and its bullyboys were the spineless few.

And so I sat out the brief remainder of the war, picking up a little paid work here and there, in bars and restaurants, and volunteering at the medical stations to give respite where I could. In those early days, I never stopped hoping I would round a corner and he would be there, or that I would turn to serve a customer in the bar where I worked and he'd be looking back at me, asking for a drink with his engaging grin.

In the end, we got our Berlin back for a time, limping and disabled. The fog of war was replaced by shame, first about defeat, and then, as the news about the camps spread out to the wider population, about the events of the war itself. There were those who hadn't seen or known about the killing and the inhumanity, at the hands of *that* man, and of those who claimed they were doing it for Germany, the greater good. When we heard about Auschwitz, Dachau, Birkenau and more, I realised there were layers to hell, and that perhaps I had not sunk to that bottomless pit. Sad to say, many had.

In those strange days of invasion, relief and renewed pain, I searched high and low for my family – in every Red Cross station, hospital, resettlement point, skimming my gaze over the women who still had flesh on their bones, plump faces and full heads of hair, to those who were wan, with thinning strands and empty eyes. I found them at last, my sister and my mother, clinging to each other in a community hall, and looking for hope. We hugged wordlessly for an age.

We found Franz eventually, on a list of the missing at Auschwitz – a name scratched amid a long list, and we knew there was little hope of finding him, knowing his only remains were his fighting spirit in our hearts. Franz was lost, and I had to tell Mama about Papa, but with the sure knowledge that he didn't die by the gas. I trusted Dieter to have told me the truth on that. I ghosted over other truths – the camp births, and my time at the Berghof. A small element of shame, yes, but also some things were hard to explain unless you were there.

When I heard about the end for them both – the newly betrothed Herr and Frau Hitler – I wasn't surprised or shocked. She would have followed him to the ends of the earth, and she did. I only wonder if Eva thought about her boy, in that moment when she bit down on the cyanide pill, whether he was lodged in her heart the moment it stopped beating. Magda, too, surrounded by her clutch of perfect babes. How can we ever know what she thought of as a mother, at that moment – beyond the lipstick, the gloss and her utter devotion to the Reich?

It was the pictures of the mountain top that upset me

most. I remember once chiding Dieter for investing so much emotion in mere bricks and mortar, for revering buildings over people. But seeing the Berghof reduced to rubble, bombed beyond recognition, muddy Allied boots stepping over places I had walked, it brought out feelings I didn't want to surface. I shouldn't have felt like that about the Hansel and Gretel house of evil. But I did, and that remains my own dirty secret.

We rebuilt our lives, Mama, Ilse and I, in a sea of fellow nomads. My crimes against the Reich were erased, and I went back to being a midwife; my work was my saviour and my solace, helping healthy babies. And no, I didn't think that for every one born robust and pink, every mother smiling and happy, that it made up for the ones we lost. I didn't tick them off. You couldn't think like that, or you would end up mad. Infected. But their faces, tiny and inno-cent, they remained a ghostly negative in a far corner of my memory for many years after.

Then, the Wall. I fought to remain a Berliner, on the West side. I'd had enough of dictatorship for one lifetime. I met my husband, Otto, in a cafe, another vital encounter among the chink of cups and the headiness of beans. He had been a regular soldier on the Russian Front, and so our wars were very different. There were only a few times in our thirty-year marriage when we talked of our shadows; we agreed on having been different people then. War had moulded us, but could never define how we emerged, as humans.

And, of course, it gave me my babies – a boy and girl. Finally, I could experience the agony and ecstasy of child-birth, of being at one with something outside of yourself, of that guttural and glorious push, the delicious wet head, the cry. The crazy, undying love. It was in that moment I thought of the Irenas, the Hannas, the Leahs, the Dinahs . . . and the Evas. I sobbed huge, rolling tears, for them and for my own relief and joy. For the lost ones, and the precious gift I held in my arms.

It was my son, Erich, who helped me search for the answers, years later. It took thirty years for some truths to come out – details of the camps, survivors, the stark truth. Graunia emerged with an astute, lightning pen, although her honesty was too bitter for some to swallow. Rosa, sadly, didn't make it out, but we tracked Christa to a town near her father's old farm. Our reunion was swamped with tears and furious conversation – she had become what she was always destined to be, a midwife, and we talked birth and babies, practice and home life. Her flaxen hair was lighter with age, but those eyes were as bright as in the Berghof days, and she was dressed in style, her skills with a needle and thread still evident. She'd had her own babies by then, and we came together as mothers and midwives. We never once talked of the baby, that birth. There seemed no need.

Erich was a keen historian, spending hours writing letters and peering at documents in the municipal halls, looking up articles about his grandfather, the revered professor of politics. He found little evidence of any attempted coup at the Berghof, the evidence perhaps burned in the rubble, and only a brief mention of a familiar name: Daniel Breuger, chauffeur to the Führer's staff, shot for 'actions against the Reich' in June 1944, reason unknown. Details of attempts on Hitler's life were well documented after a time, but there was no mention at all of the brief skirmish one May day in

1944, a tiny drop in an ocean of hatred, which might have proved to be a tidal wave in the enormity of war – it was buried, along with any evidence of its existence and the people engulfed in it.

Erich found one other name for me: Dieter Stenz. Shot for desertion in late May 1944, two weeks to the day after Eva's birth. The day I left the Berghof. There was little other detail. But Erich found an address: his elderly mother, still alive.

I wrote to her – a short letter but which took me days to compose – simply saying that I had known her son in 1944, that despite the official reports he was a hero, a saviour, and not the coward the records painted him as. That he was kind and human, and everything the SS wasn't. He was the son she would have wanted him to be. And in return, her spidery hand saying 'Thank you,' and a photograph of him without the uniform, next to his father, and in between them an engine, no doubt being dismantled or put back together. You can't see their hands, but I'm certain they are covered in engine oil. I have it in my drawer, alongside those of Otto, and my children. And the watch, its hands frozen in time.

I didn't tell her about the baby, the tiny, glowing element of Dieter nestled inside me that slipped out too soon, before I had much chance to welcome him or her into my body or my future, become part of my hope. Proof positive of our time together. The lovely Helen – she was with me as I bled grief and tissue, never asking awkward questions, but holding me as my mother would have. Dieter's own mother – she didn't need to know there could have been something of her son to adore, to hang on to. Too cruel to offer a hand,

and then snatch it away. But it's always part of me, one of those jewels wrapped safe in my heart. My Dieter. My war.

As for the other baby, I have no knowledge. And I'm glad. I only know that he left my uncle's farm three days after his arrival in the dead of night, driven away by a young man and his wife, who Uncle Dieter described as 'kindly'. There are times when I look at my television set, at the evening news, and curiosity causes me to peer a little longer. I think I might see a politician with a likeness, and my eyes immediately search for the hand, for something not quite right. Because, of course, with medicine − prosthetics they call them − being so good these days, you might not know.

But maybe he isn't a politician − he could easily be a farmer, or a carpenter, an artist. Who knows? It's good that he doesn't. He need never carry the burden of shame, of the genes in his blood. He only needs to know that he was born out of a mother's love, into an uncertain world, as one of thousands emerging under the awning of bombs, rubble or threat.

A child of the time, a war baby, and not the Reich's child.

Acknowledgements

So many people have contributed to this book's appearance, not least my long-suffering family – Simon, Harry, Finn and Mum – who have allowed me precious space to write. I say a huge thanks to my readers: Micki, Kirsty, Hayley, Zoe, and Isobel, and to my colleagues at Stroud Maternity, who have borne my bleatings about 'being a writer' with true encouragement. A special thanks goes to fellow author Loraine Fergusson, without whom I wouldn't have a publisher, or my sanity – her advice has been valued and constant. And to writer Katie Fforde – it was she who recognised the idea as more than a novella, and told me in no uncertain terms it was my first novel. How right she was! I also have to pay tribute to the wonderful crew at 'Coffee 1' in Stroud, who have kept me topped up with smiles and caffeine, and where a good portion of this book was written.

Thank you to all who have supported and shaped – Molly Walker-Sharp and the lovely team at Avon who have guided a novice through the process without losing patience. I was also reliant for the camp setting on Sarah Helm's excellent book, *If This Is a Woman*, chronicling the precise, human detail of women who survived with dignity under such conditions, and, for the first-hand accounts of survivors, the anonymous author of *A Woman in Berlin*, who illustrates that suffering is no respecter of culture or creed.

As a lifelong bookworm, I am so delighted to finally make it to the 'other side', and I say thank you to any reader who wants to flip the pages and forge on.